TO
BREAK A DARK
CAGE

BOOKS BY KATHRYN ANN KINGSLEY

KATHRYN ANN KINGSLEY

TO
BREAK A DARK CAGE

SECOND SKY

Published by Second Sky in 2024

An imprint of Storyfire Ltd.
Carmelite House
50 Victoria Embankment
London EC4Y 0DZ
United Kingdom

www.secondskybooks.com

ISBN: 978-1-83525-042-6
eBook ISBN: 978-1-83525-041-9

ONE

Avalon was about to be set ablaze.

Mordred stood upon the parapet of his keep and gazed out at the world before him. At Avalon. The field between his home and the line of trees that marked the forest was no longer filled with tall grass. It was a sea of mud and iron armor. His soldiers were working to clear away the fallen. Most of them were his own iron soldiers. They would be melted down and reused if they could not be repaired.

As for the elementals? Their corpses had turned to dust, their magic returning them to the ether of Avalon. He could see the shimmering dust rising into the air, catching the sun. Elemental corpses did not linger at least.

He rested his metal gauntlet upon the stone balustrade. Out there, lurking and gathering his strength, was a demon who wished to burn the whole world down. Who wished to destroy every life here and turn the isle of ancient magic into nothing but char and cinders.

Not for glory. Not for righteousness. No. Out of *spite*.

No one would stand in opposition to Grinn. No one but

Mordred would dare. It seemed that history was forever doomed to repeat itself—no matter how hard he worked to break the pattern.

For these events had played out once before.

And they had led to tragedy.

A thousand years ago, he had waged war upon the demon, with the elementals biding their time, falsely pretending to be *neutral*. When they were in truth waiting for Mordred and Grinn to kill each other—or at least for one to fall, so that they could deal with the other in a weakened state.

In the eyes of the elementals, Mordred and Grinn were equal—equally dangerous and equally abhorrent. Neither of them was meant to exist in this place.

Mordred was alone. As he always was. Backed only by the knights who were forced to serve him.

And one now-mortal woman who had betrayed him not once but *twice*.

Shutting his eyes, he took a deep breath and let it out in an equally deep sigh.

A woman he loved.

He clenched his fists. History was doomed to repeat itself, but for one difference this time around. Gwendolyn. And for the life of him, he could not seem to determine whose side the young woman was on. Him? Or the demon's?

Had he fallen in love with a traitor? Was she simply toying with him? Was it all a manipulative game? She would be a lauded actor if so, but it was not without question.

He could not trust the woman he loved. What a tragic and terrible gift the Ancients had given him in the form of a bright-eyed, smiling, empathetic creature.

What was he to do?

There was only one choice before him—seek the demon and put him to the blade.

What other path forward could there possibly be? Was he

truly doomed to walk the same road as before? An endless cycle of war? He knew the demon would not retreat to some far corner of the island and bide there in peace. Grinn's hatred was too strong for that.

Wronged as the demon might believe himself to be, there would be no quenching his thirst for revenge by any means other than blood. The monster *had* to die—laws of Avalon be damned. It was the only way that Mordred could see that might stop the pattern. There would be no mercy for him; no quarter would be offered.

The question merely remained—what would the elementals of the island do in the meanwhile now that their meager attempts to overthrow Mordred had failed? Would they seek to oppose him a second time? Or would they understand Grinn as the threat that he was, and seek to help him? He snorted in laughter. Unlikely. No, they would do as they had done before.

The other elementals would choose to linger by the edges, watching in wary anticipation to see who might stand victorious.

But in the end, he supposed it did not honestly matter. It changed nothing. It was war that Grinn wanted, and it would be war that he received. But one matter had to be solved first. The matter of Gwendolyn Wright. What was he to do with her?

She had been beautiful as an elemental. And she was just as alluring as a mortal. But what would become of them now? She was fragile. Mortal. Powerless in a world of creatures who could end her with a thought. The forests were filled with beings of all kinds—not just elementals. Any of them would be happy to snap her up and make her a meal.

And even if she swore her fealty to him and he believed her, and they mended their situation—what then? She would age and die. He would not.

Releasing her was just as foolish as setting her free in a town was a doomed proposition. What kind of life could she lead, alone in a world she did not understand? How could he go on, knowing that she was alive, on the island, but not with him? How could he resist the temptation to watch her as she found another to love and... perhaps even raised a family?

No.

He would be too tempted to keep her, as he had vowed to before. But she did not *belong* on Avalon. Worse still, she was a known weakness of his. Grinn had already used Mordred's obvious feelings for Gwen to his advantage. It would happen again. And if it meant laying down his life to save her, he could not promise that he would not do so, at the cost of Avalon.

There were only so many choices ahead of him. He could keep Gwendolyn as his prisoner while they... what? While they *what*? Sought to find a way to continue their doomed romance? Could he even forgive her for hiding the truth? Could he learn to trust her again? It was laughable that he was even tempted to try. It would end in more tragedy—more death—he was certain. Most likely hers.

Letting her live out her days on the isle was already a choice not worth considering. There was only one other option. Shutting his eyes, he knew it was the right decision. For her. For him. And for Avalon.

The very least he could do would be to do her the service of telling her in person.

Letting out a breath, he headed off into his keep. He was never one to let matters linger for long. He braced himself for the shouting that was shortly to follow.

He would have to send her back where she belonged.

He would have to send her home.

He loved her. He had vowed that once he had her back, he would never, ever let her go. But to protect her... he had to send her away.

And he would be forced to say goodbye.

* * *

Just when Gwen thought her life couldn't get worse or more complicated, it did.

She stared at Mordred in confused silence.

He had woken her up and sent Eod from the room, shutting the door behind the dog.

Gwen couldn't process the words that had come out of Mordred's mouth. It must be because she was still half-awake, sitting up in her bed. "I'm... I'm sorry, what?"

His expression was cold and stern as he watched her. "You are to return to Earth in the morning, Gwendolyn."

"You—you *can't*—" She got out of the bed, her legs still a little wobbly from having Grinn's elemental power ripped out of her. Everything that had happened the day before was still kind of a blur—the destruction of Caliburn to split Grinn and her apart, the death of Lancelot at Mordred's hands. None of it felt real. To be fair, none of this had felt truly real since the moment she showed up to Avalon. It was just one impossible event after another.

"Trust me. I can." His voice was as icy as his expression.

This couldn't be happening. This couldn't be real. She had to be dreaming! "Don't send me away, Mordred. Because I..." She needed to tell him how she felt. She needed to. Maybe then, he would understand. Working up the nerve, she decided it was time. She would just rip off the bandage. "I—"

She never got to finish her sentence. She never got to say the two other important words in that powerful three-word sentence.

Because he was having none of it.

"And why should I listen to you, who have betrayed my

trust not once but *twice?* Most do not see enough mercy to survive the first time, let alone a second." His hands clenched into fists, the metal creaking. He stalked to the window in her room, turning his attention outside as if he couldn't even stand to look at her.

"Because—" She felt small. Young. And like an idiot. "I—I didn't—I was afraid that—"

"You were afraid that I would sacrifice your life to save all of Avalon from a monster. And yes, perhaps you should have been, Gwendolyn. You do not understand with whom you have thrown in your lot. For all that I am—for all that I am capable of —I am a far better fate for this world to suffer than the demon." He clearly forced his hands to relax before placing them on the stone sill of the window. But she didn't miss how his claws dug into the stone, leaving small trenches on the surface.

Sometimes, it was easy to forget how strong he was.

Sometimes, it was easy to forget who he really was. Gwen shut her eyes, biting back tears. "Grinn—he—"

"Whatever story he told you of his life, he was using to manipulate you. To play your empathetic heart like a lute. He is *using* you. And how am I to believe he will not do so again? How am I to believe that you would not betray me a third time?" He lowered his head, his shoulders locked, his voice strained.

It was clear he was doing everything he could to keep from charging at her.

"I—I'm sorry, Mordred, I didn't—I didn't know what to do."

"You should have told me the truth. You should have *always* told me the truth. That is all I have ever asked from you!" He smashed a fist into the stone, cracking the surface. When he spoke again, his voice was lower. Haunted, almost. "Not your loyalty, not your affection—simply that I might, through all of this, dare to *trust* you." He lifted his head slowly, staring out the window in front of him. "Tomorrow, you shall return to whence you came."

Gwen was shaking. The silence felt like a death sentence. She had fucked this up. This was *her* fault. He was going to send her home, and it was because of her. Swallowing the brick in her throat, she struggled to form words once more. She struggled to tell him how much she loved him.

I love you, Mordred. I love you, please don't send me away. I don't think I can go on living without you.

"I—"

Yet again, she didn't even make it to the second syllable before Mordred cut her off.

"*Enough!*" He stormed up to her suddenly, backing her knees against the edge of her bed. In one movement, he grasped her by the jaw, tilting her head up to him.

For a moment, she worried he was going to snap her neck.

But it seemed he wanted to take his rage out on her in a different way.

She never got to say those three words. This time, because he was kissing her with a fury that threatened to devour her.

And damn her to hell, she *wanted all of it.*

Part of her wanted to surrender to it instantly—to give in to him, to let him just have whatever he was here to take. She loved the warlord and everything that came along with him.

The other part of her was *pissed.* Yeah, sure, fine. She had betrayed his trust, or at least not told him the whole truth twice now. But she hadn't had any other good options at the time that didn't wind up with her stuck in the Iron Crystal or used as bait for a demon.

It left her with anger and love, in equal measure, both at the same time. Two very different emotions merged and formed into one. She snarled in frustration and pushed on his chest, but the iron of his armor might have been the wall behind her. He wasn't going to budge. So she did the only thing she could think of—she bit his tongue.

Not hard.

But enough.

He pulled his head back in surprise. She expected him to be angry—but instead, his lips turned up into a grin and he chuckled. As if she had just done something extremely silly and didn't quite understand the ramifications of it.

If there was one skill in life that Gwen didn't have, it was knowing when to stop digging a hole she had found herself in. Glaring at him, she decided that if he was going to rip her to shreds, she might as well make it count.

She slapped him.

His face barely moved, and she was certain it had hurt her palm way more than it had hurt his face. When he only laughed again, she went to repeat the motion. He caught her wrist before she could land the strike and quickly pinned it to the wall over her head. When she struggled and tried to push him away with her other hand, it quickly met the first, both wrists pinned under his single hand.

"How *dare* you, you—" She went to lay into him. But another searing, desperate, *furious* kiss cut her off again, swallowing her words and robbing her of her breath. God, it felt so good.

She moaned. She couldn't help it. Need and desire lit in her instantly like she was still a fire elemental, sending all her nerves crackling to life.

She knew if she screamed or if she demanded he stop—he would. He wasn't that kind of monster. She was ultimately in charge of this dance of theirs.

Maybe she should. It would be the intelligent thing to do.

The really intelligent thing to do.

But she needed him—needed *this*. Needed to feel his wrath

and needed to take her own out on him in return. Needed to feel him one last time.

Even if she wanted to beat him with a baseball bat at the same time.

When they parted, her head was swimming, and her chest was heaving in a desperate attempt to catch her breath. He watched her, waiting for her to protest. Waiting for her to strike him again or tell him to stop.

It was the farthest thing from her mind. Reaching up, she dragged him back down into another kiss, needing to feel him against her. Needing him to understand that he *couldn't* be serious. Not when they had each other.

Mordred broke the kiss before he slid his hand to her throat. He tightened his grasp, restricting her air just enough to send another dangerous thrill through her body. "I have come to procure an apology, Gwendolyn."

"I said sorry," she squeaked out. God, he was so painfully hot when he was scary.

"Not like that." He smirked.

She should try to pretend that this didn't turn her on. She really should. And she did her best to continue to glare. But when he tightened his hand just a little bit more, she let out a whimper that must have told him everything he needed to know.

She squeaked as he suddenly grabbed her by the hair and half threw her across the room, sending her staggering. She caught herself on the bedpost, her head spinning.

"Kneel."

The one word from him almost sent her straight to the floor. It was an order. It was a command. And it was obvious what would follow if she did.

But she wasn't going to go down without a fight.

Instinct took over. Turning, she picked up a metal candelabra from the nightstand and threw it at his head. He deflected it with a wave of his arm, the projectile clanging off his armor harmlessly before clattering to the ground.

The smile on his face was as cruel as it was joyful. "I see. Good. I was hoping to get a chance to spar with you one last time."

Oh, no. *Oooh, shit.*

"Come." He turned on his heel and stormed from the room, throwing the door open and disappearing out into the corridor.

She shouldn't follow him.

She shouldn't. She should sit right down. She wasn't feeling well, still, and he was about to kick the shit out of her—and then do *other* things to her. Clearly.

But she was mad. And she wanted him desperately. And she loved him.

So she did the stupid thing.

And followed.

* * *

Mordred had never wanted someone so desperately in his life as he watched Gwendolyn the mortal step into the courtyard where he had attempted to train her to fight with a sword. Finally, their lessons would end the way he had wanted them to from the very beginning—the thoughts that had twisted in his head as she had struggled to keep her footing.

Images of her on her knees, lips parted around his length, paying the price for her folly.

On her back in the sand, spread wide, begging him for mercy and for more.

Bent like an animal as he took her for all he was worth.

The woman he loved.

The woman he didn't trust.

The woman he *needed.*

She was shaking, her cheeks flushed, doing her best to hide

her equal desire as she stepped into the sand circle. She was glowering at him like an angry cat. Feisty but small. *She will use those claws of hers if you are not careful. Even a kitten can take out an eye.*

He summoned two swords and tossed one into the sand in front of her before vanishing his armor. It would make it more of a fair fight, and, truth be told, he wanted to feel those nails of hers digging into his skin.

"You may surrender at any point, and I will stop." He spun the blade idly in his hand, watching the moonlight glint off the steel.

"Fuck you." She picked up the sword, and did her best to take a defensive stance, just as he had taught her. "If you think I'm going to just let you—"

"Good." He jumped at her, swinging the blade. She dodged the strike, ducking under his arm. She was moving slower than usual—she was still recovering. But he gave her the time to escape the blow, even if he could have easily swept her legs out and ended their fight then and there.

No, this was about the dance.

This was about their frustrations.

This was about their desire.

Bless her heart, she even tried to attack him, swinging the blade with a furious shout as she sought to open a gash in his chest. He stepped out of range of her swipe. He laughed, a sound that only infuriated her more.

He let her slash for him a few more times before he kicked out one of her feet, sending her staggering, trying to catch her balance. "You will kneel for me. Defiant as it might be. I do hope you glare at me as you are now. I do love you when you are so pointlessly angry." He could not help but grin.

"You're such an egotistical piece of *shit!*" She ran at him, adrenaline clearly fueling her. He let her knock his blade from his hand—the look of shock on her face his opportunity.

He snatched her wrist, twisting it, forcing her own blade from her hand with a yelp before pulling her arm behind her back. With his other arm, he caught her throat in the crook of his elbow and pulled her to his chest, facing away from him. She squeaked and struggled.

"You used me. Manipulated me. Dared to twist my affection for you to benefit my sworn enemy. A creature that you sided with against *me*. I have every entitlement to an... apology." He leaned his head closer to her ear, scraping his teeth along the skin. She shuddered in his grasp. "If my choice for your method does not please you, by all means... say so. Tell me to stop, and I will stop."

She shut her eyes, her body still quaking in his grasp. By the Ancients, she was an intoxicating drug. "Fuck you, Mordred."

"That is, I believe, entirely the plan," he whispered, before chuckling quietly. "Kneel."

"No."

"*Good.*" He tossed her forward, sending her staggering.

She scooped up her fallen sword and turned to face him, blade at the ready.

He did not bother to retrieve his. He would do this with his bare hands. He stepped toward her. "I want you to fight me. I want to feel you kick me. Struggle. Punch and claw. I want you to scream out your wrath, your anger—for I plan to eke out mine on you in return."

Her cheeks turned a deeper shade of pink as she reacted to his words, her eyes going wide. But still, she remained defiant, even if she was grasping her sword now with trembling hands.

Beautiful. So beautiful.

She hollered in rage and ran at him, making what she realized might be her last desperate attempt. She wanted this to be a brawl, and he would give her a brawl. He stepped aside, and she pivoted—correctly predicting his move. He blinked in surprise, looking down at his shirt, at the cut on his arm that was slowly turning red before oozing with blood.

Mordred laughed. "You *have* learned."

Her eyes were wide now for another reason—fear. Did she still not understand that he could no more hurt her than he could tear the sun from the sky? "You—I'm sorry—I didn't mean —I didn't think I'd actually hit—"

"I am impressed. Forgive me for having treated you gently thus far." He took a step back and held his arms out at his side. "I will give you one more attempt to strike me down, Gwendolyn. And then you *will* apologize to me."

She hesitated for a moment, her gaze flicking between his eyes, searching for something. It was clear that she understood what was about to happen. That this was her last chance to drop the blade and walk away. To tell him that she did not wish to *apologize* to him in the fashion he was demanding.

It was her choice.

She dove at him with the blade.

And Mordred could not have been happier.

* * *

It was a lot harder to fight when Gwen was so violently turned on. Or turned on violently? She didn't know which. It didn't matter. She yelped as Mordred knocked the sword from her hand like it was a toothpick. He had been going easy on her— which was making her even more furious—and it was clear that now that she had drawn blood, the gloves were off.

He wanted to end it.

Well, it was clear he wanted to *start* it. Their "fight" had only just begun.

The Prince in Iron was terrifying, even in his black linen clothes and without his armor. It made his towering, muscular form no less intimidating. And even if he were just a normal human, he'd have outclassed her instantly.

It didn't come as a surprise when he fisted her hair in his hand and yanked backward, sending the stinging pain through her scalp.

It didn't come as a surprise as he nudged the back of her legs with his, sending her toppling to her knees.

He kept his hand fisted in her hair as he watched her, smiling in victory. And she did her best to glower up at him like she was trying to set him on fire with her mind.

"Unlace your dress," he murmured, his voice raspy. "I want to see your flesh as you lavish me with your sorrow over your actions."

"F—" She was about to tell him off again but broke off in a yelp as he clenched his fist tighter and tilted her head back. It didn't hurt. Not really. It did something else extremely dangerous to her instead. *I like this. No, I love this. I want him to wrestle me to the ground.*

God, she wanted it.

Needed it.

"I will tear it from you if you wish." Mordred began to undo his trousers—which was an extremely distracting sight. "And you can walk back to your quarters in shredded, stained clothes. I have sent the servants away, but... if you prefer to parade your shame to them, it can be arranged."

Gwen swallowed the rock in her throat. He'd do it. Letting out a wavering breath, she began to unlace the front of her dress. He drank in the sight of her, his gaze raking over her body like he hadn't ever seen it before. Or like he was trying to burn it into his memory.

When it was untied, she parted the panel in the front, revealing her breasts.

"More."

Another command that ran to the very core of her. She

shrugged the dress off her shoulders, letting the fabric pool at her waist.

"Good." He loosened the grip in her hair, just a little. "Now... apologize to me for your betrayal." When she punched him in the thigh as hard as she could, he chuckled. "Very well." He freed himself from his pants. She was in awe of the sight of him—she always was. The sheer girth of him. She wasn't allowed to admire him for long, however, before he pulled roughly on her hair.

When she gasped, it wasn't just air that filled her.

Mordred wasted no time in procuring his apology.

He grasped her head tight in his hand and began to pump himself into her, slow but unrelenting. His deep, guttural moan tangled with her own sound of bliss as he worked himself against her tongue.

She pressed her hands to his thighs, desperately trying to control the pace—but he wasn't having it.

"Good." He pulled on her hair again, causing her to wail, muffled against him. He pushed himself another half an inch deeper, threatening to gag her on his length. "I plan to make you take it all."

He had to be kidding.

Had to be.

"Such is how I wish you to make amends,' he snarled, grasping the back of her head with both hands, pulling her closer to him. "I suggest you relax as best you can."

Was he really trying to coach her through—

Her body rejected him, sending her coughing. He pulled away from her, allowing her to breathe. "Wait—" She coughed.

"You can and you will. Relax. Focus." He ran a thumb along her lower lip. "And breathe before you are unable to do so." His voice softened briefly, revealing the game for just the moment. "Punch my thigh if you need me to stop."

She tried to draw her head back as he pulled her forward

again. But this time, he didn't force her mouth open. This was her choice. It was always her choice.

She shot him a withering stare. "I really hate you sometimes."

He smiled in a devious victory. "Deep breath, firefly."

For once in her life—for survival reasons only—she did as he told her. She took a deep breath and did her best to focus on suppressing her reflex. And she opened her mouth.

And slowly, but surely, like the inevitable force of nature he was—he proved her right. He slipped farther and farther into her with each pull of her head onto him. It seemed impossible. Wholly impossible. But it might have only been a matter of minutes, breathing between each stroke as she was able before her nose touched his body.

It was the single most erotic moment of her life.

He moaned above her, a broken, almost euphoric sound. "Yes, my firefly—*ah*—" He relented, letting her breathe, if only for a second, before plunging back in, this time seemingly trying to find a way to bury himself even deeper.

It felt so good.

It had no right to.

But her head was reeling with the sheer bliss of it. She couldn't make a noise—didn't dare—but she had never felt anything like it in her life. He kept at it, slowly inching her off before pulling her back to him, again and again, until it was clear he might not be able to handle it anymore.

And this apparently wasn't the end of his plans for her.

In a blur of a moment, she found herself on her back in the sand of his sparring pit, her dress pulled off and discarded. He was over her, hands grasping her thighs and forcing them apart and her knees to her shoulders.

With a snarl, he rammed himself to the hilt in one stroke.

Her mind went white in ecstasy from that one movement. Already at the brink, the sudden sensation of being filled sent her toes curling and her body spasming as he wasted no time in eking out the rest of his anger on her.

And she couldn't stop begging him for more.

She didn't know how long it went on—time lost all meaning as he ravaged her. As he made sure that nobody would *ever* be able to hold a candle to him in the future.

When her body couldn't take it anymore and sent her into another frenetic crash of ecstasy, he was also pushed over the edge. He roared, slamming his body into hers, surging deep inside her. The heat of it sent her into another wave of bliss. Her head swam, and she swore she was going to black out.

After a moment, his weight shifted, letting her fill her aching lungs. Between ragged breaths, he murmured to her, "Apology... accepted."

"Fuck you," she muttered back, her eyes shut as she struggled to gather her wits.

He kissed her then. The tenderness in it shattered what was left of her already broken heart. It was a kiss filled with an emotion that she refused to believe was real, given the situation.

As quickly as it came, it was gone. He parted from her and sat back on his heels. His expression was once more as cold as the iron he embodied. "This changes nothing."

She knew what that meant. It meant she was still going home. She tried not to let the tears come back. She didn't regret what they'd just done—not in the slightest—and she hadn't gone into it thinking it'd change his mind. But it still hurt. "I don't mean anything to you, do I?"

"Yes. You are a traitor to me, and nothing more."

Meeting his cruel gaze, she straightened her shoulders and lifted her chin in defiance. "Someday, I hope you realize that all the betrayals in your life have one thing in common—*you*."

The harshness in his tone was the worst part about it all. "Get dressed. Sleep. You leave at dawn."

Yeah. Yeah, that hurt a lot.

Letting out a wavering breath, she did as she was told without a fuss. It wasn't until Mordred put her back into her room and shut the door behind her without a word—or even a kiss—that she finally let herself cry.

And she vowed it was the last time she'd cry because of him.

If this is what he wants?

Fine.

TWO

Mordred destroyed two pieces of furniture when he returned to his room, smashing one wooden chair and one end table against the wall. Once he had vented his anger, he let out a long, shuddering sigh. He, too, was on the verge of tears once more.

Because while Gwendolyn was so very wrong about what she meant to him, she was also so very right. And her words had cut deep.

Picking up some of the bits of wooden shards from the ground, he tossed the shattered furniture into the fireplace one piece at a time, watching the remains burn.

And could not help but picture himself atop a pyre.

Grinn was no easy foe. How could she not understand that Mordred had barely defeated him the first time in battle, and that she would likely be a casualty in the terrible war?

And that if she died, he would follow her to the grave?

It was inevitable that Mordred would be the ultimate cause behind her demise. It would just be a matter of time. Putting his head in his hands, he let the tears roll down his cheeks. He loved her. And to honor that love, he had to send her away.

She would go to her grave thinking that he despised her. That she was no different to him than one of his dogs.

Once more, Mordred seemed doomed to play the villain. To Gwendolyn, to Galahad, to Avalon, to everyone he cared about. It was his lot in life—forever to be despised for his actions. To be reviled for doing only what he could to protect them all.

A life with him would be short and painful for her. Grinn would not hesitate to kill her in front of his eyes, simply to cause Mordred pain. It would not be a quick death. Long ago, the demon had lost his mate and his love to the wrath of the elementals. Mordred knew that Grinn would not hesitate to cut pieces off Gwendolyn one by one and send them to him as trophies. As reminders of what had been done to his own love.

And yet, Mordred would be despised for sending Gwendolyn away by all those who had come to care for her as well— the unfinished guard, Maewenn, Galahad—who knows who else. They would label him as heartless, callous, and cruel.

Always the villain.

Always.

So be it. If that is what they wish me to be?

Who am I to deny them?

The hour was late, perhaps two or three in the morning. He knew he would not be able to sleep. His thoughts would not stop racing, tracing back through what would be his last interaction with the woman he loved.

The idea of never knowing if she was all right, never feeling a connection to her again, was too much for his selfish soul to allow. There was one way to keep them linked—or at least one way to try. He was unsure if it would work once Gwendolyn had returned home to Earth. He had never tested the connection in such a way.

But it was his only hope at keeping some part of her close to him. Or rather, some part of him close to her.

Entering her chambers like a thief in the night, he found her asleep in bed. Eod was curled up beside her, and the long-legged dog lifted his head in curiosity at the entrance of his master. Mordred walked up to the edge of the bed and stroked the dog's head as he settled down on the edge of the mattress beside Gwen, careful not to wake her.

Touching his hand to his chest, he summoned a small piece of iron, pulling it from his own body. It resembled the Iron Crystal with the way it glowed at the seams with brilliant, opalescent magic. It was only about the size of a grape. She would not notice its existence—nor would he tell her it was there.

The same fashion of metal shard that kept his knights bound to him. But it was a different kind of will that he infused into the iron. A different command.

He placed it to the skin of her collarbone. The shard sank into her, disappearing into her form, finding somewhere unobtrusive to exist within her. While he could not rip his broken heart from his chest and send her home with it in a basket—it would be good enough. A piece of him would travel with her, wherever she went.

Now and forever.

Until the day she died.

On Earth.

Without him.

* * *

Morning came. Mordred, for the second time in recent memory, did not quite know what to do with himself. He sat there in his war room, staring down at the iron map of Avalon, doing his best to focus on his impending war against Grinn.

Instead, his mind would not stop wandering to Gwendolyn Wright. And how close he had been to confessing to her how he felt.

How much he loved her.

And that he had to send her away *because* of that love.

A polite but heavy knock on the doorjamb told him who was intruding into his thoughts. For once, he did not mind, although he was certain he was about to be scolded like a child. He shut his eyes wearily. "Enter, Galahad."

"What are these rumors I hear?" Galahad entered, his steps surprisingly light for a creature of his size. "You cannot be seriously considering returning her to Earth."

Mordred eyed the slash on his own arm where the young woman had managed to catch him with her blade. It was already healed, nothing more than a smear of dried blood. "She returns shortly. I have the skiff prepared."

The dreary sigh that left Galahad told Mordred all he needed to know of the Knight in Gold's opinion.

Well, he might as well finish digging his grave. "And you will be the one to send her back."

"Excuse me?" Galahad's disbelief was understandable. "*Why?*"

"Because if I look her in the eyes one more time"—he clenched his metal gauntlet into a fist—"I will lose my resolve." There was no point in hiding from Galahad what ached in his heart. The knight had known him too long—and shared too much of a similar pain. He would see it for what it was. "It must be done."

"You have yet to tell me why."

Mordred leaned back in his chair. The wood creaked under his movement. "I cannot risk her safety or mine. The demon knows what she means to me—and that means others shall as well. If they were given the chance to wield her against me, what do you think would happen? I would be forced to sacrifice her life or mine. I cannot risk either."

Galahad went silent for a long moment. That meant he was attempting to formulate an argument but could not. When that approach did not work, he clearly chose another. "And you are forcing me to do the deed *why* precisely?"

"Better she loathe me than love me. Better she return to Earth believing that our time together was of no consequence to me." He dug his claws into the armrest of the chair, knowing that he was marring the surface and not caring in the slightest. "Let her believe me to be the cruel tyrant I am to everyone else. It will set her free. I cannot stomach the idea of her tethering herself to a memory as her mortal years tick by."

Galahad walked to a table by the wall and, picking up a jug, poured himself a healthy-sized cup of wine. He downed it before pouring himself a second.

"I shall take that as a sign that you see my logic."

"I do." Galahad grimaced. "But at what cost? Love is a rare gift, especially for those like... well, you."

"I am quite aware." Mordred propped his elbows on the metal table and stared down at the metal map once more, attempting to will the knowledge of Grinn's location into his mind. "What would you have me do? What choice would you make? I cannot hunt the demon and leave her here. The keep is not secure enough—traitors are everywhere. I cannot take her with me, it is too dangerous. I cannot set her free upon Avalon."

Galahad's shoulders slumped. "I do not have a suggestion. Only that I would not give her up."

"You have always sought to lay your sword down for your morality. I am well aware." Mordred reached for his goblet of wine—another old friend—and sipped it. "Pardon me if I do not wish to suffer such a tragic and melodramatic death."

"I am simply stating a fact. I do not think my heart could survive the loss. With Zoe, and the Iron Crystal, I always held onto hope that I might see her again. But to return her to Earth is ensuring that is no longer a possibility." Galahad poured himself a third cup of wine.

Mordred would be concerned if he had not seen the fae put

down an entire cask of wine in a sitting and be hardly the worse for wear. "I spoke naught of the survival of my heart. It goes with her." He turned his attention back to the map of Avalon. "This shall be my last stand. I have lost my desire to fight for a land that despises me."

Galahad watched him, the wrinkles at the edges of his eyes creasing deeper than usual. Mordred had no concept of how old the Knight in Gold was. He had been an elder fae when he had found Arthur and his ragtag group of mortals. And fae, by Mordred's knowledge, hardly aged at all—if at all. The man might be as old as humanity itself.

And yet he looked up on Mordred with... empathy. Sadness. *Pity*.

Some of him was thankful for it.

But most of him despised it. Mordred stood from the table and headed for the door. "I am tired. You shall see her home." After a pause, he added, "Tell her she can take the dog with her." He did not wait for Galahad to reply.

There was no point.

* * *

It was just as the sun was starting to peek over the horizon that Gwen sat down at the small desk in her room, picked up the quill pen there, and wrote Mordred a letter. There was no way she would be able to form the right words to him on the cusp of going home.

She didn't know how she was meant to get back home. Maybe it was a portal. Maybe it was giant eagles—honestly, it didn't matter.

This was farewell.

And even if she didn't have the nerve to tell him face to face how she felt, she knew that if she didn't tell him, she'd never forgive herself for as long as she lived.

Eod, sensing her dismay, was sitting at her side with his giant, heavy head plonked on her lap, those big eyes watching her with a look of innocent concern. She petted his head as she wrote. Quill pens were annoying, and she left little blots of ink all over the page, but she managed to figure it out and still make the letter legible. She noticed pretty quickly that there was a powder she could shake onto the page and then shake back off that took care of all the excess ink. And she had a lot of excess ink.

All in all, it was an awkward and messy process. No wonder ballpoint pens were invented.

After making sure the ink wasn't going to smear all over the place, she folded it up and added "To Mordred" on the outside of it before using the fancy wax sealer to hold it shut. How cute. She'd never got to use one of those before.

Her mind was focusing on every little thing. Every small action. It was like she was about to go in for surgery—or for execution. In an hour, her life would change drastically again, and she would never see her friends or the man she loved, ever again.

It took every ounce of willpower she had not to burst into tears. So, she latched onto the little things. Getting dressed. Brushing her hair. She decided she was going to steal the small hand mirror that was in the room as a memento. She'd have the dog as proof of her visit, but animals... weren't permanent, no matter how much she wished they were. Tucking the ornate hand mirror into the back of her dress, she sat on the edge of the bed and petted Eod until there was a quiet knock on her door.

"Come in."

It was Galahad. He had to duck under the jamb to enter the room. He was dressed in his full golden armor, his white cape draping elegantly down his back. He carried his helm underneath his arm. There was a grim and sad expression on his wizened features.

Letting out a breath, she stood, feeling like she was walking to the gallows.

"It is time," Galahad said simply, standing aside to gesture to the door.

Part of her was glad that the Knight in Gold was going to be there. She walked up to him and hugged him. "Thank you. For being a good friend."

He returned the gesture. "My soul weeps at your departure, Lady Gwendolyn."

Lady Gwendolyn. *Princess* Gwendolyn. But pretty soon? She'd just be Gwen Wright. Lost and returned home with a lot of explaining to do. Taking in a deep breath, she let it out in a wavering, shaky exhale. "Let's get this over with."

"Of course."

Eod walked up to Galahad, his tail swishing hopefully. He licked the knight's hand, as if to ask, "*Galahad make better?*"

No, Galahad no make better.

"Mordred has given you a mighty task, Eod. He has declared you the guardian of Lady Gwendolyn upon her journey." The enormous knight knelt to pet the dog before placing a kiss to the top of the animal's head. "She is your responsibility now. You are her knight and her protector."

Sniffling, Gwen stared up at the ceiling in hopes of making gravity work to her benefit. "Don't make me cry, man."

"Forgive me." He stood, his expression somehow even more grim than before. "Come. The skiff awaits."

Ah. It was a boat. Great. She nodded and followed him from the room. He led her down a flight of stairs that seemed to go on forever. She realized it was taking her through the cliffside to the rocky shore below the keep. When they finally emerged from the darkness, she had to blink and squint in the sunlight.

Pulled onto the rocks was a boat with an ornately carved wooden dragon's head as a mast. It wasn't very big, but then again, it didn't really need to be. Maewenn, the metal cook, was standing at the shore, her hands clutched in front of her. Tim, the broken but adorable iron soldier was there as well, staring aimlessly at the boat.

But someone who was missing was Mordred.

Her shoulders fell. Looking up at Galahad, she didn't need to ask her question for the Knight in Gold to understand.

"He opted not to see you off."

Cringing, Gwen turned to look up at the keep, and shouted at it. At him. "You fucking *coward!*" She grimaced, deciding she really was done crying over him. Was that how he really felt? Did she mean so little to him that he couldn't even say goodbye? Fine. Fine! Whatever. "You're such an asshole!" she screamed up at the keep, knowing he likely couldn't hear her. "If this is what you want? Sure! Fuck you!"

Cracking her neck from side to side, she threw up her hands. If that really was how Mordred felt, then that made things simpler. Taking her letter out from the fold of her dress, she held it out to Galahad. "Give this to him. I wanted to give it to him personally, but the rusted shitstain apparently couldn't be bothered."

Galahad took the letter and bowed his head. "It shall be done."

Maewenn let out a sob and rushed over to hug her. "I told that idiot—I told him—"

"I know, Mae. I know." She hugged the cook. "It's okay. This is probably for the best." It wasn't, but that was what she was supposed to say, right? "If this is how he wants it, then fuck him."

"I—I made you a basket of snacks for the journey—just in case." The cook rushed over to the rock where she had placed a wicker basket. It was filled with meat pies, cheese, bread, vegetables, and fruit. Gwen also saw a bottle, one she hoped was water and not vodka. That was all she would need—retching overboard.

Eod started sniffing the basket, his tail wagging. As long as there was food, he was happy.

Smiling through the tears that were threatening to overtake her, Gwen hugged Maewenn again. "Thank you. Thank you for everything. Thank you for being such a wonderful friend."

Maewenn was crying—tearlessly, as she was made of metal —too much to speak. She simply hugged Gwen hard enough that it hurt a little before finally stepping away.

Next was Tim. When Gwen walked up, the unfinished guard's shoulders slumped.

"Hey. It'll be okay. At least you have a name now, right, Tim?" She reached out and took the guard's hand. He squeezed hers gently. "Thanks for trying to help me so much."

He nodded slowly but didn't look at her. She let his hand go a moment later, put the basket of goodies into the skiff, and then went up to Galahad. Taking a deep breath, she held it for a moment before letting it out.

"Tell him..." She didn't know what to say. "Whatever. Just fucking whatever. It's all in the letter."

Galahad reached out and pulled her into an embrace, careful not to crush her against his golden plate armor. "I am so very sorry for how this has played out."

She hugged him back, though she couldn't reach her arms all the way around him. "Could I have done things differently?"

"I do not believe you could. You did your best and stayed true to yourself. And sometimes, that is all that we can take with us in the end. That we tried." He stroked a hand over her hair. "You are a kind-hearted soul, Gwendolyn Wright. You will live a long and happy life on Earth."

She sniffled. She wasn't so sure about either of those things. "I'm surprised Doc isn't here."

"He vanished yesterday. Said that Mordred had made 'the boring choice' and walked off into the woods." Galahad grunted. "Wizards."

She chuckled. That did sound like Doc. Oh, well. She supposed it was better that way. One less teary goodbye. "So—how does this work?" She looked back at the skiff.

"It will take you wherever it is commanded to go. I have been instructed to tell it to send you home." Galahad frowned. "When you are ready, please climb in."

There was no point in delaying the inevitable. With one last hug for each of the three of them in order, she climbed into the skiff. Eod joined her a second later, still eagerly nosing at the food, oblivious to the seriousness of the situation.

Sitting down on the bench in the center of the boat, she noticed there were no oars. It wasn't like she needed to row it if it was magic, she supposed. At least she wouldn't have to row her own ass home. That just sounded like adding insult to injury.

"This sucks."

"I know." Galahad reached out a hand and placed it atop the carved dragon's head. Its eyes flickered and came to life, glowing the same eerie whitish opal color as the rest of Mordred's creations. "Take her home."

It lurched, and the skiff shoved off the beach backward. It wasn't until Gwen was a foot away from the shore that it all sank in. This was goodbye. She was never going to see them again. Mordred was sending her away, and he didn't even have the balls to do it himself.

Maewenn was weeping on Tim's shoulder, the unfinished guard seemingly unsure of what to do with the hysterical cook. Galahad was watching her with the same, dreary, heartbroken expression.

A mist came from nowhere, quickly swallowing the boat. They were moving, she could tell by the ripples in the water next to her. But there were no waves. Nothing but calm waters as they sailed *somewhere*.

Home.

Whatever that meant.

* * *

Mordred watched from the top balcony as the skiff was swallowed up by the mist that had appeared to take Gwendolyn home. Back to where she belonged—back to where she would be safe from the mayhem and inevitable war. His inevitable war.

There had been no other choice.

Yet he still wondered if he should not throw himself from the balcony and end it all. Whether that would be less painful than what he had just done.

The mist dissipated. Mordred stood and watched, waiting for its return. Perhaps a half hour later, it did just that—the mist appearing magically, and the boat returning to the rocky shore. This time, it was empty, devoid of its passengers.

The deed was done.

Gwendolyn was gone.

It was until precisely that moment he had almost managed to fool himself into thinking this was all a terrible dream. But as the wooden vessel beached itself without her and Eod on board, the reality of what he had done sank in.

Lowering his head, he shut his eyes and allowed a tear to slip down his cheek. How long he stood there on his own, he did not know. But the sound of heavy steps behind him jarred him out of his dark thoughts.

It was Galahad. The Knight in Gold wordlessly produced a letter from his breastplate and handed it to Mordred.

He took it. The letter was addressed to him in simple, somewhat sloppy handwriting. It must be from Gwendolyn.

Galahad turned and left Mordred alone. But not before casting a disapproving, hateful, and mournful expression his way. Mordred deserved that. That, and more.

Once Galahad had gone, Mordred looked down at the letter in his hand. He was tempted to crumple it into a ball and let the wind have it—or perhaps to burn it. Whatever it contained would only make his agony worse. It was likely a diatribe, scolding him for being too cowardly to send her away personally.

Perhaps it was berating him, carefully outlining all his many failures as a tyrant of the realm. Explaining how he deserved whatever horrible fate befell him in the end. Resigning himself to whatever she had to say, he broke the wax seal with the end of his jagged pointer finger and opened the letter.

Whatever he had been expecting her to say, however much he had expected it to hurt, he had sorely underestimated its magnitude.

> *Dear Mordred,*
>
> *I'm sorry I didn't have the spine to tell you this in person. I guess I just couldn't handle your rejection on top of everything else. But I knew that if I left without ever telling you the truth, I wouldn't be able to live with myself.*
>
> *I know you'll brush this off as childish and I know I shouldn't feel this way, but I do. I will spend every day of the rest of my mortal life thinking about you.*
>
> *And I will spend every night dreaming of the time we spent together.*
>
> *I love you.*
>
> *Gwen*

What a wretched creature he had become.

To not see what was before him. To be so set on his righteous path as not to recognize—not to *believe*—

Mordred folded the letter and tucked it away. Though he was once more tempted to destroy it, he opted to keep it instead so that he might read it a hundred thousand times.

He had made a terrible mistake.

But like all his errors in judgment... it was too late to change.

Gwendolyn was gone.

And Mordred was alone.

Now, and forever.

THREE

"I wonder how exactly this thing plans to take me 'home' to a landlocked state." She petted Eod, scratching the fur at his shoulders. At least she wasn't alone. "Maybe I'll wind up in Mr. Foster's swimming pool." She chuckled at the mental image of the skiff just appearing out of nowhere like that. It at least made for a funny scenario, even if she was trying to keep from crying again.

Eod tilted his head to look at her upside down, his tongue hanging out of his mouth, doing his best derp routine to cheer her up. And damn it, it was working. She might have had to say goodbye to Avalon, but at least she got to keep the dog.

How exactly she was going to explain this all to her parents, she had no idea. But hey—at least her panic issue seemed to have calmed down a bit. Well, she hoped it'd stay calmed down, anyway. She wasn't sure if it was the magic of Avalon that had cured her panic attacks. In a few hours, she'd have the answer to that question.

Gwen watched as the mist parted, the sunlight peeking back through the haze. She could see a sandy shore ahead of her —definitely nothing that Kansas owned. Great, maybe it was just going to drop her randomly somewhere on Earth with no care of where she wound up exactly.

That meant she was going to have a lot of super-awkward conversations with cops. Had she been abducted? Sure, *kind of*, but not in the way they would probably assume. Letting out a huff, she braced herself for also explaining why she was in some weird medieval dress. Everybody was going to assume it was some weird sex thing.

Didn't you know, guys? Medieval abduction orgies are all the rage right now. Think Eyes Wide Shut, *but with more typhus.*

The idea of it made her snicker again. At least she could laugh at her terrible situation—and laughing was better than crying. Hugging Eod again, she let out a long sigh. "Okay, buddy. Ready to go? My dad is going to love you. My mom'll be horrified at first but then won't stop sneaking you table scraps." She was dead set on trying to find the bright side of the situation.

Somehow. Some way. She had to cheer up.

The trees didn't look like anything Kansas had to offer either, and it was far too hilly to be home. That meant she had probably been dropped somewhere in New England or maybe Virginia. She hadn't been to either place in person, but that was just her best guess.

As soon as she'd hopped out of the skiff with the basket, Eod jumped out and instantly began happily splashing about in the water. That was, until he caught sight of something just by the edge of the woods. He barked, tail wagging, and ran up to whatever it was.

Not whatever.

Whoever.

Gwen stopped on the sand, staring at what she saw in front of her.

Nope, she definitely wasn't in Kansas.

Hell, something told her she definitely wasn't on Earth.

Now she was *super* confused.

Eod was licking the face of Doc the mad wizard, who was sitting on the sand with his legs stretched out in front of him. A pair of dark tinted sunglasses sat perched on his face.

"Good to see you too, friend." He laughed and patted the dog.

Walking up to him, she stared. "The *fuck?*"

Doc reached for the basket of food without responding. She let him take it, too perplexed to do otherwise. She sat down next to him and stared out at the ocean, watching the skiff sail itself back into the mist that reappeared from nowhere.

She tried to make sense of what was happening as the mad sorcerer started rooting through the goodies. He uncorked the bottle of wine first, which didn't come as a surprise to her.

Furrowing her brow, it finally clicked. "Galahad told the boat to take me home."

"That he did." He handed her a clay mug filled with wine.

"Isn't it, like... still morning?" That didn't stop her from taking it.

"It's afternoon in some reality, right?" He snickered and shoved a hunk of bread into his mouth before ripping off another small piece and giving to Eod.

Letting out a sigh, she sipped from the mug. Whatever. "Also, where the hell did you get sunglasses?"

"Where the hell do *you* get sunglasses?"

She wasn't sure in what fucked-up reality that sentence made any sense at all, but she let it slide. No wonder everybody kept warning her about trying to figure out the wizard. She reached for the cheese, deciding that if she was going to start her day drinking at ass early in the morning, she shouldn't do it on an empty stomach. "Now what do I do?"

"Don't know. I'm just here to watch. It's not my place to change things."

"Don't you change things all the time? Just being here is changing things."

"No, it's speeding things up. There's a difference between *skipping ahead* and *changing course*." He waved his own mug of wine as if he were lecturing to a class. "Think about it—if I wasn't here to confirm that you were still on Avalon and Galahad used a wonderfully un-specific turn of phrase to roll the dice and hope that the magic of the isle knew where you belonged better than Mordred does, you'd be wandering around the woods right now thinking you were in Maine or some shit. Right until you met some sort of magical creature and then you'd figure it out on your own." He shrugged. "I've been bored out of my mind since the battle. So we're skipping that section and jumping ahead. But I'm not altering the course of anything."

Rubbing her forehead, she decided that Doc was going to give her a headache. "Sure. Whatever. I guess that makes sense."

Eod had decided that digging a hole in the damp sand was way more entertaining than begging for scraps at the moment, as he was currently half a foot deep and wagging like a maniac.

She was still on Avalon.

She was "home."

Home. What a funny word. For the longest time, she had known what it meant. A farmhouse in Kansas, with her mom, dad, their farm animals, and one crochety old stray cat. It had been her friends, her school—and a complete lack of a future.

Then all this happened. Avalon. Fire powers. New friends. And Mordred, the man she loved. The man who had tried to send her away. The island wanted her here. But why? What *for*?

But now she really, really didn't know what to do. Going back to Mordred meant that he'd probably try to send her away again with far more specific instructions that time. She was human—*aka fragile*—and the world was filled with elementals and magical monsters that would probably try to eat her face.

Then there was the fast-approaching war between Grinn and Mordred. One that would guarantee that either or both were going to die. She was pissed at Grinn for what he had done, but she also couldn't say that she was entirely surprised. It's not like the demon had been subtle about his mission to separate them and regain his power. He'd only done exactly what he had said he was going to do.

She didn't want Grinn to die, even if he was a massive asshole. And she certainly didn't want Mordred to die.

"I have to find a way to stop the war."

Doc snorted as if to say "Good luck with that." He topped off his mug of wine and shoved a hunk of cheese into his face.

But that wasn't exactly how she should start things off. She needed a way to defend herself. Figuring out how not to get herself killed was an important first step before thrusting herself into the middle of a fight to the death between two veritable demigods who hated each other.

Gwen twisted to face Doc. "Can you teach me to use magic?"

"Oh, boy." He scratched his head. "Fuck. That's how you want to do this? I gave that option super-low odds."

"I can't walk around here with a target painted on my back. Half this place probably wants me dead just for fun, and the other half would probably want to use me to hurt Mordred—Grinn included." She shook her head. "I need some way to protect myself."

Eod barked.

Yeah, she was starting to really suspect he could understand more English than he let on. She chuckled. "I know, hon—but you're just one dog. And if anything happened to you—" She didn't want to even think about it. It'd get her crying again.

Eod just wagged his tail slowly, and then went back to digging in the sand.

Doc sighed hard and lay back on the beach, staring up at the sky. "You want to learn to tap into Avalon's magic? Do you realize that's like asking to lick an electrical transformer? You're asking me to plug you into something that might kill you. Or worse, you might wind up like me."

"Bonkers and alcoholic?"

"More or less."

"Well, I'm shit with a sword."

Doc snickered. "Yeah, you are."

She shrugged. "I might not be any better with magic, but it's worth a try. Either that or I'll get eaten by some weird frog-eyeball-shrub-thing."

"They're harmless unless you're a bird or a bug. But I get your point." He stretched his arms out and let out a long, heavy sigh. "Learning magic isn't like snapping your fingers. It doesn't just happen."

"I don't know if I'll have much time to practice. I don't think Mordred or Grinn are going to wait around for long before they try to murder each other. I just don't think I have any other choice. Option one—I try to stop Mordred and Grinn without anything to back me up. Option two—I try to learn some magic to help me." She sipped the wine.

Eod had found a clam in the sand and was pawing at it curiously. When he picked it up in his mouth, it must have moved or squirted water at him, as he dropped it immediately and yelped. He jumped back a few feet before deciding that the clam needed to be barked at for its transgression.

Doc sighed. "It's risky, Gwen."

Gazing out at the ocean, she took a moment to think it through. "Avalon wants me here. It thinks this is my home. I have to try to save it—from both of them."

With a grunt, he pushed himself up to his feet. "Well, then let's get going."

"Where?"

"To the heart of Avalon's magic." He walked off into the woods down a path without turning to look back at her.

"Which is where, exactly?" She arched an eyebrow.

"Does it matter?"

No, it probably didn't matter in the slightest. Shaking her head, she picked up the basket of food, dumped out the rest of her wine and, just like she had with Grinn not too long ago, followed a deranged madman into the woods of a magical island.

I'm starting to sense a pattern here.

And I'm also starting to take this personally.

Screw you, Avalon.

* * *

Mordred stood atop the rampart of his keep and watched as two of his knights set out upon their dragons. Bors and Percival, the Knight in Nickel and the Knight in Copper, had simple enough orders.

Find the demon, but do not engage.

For even two of his knights were no match against that bastard.

But no matter how simple the orders might have been in theory, he knew in practice they were still in danger. Not only from Grinn—but from the elementals of the isle.

How many more of his knights would he lose in the coming fray? How many more would be reduced to ashes? How much else would he have to lose in the end?

Shutting his eyes, he lowered his head and braced himself for what was to come. It was time. Turning from the rampart, he headed back into his keep, his thoughts growing dark as he walked down the long stairs that led to the chambers beneath his home.

On his deathbed, Arthur had made Mordred swear to protect the isle and all those who lived within it. He had entrusted him with Caliburn. He had entrusted him with his knights.

Lancelot was dead by his hand.

Caliburn had been destroyed.

And the woman he had sacrificed it over was now far away from him—returned to Earth. They would never meet again. With her went his heart.

His love was gone. His blade was shattered. And his knights would likely soon join their fallen comrade, one way or another.

There was a deep grief that ran through him, that cut to his soul like a knife.

But there was also a strange sense of freedom in it all.

With a gesture, the enormous doors of the chamber that housed the Iron Crystal swung open, silent and ghostly despite their size.

And there, suspended from the chains that attached to the pillars, was his inevitability. Gazing up at it, it was dormant—the opalescent glow of contained magic was absent. The prison was empty.

For now.

If he was lucky—if the Ancients smiled upon him—it would remain that way. There would be no quarter for Grinn. There would be no second chance. But as for the others who would likely stand in his way? What of those who would obstruct his army's path to the demon?

He took in a deep breath and let it out slowly. Lifting his hand, he summoned all his strength. The chamber rumbled around him. Stones that had been placed some three hundred years ago began to crack and shift as he willed his creation to rise. To be free. He had put it to rest long ago—and he had hoped there it would remain.

But the Crystal was needed once more.

One by one, the stone pillars that suspended the Crystal split and fell, the blocks tumbling to the ground in a rain of rubble and rocks. Inside each, hidden away by Mordred's handiwork, were the legs of his most horrifying creation.

And from the walls itself, it emerged. Twisted and cruel, like a vision from a nightmare, the spider-like monstrosity freed itself from the stone of the walls. From its rib cage hung the Crystal, suspended there between jagged metal bones like a corrupted heart.

The sound of metal screeching on metal was its greeting to him as a dozen, glowing, opalescent eyes flickered to life and it awoke from its slumber and fixed on him.

It awaited its orders.

As it always had.

Mordred's jaw ticked. "It is time."

The amalgam turned, its long, pointed legs making quick work of the far wall of the chamber. It was the outside wall of the cliff, the stones placed there to block the room from the outside, closed off for so many centuries.

But it knocked them loose, the sunlight streaming into the room for the first time since its creation—breaking free of its resting place. Its *lair*. Without a moment's hesitation, the iron arachnid climbed free. It would scale the surface without a problem. He could hear more crumbling stone as his creation lumbered its way to the field where his army awaited.

How he had hoped to never raise his creation from its slumber.

How he had hoped it would remain there for the rest of time.

But like his resting army, there had been no guarantee of permanent victory.

Cracking his neck from one side to the other, he turned from the desolate chamber that stood in ruins, and knew that this time, there would likely be no returning to that place. The odds were likely that he would fail in his mission. And with him, would go the Crystal.

For the first time in centuries, Mordred was tired. Tired of the cycle. Of standing forever vigilant in the name of upholding his vow. He had lost so very much—and he knew more would be taken from him before all was said and done.

All in the name of protecting a people who despised and feared him.

Perhaps it would be for the best if this was his last stand.

For Mordred had nothing left to lose.

* * *

Doc and Gwen walked along the path through the woods in Avalon like it was just a normal late summer day and they were out walking the dog. Eod was crashing through the underbrush, occasionally pouncing on shrubs in an attempt to spook out rodents. Fortunately for the rodents, he was slow.

The path took them along the edge of a gorge, with a rushing river down at the bottom of it. The rapids created a white foam against the rocks. When one of the rocks moved, Gwen realized it was actually a giant turtle. Made out of rock.

As frustrated as she was with the island for jerking her around so much, she had to admit it was pretty damn cool.

They walked along in silence for a while longer before she had to ask a question. "So..." Gwen started.

"I'm not going to tell you what's going to happen." Doc shook his head.

"For once, I wasn't going to ask."

"Color me shocked!" He placed his hand on his chest in mock surprise.

She rolled her eyes.

"Anyway, what were you going to ask?" Doc grinned.

"I guess I'm just kind of confused. Not like that's anything new." She ran her hands through her hair. "But why does Avalon think this is my home now?"

"Because it decides who it wants to keep, in the end. It isn't sentient—not really—but there's a will to it all the same. Some people believe that this island was formed from the dreams of ancient gods. That there are *things* that exist between worlds, that are made of the void itself. Of darkness and emptiness. But that from time to time, they dream of happier things—of life." He gestured to the forest on either side of them. They had found a path leading through the woods, and Gwen had just been content to follow wherever Doc wanted to go. It wasn't like she knew where she was supposed to be going.

"I guess that makes sense. As much sense as anything makes around here." Frowning, she looked up at the sky. It was afternoon, now, and she wondered how long they'd be walking before they came across someone or something. And if they'd be friendly. The last few times she had bumped into the locals hadn't gone well, to put things mildly. "But why me?"

He went quiet for a moment as he thought over his response. "You've already been touched by the power of the island. Even if your elemental powers were borrowed, they were still yours for that time. It doesn't like to let go of the people it collects." He ran a hand over his head, ruffling his scruffy hair. "It's why you stand a decent chance at tapping into its magic. You've already been connected once."

That gave her some hope, small as it might be. Maybe she could become some kind of badass sorceress. Then, once she could handle herself, she'd kick in Mordred's door and tell him exactly how much of an asshole he had been.

The thought of Mordred ruined her mood. Her heart ached. She missed him—she wished—she just *wished*. Wished that he hadn't sent her away. Wished that she had been brave enough to tell him how she felt to his face.

Wished that he loved her back.

God, she loved him. She wanted to stay with him, to stay by his side. As much as she missed her parents, she didn't *want* to be without him.

But if he felt the same way, he wouldn't have tried to send her back to Earth. No, he probably believed that she was back in Kansas with Eod and that they'd never see each other again. Which seemed to be what he wanted.

And that *hurt*.

As if sensing her line of thought, Doc patted her on the shoulder. "There, there."

"Seriously?"

"What?"

"That's the best you've got?" She arched an eyebrow at him.

"Look—" He pointed a finger at her face. "It's not my job to do *feelings*. I don't do the squishy whatever-the-fuck you idiots have going on."

"What *is* your job, anyway?" Eod bounced up to her with a stick in his mouth, wagging his tail happily. She pulled it from his mouth and lobbed it as hard as she could up the path, sending him tearing after it.

"I don't know." Doc barked a laugh. "But it ain't that."

Great. She was surrounded by sociopaths and emotionally stunted man-children. Rubbing a hand over her face, she sighed. "How do I learn magic?"

"Don't know."

"What?" She blinked. "I thought you said you could teach me."

"Don't look at me like that. I never technically agreed to help you with magic." He planted his hands on his hips.

"But—"

"I never said *yes*. Technically. You just inferred a yes. And that's on you." When her shoulders slumped, he grumbled, "Look. Okay. Fine. I'll try to help you, but here's the thing—I don't know how you'll tap into it. It's different for everybody. You have to figure out how to wield it on your own, then I'll help you learn to control it. Before it melts your face."

"Melts my—seriously?" She grimaced. That didn't sound like fun in the slightest. Of all the ways to go, face-melting seemed pretty terrible. Or at least it looked like it in the movies.

"Only partially joking. I once watched someone immolate from the inside out." He made a *bleh* noise. "And it somehow smells worse that way."

"That was way more info than I needed, thanks."

Eod came out of the woods carrying a stick that was far too large for him, looking pleased as punch, his tail wagging behind him.

"Just trying to give you an idea of what you're signing yourself up for. We're going to a place where the magic is stronger, to give you a better chance of digging into it. But first, a stop at an inn. I need a fucking nap." Doc's tone made it sound like this was all perfectly normal.

Not that they were going to try to teach her how to use magic that may or may not melt her face off and/or set her on fire from the inside out. "If you see me melting in the near future, would you warn me?"

Eod dropped the enormous stick to rush ahead and start snuffling underneath a tree that had fallen across the path.

Doc hopped over it without a problem and didn't even look back to offer her a hand. "No. Sorry. Can't."

She rolled her eyes again and hopped over the tree. "Can't, or won't?"

He paused as he thought it over. "Won't. I mean, I could tell you everything I know—but then I'd be changing things, wouldn't I?"

"Again, then, I don't know what you're supposed to be

doing." She really wanted to shake the wizard sometimes, but she supposed it was much better than being alone when it came down to it. She'd prefer to have someone to talk to than nobody at all.

"If you do happen to figure it out, let me know." He kicked a pebble up the dirt road, sending it skittering along. "It's not like I asked to be this way. Or if I did, I clearly didn't understand what I was in for. Not remembering who I am—where I came from—what my damn name is. But knowing *literally* everything else."

It did sound more than a little miserable. "It must get very lonely."

"It can." He let out a breath and stared up at the sunny sky. "But then, I can distract myself by focusing in on other people's lives. I can tell myself a billion stories through the eyes of others. It's easy to pass the time when you have that many stations to choose from. It's like having a cable subscription with like four million channels." He paused. "And sometimes there's still nothing good on."

She snorted. "How do you know about modern things? Can you see Earth?"

"Ish. More or less. Sometimes. It's... vague and weird. Think about it this way—Avalon and Earth aren't stuck together like soap bubbles. We're like planets in orbit. Sometimes we're closer together, sometimes we're farther apart. That's true for all the other worlds, not just Earth."

"Huh." She blinked.

"When we're closer, I can see through to the other side. I can reach through and grab small things too." That explained the sunglasses. He gestured up at the blue expanse through the cover of the trees. "Sometimes I can see sunlight, sometimes I can't."

"Can... do you know if my parents are okay?"

Doc went very quiet. She didn't know if it was because he was trying, or if he was preparing to lie to her. "No."

She decided she was happier probably not knowing if that was the truth or not, so left it alone. "If you ever get a glimpse, would you tell me if they're okay or not?"

"There's nothing you could do either way. Why do you want to know if they're not?" Doc shook his head. "Mortals. You seem to love to go from one tragedy to another, with no space in between."

"Some of us don't live forever. We have to make the time count."

"Hm." He tilted his head to the side slightly. "I suppose that's true. Fine. If I get a glimpse of your parents, I'll let you know if they're all right or not."

"Thanks." That was a comfort, even if she didn't know if she could trust him. He was the closest thing she had to a friend at the moment, and he was going to *potentially* teach her how to use magic, and/or be involved in her dying in spectacular fashion. "How long do we have to walk?"

"Eh, not too far. A day or so. Which is good, because there's nobody around to make me a horse that doesn't make my eyes water, and I don't want to fucking walk more than I need to." He made a face. "I hate walking."

She chuckled. "I guess I'm not super fond of it either, but at least Avalon is gorgeous. When it's not trying to kill me." She paused. "Which is like, every other day at this point." She scratched her side where the arrow had gone straight through her. The mental image of staring down at the tip of the arrow as it had stuck through her stomach made her shudder, though the villager who had shot the arrow in the first place had fared far worse than her. The wound had healed, but now and then she imagined it itching, which absolutely made it itch.

"Eh, if people don't know who you are, you're just any other normal villager. I don't think you'll have a problem with the locals. You had a target painted on your back when you were an elemental. Now, the forest critters—the monsters? Like the s'lei and the rest? Yeah, those you have to worry about." He peered off into the woods, as if checking for some of the monsters in question.

"How many species of monsters live in Avalon?"

"It's impossible to know. They come and go—appearing as if from a dream, and then disappearing just as quickly. I once had an enormous, spined, soul-eating rock golem disappear right before my very eyes because the island just decided it was bored with it." Doc scratched the back of his neck. "Which is probably for the best, since it was about to flatten me into pulp."

"Maybe the island did it to save you."

"It doesn't like me. I doubt that."

"Why doesn't it like you?"

"Couldn't tell you." He smiled at her and batted his eyes. "I'm just so *sweet* and *caring*. And not a deranged wiseass in the slightest."

Laughing, she shrugged. "You don't seem that bad to me. I mean about the deranged bit. You are a total wiseass."

"When you've seen as much life as I have, when your head is full of a million stories, you learn to rely on one thing to get by —snark." A beat. "Well, okay. And alcohol. And caffeine."

"And magic."

"Fine." He counted the items out on his hand. "Alcohol, caffeine, magic, and snark. But mostly the snark."

He might be a wiseass, and he might be insane, but Gwen couldn't help but laugh when she was around the sorcerer. Laugh and smile—and feel like there might just be a shimmer of hope that everything was going to wind up okay in the end. Maybe he *was* Merlin—guiding people through their adventures, helping keep them on the right path.

Or maybe he was just a crazy hobo who was plugged into the universe in a really fucked-up way. She supposed it really didn't matter in the end. He might not be the real Merlin—but he was her wizard all the same.

And she would be happy with that, even if it resulted in her having her face melted off.

If she didn't get her face melted off, she'd finally be able to stand toe-to-toe with Mordred and the other elementals. She could finally defend herself. And she was really, *really* looking forward to seeing Mordred again. And, also, chewing him out for trying to send her home.

Sounded like as good a plan as any.

* * *

Mordred climbed atop his dragon—he would never let himself call the beast *Tiny*, even if the dragon himself didn't seem to mind the name—and prepared for flight. His army was assembled; row after row of iron soldiers were poised to follow his every command.

The Iron Crystal, suspended from the rib cage of the skeletal arachnid monstrosity, stood on its seven, pointed legs, surrounded by his most elite guards. It could handle itself in a fight—it had proven that time and time again. But he would take no chances.

Galahad sat atop his golden steed at the head of the army, flanked by Gawain and Tristan. Mordred would take the strongest knights with him. Bors and Percival were still scouting. It left no one in charge of his keep—but there was nothing of value within it now.

Stopping Grinn was far more imperative than protecting his home. For everything was now on the line.

Clicking his tongue, his dragon beat his enormous wings and leaped into the air, taking flight. His army began to march.

The engine of war had begun.

FOUR

"Ew."

"I warned you."

Gwen stared down at the bowl of... she guessed it was supposed to be stew. It was vaguely potato-flavored water with a few scraps of vegetables floating around in it. To Doc's credit, he had in fact warned her that "dinner" at the little inn they had wound up finding was going to be gross.

And he was right.

The beer was almost as bad as the stew, but at least it was going to come with a buzz. It was also probably safer than the food. But beggars couldn't be choosers, and they had walked for hours through the woods before finding a place to stay for the night.

At least they had separate rooms.

And it wasn't sleeping outside in the drizzle that had over-taken the area about an hour before. Eod's scruples were far fewer than hers, and he was eager to gobble up whatever bits of food or bread she gave him. She'd feel worse for him, if he hadn't murdered a squirrel earlier that afternoon and eaten it before she could pull the remnants of the poor critter out of his mouth.

But the tavern was dry-ish, it was warm, and there was a bed for her to sleep in. Hopefully, it was better quality than the food.

"Remind me to compliment Maewenn if I ever see her again." She nudged a floating block of undercooked-yet-some-how-mushy potato around with her spoon.

"I'm sure you'll see her again." Doc had given up on the food and decided he was going to drink his dinner. He had purchased a bottle of hard alcohol from the innkeeper and was putting it down by himself. She opted not to partake. It smelled like paint thinner, and she didn't want to throw up what little she was putting into her stomach.

Her thoughts were still miles away as she stared down into her pathetic dinner. They were, namely, on one person in particular—Mordred.

He didn't know she was still on the island. And if he did, he'd likely try to round her up and send her away again. She had to lie low. As much as was possible, traveling with Doc. The mage seemed to have a reputation, and everybody in the small inn kept glancing at them nervously.

"How far away are we from wherever this super-magical place is?" She took a sip of the warm, flat beer. *Bleh.*

"Should be there by midday tomorrow." He shrugged. "Then we'll see how you do with Avalon's magic. It might not work, you know. You might not be able to tap into it. What then?"

"I don't know." She sighed. "Find Grinn and... ask him nicely not to torch the island." When Doc started to snicker, she joined him. "I know, I know. I'll just end up being barbeque."

"Eh, he wouldn't kill you. Not right away. He'd probably rather use you to torture Mordred." Doc sniffed dismissively. "Send him body parts in boxes, that kind of thing."

She went a little cold as she felt the blood drain out of her face. "You're... joking, right?"

The sorcerer's expression was flat as he sipped the alcohol out of the bottle. "Sure."

Shaking her head, she stared down at the bowl of food. "I guess I don't know what I was expecting. Of course he'd do that. He doesn't like me. He made that very clear."

"He doesn't like anybody, kid. It's not personal."

"I guess. I just figured—I don't know. It's stupid." Looking out the window, she watched as the gray sky grew slowly dimmer as the sun set behind the clouds. The panes were diamond-shaped and small, the waves in the glass distorting the scene beyond. The whole inn was made out of unpainted wood panels. Despite the lousy food, it had a wonderful smell of woodsmoke. It was cozy, if incredibly dark. But that was probably for the best, so she couldn't see how gross the floors probably really were.

"It's not stupid. You saved his life, took care of him for a decade—you thought he was your cat. It's not your fault you got attached to him and the feeling wasn't mutual. How were you supposed to know he was a deranged, megalomaniacal, murderous, sadistic demon, bent on the total destruction of the magical land of Avalon?" He smiled, as if the idea were the most benign thing in the world. "He was just a mean lil kitty cat."

"It explains why I could never get him to like me." She couldn't help but smile at Doc's way of phrasing things. It was sarcastic, but it was always funny. "I'm good with animals. But that cat always *hated* me."

"See? There you go, looking on the bright side. You weren't failing at winning over a cat, you just had a serial-killing despot hanging out in your barn." Doc wiped his nose with the back of his hand and then took another deep swig from the bottle. He had long since given up on the bowl of dubious food.

She let out a heavy sigh. "Yeah."

How did she keep winding up in this scenario? Missing Mordred, unable to actually be with him. Twice now, they had played this stupid game. Now that it was the third time, it was probably going to end very poorly. And this time, if she got shot with an arrow, she wouldn't be an elemental. She'd die.

"If it's any consolation, I'm sure he misses you too."

Looking up, she arched an eyebrow at him. "Mindreading, now?"

"No. Just obvious. You get that doleful woe-is-me look on your face." He wrinkled his nose.

"Right. Like you've never missed anybody before."

"I don't remember if I have or not. Which is why I want you to be absolutely sure about this whole 'learn magic' thing. Like I said, you might end up like me. And nobody wants that." He pointed at her. "Especially me."

"If I'm going to try to stop those two from murdering each other, I don't have any other options. I don't want to go home."

"You could just let Mordred kill Grinn. Or try. You haven't brought that choice up yet."

"I—" She blinked. He was right. It hadn't even been on her radar. "I don't want Grinn to die either."

"He hates you. Wants everybody dead. And you don't want him to die?"

"No. I don't." She knew she probably should, but it just felt wrong. "I don't agree with what he wants to do, but I know why he feels that way."

"What if he can't be convinced to stop? What if it's his death, or the death of everybody on the island?" Doc leaned his elbows on the table. "Which would you choose?"

Frowning, she fidgeted with the mug of beer, spinning it around in a circle. "It's not my choice to make."

"But what if it *was*?"

"That's the stupid trolley problem thing. Do you save one

life or save ten?" She rolled her eyes. "It never really comes down to that."

"You'd be surprised." He hummed. "Well, think about it. You might have to make that choice someday. Whelp, I'm going to go get drunk in my shitty inn room and pass out." And without any more ado, he got up and went up the stairs, swerving a little as he did.

Weirdo.

Shaking her head again, she fed Eod the last of the stale, dense bread that she'd been served, and chugged the rest of her warm, gross beer. Hopefully, it'd be enough to help her sleep. Heading up the stairs after the wizard, she found her own room and opened the door. The room was better than she was expecting, but then again, she hadn't been expecting much.

But the bed looked relatively clean and proved to be somewhat comfortable—not much better or worse than camping. Eod jumped up next to her, turned around a few times, and settled down with a heavy *harumph*.

"At least I've got you, puppy." She rolled onto her side and slung her arm over him, shutting her eyes and trying to pretend she was still in the keep. And that Mordred wasn't far away.

I can't keep pining over him like a loser when it's my fault that he sent me away. If I had just told him about Grinn... well, I'd probably be dead. But at least I wouldn't be lonely.

Sleep, luckily, caught up with her pretty fast. The fact that she had been walking literally all day and hadn't slept well the night before probably did the trick more than the gross beer.

But when it dawned on her that her dream wasn't exactly normal, she realized she probably wouldn't be getting any more rest this night than the one before. She was in the keep—but she was in a place she had never seen before. But she knew—just *knew*—that it wasn't an invention of her own mind.

This was Mordred's dream.

The walls were covered in armor. Bits and pieces, stacked

and hung from chains, everything she could imagine from every style she could possibly think of. There was so much to look at, so much detail, she couldn't take it all in. It was a sea of helms, breastplates, gauntlets—big, small, delicate, rough-hewn. Some looked decorative and never worn, some looked as though they had been through a thousand wars—dented and stained with what she hoped was rust and not blood.

Standing in the center of the room, his back to her, was Mordred. He held a large metal hammer in his hand and was smashing it down on an anvil with a loud *clang*, shaping whatever piece of armor he held in his other hand. He was shirtless, sweat beading on his back. A forge was raging against one wall, making the air sweltering and thick.

He took her breath away. She suspected he always would. The way the muscles of his back moved—the strength in him. The certainty of each movement.

Clang.

This wasn't her dream.

This was *his*.

She didn't know what to say. Didn't know what to do. More importantly, she didn't know how she felt. There was a part of her that hadn't believed she'd ever see him again. And if she did, he would likely be furious with her for still being on the island. But she loved him, more than she knew how to handle.

So, she just watched him, unsure and stuck between all her options. Should she scream at him for sending her away? *No, if he knows I'm still on the island, he'll come looking for me.* Tell him that she loved him? *What if he never read the letter, and just chucked it in the fire? How would he know, then?* Start crying? *I've had enough of that.*

So she did nothing at all.

Just watched.

Clang.

It seemed he felt her presence all the same. "And here you

are to haunt me." He didn't turn to face her, but reached for a rag in a bucket of water and wiped his face with it. He wasn't wearing his gauntlets. "I suppose it serves me right."

No words came to her. Nothing useful, anyway. "Why use a forge when you can just... make it?"

He huffed a quiet laugh. "That is something you would ask. It *is* you, then. And not a simple trick of my mind. I wondered if I would remain linked to you while you were on Earth."

That confirmed it—he thought she was on Earth. And she'd have to leave it that way.

"As for why? It helps me think. Sometimes, I need to use my hands. Then, once I can see it in my head, I can finish it using my elemental power." He still didn't turn to face her. He picked up the hammer again and brought it down. *Clang.* "It brings me some kind of solace when I am alone."

It was two more blows of the hammer before she got the nerve to say something salient. "You don't have to be alone."

Clang.

A pause. "Perhaps. But I always seem to find a way to manage it." He lifted the hammer and brought it down again. *Clang.*

She couldn't take it anymore. Walking up to him, she put her hand on his wrist. He was shirtless and glistening. He looked so damn good it was kind of ridiculous, honestly. She tried not to stare. Or laugh. Or do other terrible things. "You did this to yourself."

He watched her, those molten iron eyes flicking between hers. "Yes. There was no other way."

"Because you were afraid to let me in?"

"Because I was afraid to bury you!" He turned and threw the hammer at the wall. It impacted the stacks of armor, sending several of them smashing and clattering to the ground. He reeled around to face her, grabbing her by the shoulders. He yanked her forward, and before she could react, he kissed her—as searing as the fire in the forge.

God, he was so hot when he was angry.

When he broke the kiss, he pushed her away. She didn't blame him—he didn't know she was real.

"Why would you make me watch you die? Why would you wish to put me through that? Do you not understand—" He threaded his hands into his hair, fisting the iron-gray strands. "It would be the last thing I would ever do. And this world relies on me, Gwendolyn. This is larger than my own desires."

Numbly, she shook her head.

"You would die. Sooner rather than later, by my wager. Someone would use you against me—like that bastard Grinn already did. And how—how could I keep going?"

"Why didn't you tell me? Why didn't you tell me any of this?"

"I did not know how." He turned his back to her again. "And I knew you would fight to convince me. And if I allowed myself that temptation, I could not withstand it."

"Mordred..."

"I had to send you away—a mortal woman has no place by my side. I am too dangerous. Too despised. Better you hated me, believe that you meant nothing to me—than... than force me to bury you in a crypt." He leaned both hands on the anvil of the forge, as if it were the only thing holding him up. "Better my heart go alone to the grave than to see you beside it."

Apparently, she wasn't done with crying today. Even if these were dream tears. She walked up behind him, not caring about the sweat. She hugged him around the waist, resting her cheek against his back. She felt his muscles slacken.

She had nothing to say.

"I do not regret sending you away. I would do it a thousand times again. You are safe now, on Earth, with those who love you." He placed his hand over the back of hers. It was rare to feel the skin of his palm. It was rough, but not unpleasant. "And we can dream together until death takes me."

"I love you, Mordred."

He let out a small breath. "And I shall cherish those words you wrote to me, Gwendolyn Wright. For they are a kindness not once ever spoken in this world."

She wasn't sure when the dream faded away.

* * *

Gwen felt like she had been hit by a car by the time they hit the road again that morning. She had slept like garbage. Once she had woken up from her "dream," she had tossed and turned until the sun came up and Doc knocked on the door to her room.

She was pretty eager to get going, even if she did feel terrible.

Because now she had a *plan*.

It had come to her in the hour just before the sun rose. She knew what she needed to do. She just had no idea if it would actually work or not.

Mordred would refuse to be with her until she wasn't a squishy mortal anymore, right? Okay, so she had to become something other than a squishy mortal. Which was, of course, easier said than done. Doc was going to try to hook her into the magic of Avalon, but there was no telling what would actually come out of that.

Would it work at all?

Would it *do* anything to her?

Or would she just wind up with the power to rapid-boil pasta water or some shit?

There really was no way of knowing.

But Avalon was full of magical creatures. Maybe there was a vampire somewhere who would turn her—ew, on second thought, she quickly decided she'd make a terrible vampire. Blood made her kind of nauseous. Not to mention, she'd probably end up apologizing to every single person she bit.

"Is there a way to become an elemental again? Like, willingly?" she asked Doc as they walked along the road.

"No. Avalon chooses who it wants. Sorry." He tucked his hands into his robe pockets. "Why?"

"You know why. You know the answer to everything, don't you?"

"Yeah, but I like to play dumb sometimes. I like to hear what people say." He grinned cheekily at her.

Wiseass. She rolled her eyes. "I—I need to find a way for Mordred to accept me. But he'll just send me away again until I can prove to him that I can hold my own in a fight. That I won't get used by others to manipulate him."

"You realize that even if you became an elemental, you can still be outnumbered and lose, right?" He kicked a pebble down the road ahead of them. "Same if you learn how to use some magic."

"Well, you're immortal, right?"

"Unfortunately."

"Can't I just become a wizard like you? Only, not insane?"

"That's not up to you. That's up to the island. I'm taking you to the heart of Avalon, where you can—eh—talk is the wrong word. It doesn't *talk*. It simply *is*. The island of Avalon is alive." He gestured at the forest. "And I don't just mean trees and animals. It'll decide what to do with you."

"I still can't wrap my head around the fact that the island is sentient."

"It doesn't really think. It feels. Like the way tree roots are connected. It *exists*. And it does that on a level far, far above the tiny minds of creatures like us. But it can be communed with, pardon the hippie phrase."

She chuckled. "Great. I'm gonna go commune with the island."

"Yep. And you're going to ask for whatever it is you want. And it might grant it. Or it might not. It might pop you like a water balloon, for all I know." He made a face. "I hate it when it does that."

"So, on the table of options are"—she started counting on her fingers—"face melting, going insane, and popping like a water balloon."

He paused for a second to consider her list. "Imploding is also a possibility."

Groaning, she ran a hand down her face. "Imploding."

"Yeah. Like. Getting sucked into a singularity." Drawing air in through his teeth to mime a shrinking sound, he pulled his fingers together into a point. "Like getting crammed through a pinhole."

"You're really cheering me up, you know."

"Look, I'm just here to make sure you know the risk. I don't want to hear you whining at me when you start hallucinating invisible farm animals running around." He threw up his hands.

"Chances are, I'll implode or explode, and you won't have to deal with me whining, anyway."

"You seem like the haunting type. I don't want to deal with your ghost either." He huffed. "No sense of personal space, ghosts. It's like all manners go out the window the moment someone can walk through walls."

She blinked. Ghosts were real too? Yeah, that made sense. "Well, the fact of the matter is, I have two reasons to try to become 'special' again. One, to try to stop the war between Grinn and Mordred. And two, because then maybe Mordred won't kick me off the island for my own safety. I don't know if I have any other choice but to take the risk."

"I don't blame you for wanting to try. I just want to make sure you understand that it'll probably kill you in some horrific and gruesome manner." Doc smiled beatifically, which made his sentence all the more obnoxious.

She fought the urge to smack him and opted to just glare at him instead.

"What?" His smile didn't waver. "At least it'll probably be pretty painless. Except the face-melting bit."

"Please stop being helpful."

"Suit yourself." He sniffed dismissively. "I—" He froze in his tracks. "Ah, fuck."

"What?"

He gestured his hand. A modern concrete wall appeared in the middle of the path, blocking their way ahead of him. It was like he just teleported something from Earth and plopped it into the middle of the road.

She was about to ask why when something smashed into it from the other side. Someone had hurled a projectile at them. There was a creak of wood, and vines—thick and dark with thorns the size of Gwen's fingers—began to overgrow the wall, quickly covering the concrete.

Eod took a defensive stance in front of her, his ears flat and his hackles raised. He growled at the wall and the overgrowth.

"Hello, Lady Thorn," Doc said dryly. "Nice to see your temperament hasn't changed."

A woman emerged from the thorny vines on the side closest to them, literally forming *out* of them. Gwen couldn't help but stare as the thick bands of thorns smoothed and became a young woman that looked like she had been homeless for her entire life. Dirt caked her fingers and her bare feet, her toenails black from the mud. Her clothing was simple, tattered, and threadbare. Her hair was a tangled, matted mess, and her face was streaked with grime.

She looked *mean*.

And she was glaring right at Gwen.

Gwen took a step behind Doc, not knowing what she'd done to piss off the stranger.

"I've come for that one." Lady Thorn pointed at her. "And you are going to step aside, *madman*."

"Let me think." Doc scratched the back of his head. "No."

That was a relief at least. "Why are you after me?" Gwen frowned. "What did I do to you?"

"Nothing. But you are weak and an opportunity." The woman grinned. She was missing a few teeth, and the others were pointed in odd directions. "I saw what happened at the battle for the keep."

Mordred was right.

Gwen hated to admit it, but she hadn't even made it twenty-four hours on Avalon before somebody wanted to use her to hurt the Prince in Iron. She sighed, her shoulders slumping. She supposed she should apologize for being so angry with him.

If she ever got the chance.

"You aren't taking her anywhere, Thorn. You can find your own way to needle the prince without hurting her." Doc folded his arms across his chest. "Heh. Needle. Thorn. Whatever. Anyway—you won't touch her. It's because of her you're free of the Crystal in the first place. You should be grateful."

"And I am. But if you think I will let that bastard rampage through Avalon a second time, you do not know as much as you pretend to, mage." Thorn bared her teeth like a wild animal. "He has resurrected the Iron Crystal. His abominations are on the march with it as we speak."

"He seeks the demon, you know this. If you do not interfere, he'll leave you be." Doc sighed. "But you won't listen. You want revenge. And I won't let you use her to get it."

"It is not like you to interfere." Thorn tilted her head to the side, studying him as if he had done something interesting. "Why is she so important?"

"She isn't."

Gwen tried not to take that personally.

Doc continued. "Which is precisely why I can interfere right now."

"Then I will kill you and take her." Thorn took a step toward them. But she froze when the sky overhead quickly turned black, and a loud roll of thunder filled the air. She snarled at him.

"I would like to see you try." Doc had a tone in his voice that Gwen had never heard before. Cold. Hard. And *ancient*. "Do you wish to die here, Lady Thorn?"

The elemental hesitated before taking a step back. She spat on the ground in front of her. "You will regret this, you old fool."

The sky slowly began to lighten. "We'll see." Doc was back to his obnoxiously smartass self. "C'mon, Gwen. Let's go. She won't be a problem."

"Yeah. Sure." Gwen didn't believe him.

Lady Thorn stepped back into the overgrowth and vanished —the vines following a moment later. Eod walked up to where she had been standing, sniffed and growled.

Letting out a breath, Gwen followed after Doc as he simply walked around the concrete wall like all this was perfectly normal. "How many more people are going to be trying to murder me or use me for bait?"

"Oh, probably everybody we meet from now on." He smiled over his shoulder at her. "But I'll protect you for now."

Eod barked cheerfully as if saying, *Me too.* She really was concerned that the dog spoke English. Or at least understood the wizard more than he had any right to.

"For now?" She arched an eyebrow.

"You're still mortal. And easily broken. I'll do my best, but I can't stay with you forever."

She supposed that was fair. Wrapping her arms around herself, she tried not to think too hard about what had just happened. Now she had another concern to add to her list—that she really might pose a risk to Mordred. What if somebody captured her? Would he lay down his life to protect her? Could she ever live with herself if he did? Well, that last bit probably wasn't a concern. She wouldn't live long enough for that to really be an issue.

A dog, a madman, and a mortal with a target painted on her back.

Yeah, she was pretty much fucked.

* * *

Mordred rode on his horse along the road, hearing the thud of the giant arachnid behind his armored soldiers. The rhythmic clanking of metal as his forces marched in unison was a familiar sound. Familiar, but not entirely welcome. How many more centuries would he endure of warfare? How much longer before he could lay down his sword and live in peace?

Never.

Not until the grave.

His dream from the previous night lingered in his thoughts. It was a shadow made by the magic he placed inside of her— veiled and hardly as good as the waking world. But she was safe on Earth, and he could take solace in that.

While his thoughts lingered upon Gwendolyn, another issue was closer to mind. The demon's whereabouts were still unknown, despite his knights' incessant searching. He was lying low; likely licking his wounds and building his strength.

Mordred would have to flush him out.

But how? There was nothing in the world the demon desired, save for total death and destruction.

Death, destruction, and revenge.

There was the demon's weakness—hatred. And hatred made opponents passionate but sloppy. It had been Lancelot's downfall. Perhaps Mordred could use that to his advantage. To find some way to feign weakness to draw the monster out.

But *how?*

Shutting his eyes, he let his mind turn over and over on the thought, attempting to concoct a scheme. Nothing came to mind that he could see panning out. The demon was clever and would see through any rudimentary ruse. No, the danger to Mordred had to be real.

Letting out a ragged sigh, he realized what he needed to do to draw the demon out.

First, he would need to speak with Galahad.

For any matters involving Zoe the Gossamer Lady must be brought to his attention.

It was only fair, after all.

If this does not kill me, it may work.

And if it does kill me, this world is no longer my concern.

He laughed behind his helm. *Either way, I win.*

FIVE

Gwen's thoughts were a million miles away as she walked alongside Doc and went to the "heart of all of Avalon's magic" or whatever Doc had mentioned. He was right. It didn't really matter where it was specifically. She tried to pretend they were just on a grand hike through the countryside, seeing all of its natural wonders.

But it was hard not to feel terrible. Even if the day was shaping up to be a beautiful one, her mood was in sharp contrast to the chirping of birds and the gentle rays of sunlight streaming through the trees. Doc was humming to himself as they walked, seemingly content to leave her to her sulking.

She wanted to run to Mordred and tell him that she understood now why he wanted to send her away. Maybe, if Avalon didn't melt her fucking face, she could have that chance. But that only worked if she had enough power to defend herself from the likes of Grinn and Lady Thorn.

There was no telling what the magic of Avalon would do to her.

The likelihood that I get killed during this stupid stunt is high. Mordred thinks I'm safe on Earth. I suppose that's for the best.

Eod was also none the wiser to her turmoil. He was all too happy tromping through the underbrush, chasing squirrels and sniffing every single plant he came along, to really notice. Even his usual cheeriness wasn't enough to break her foul mood.

Luckily, she wasn't allowed to sulk for long. Doc took a sharp left turn and struck off into the woods. "This way."

"Are we close?" She was partially curious. She was also nervous.

"Yeah. The heart of all of Avalon's magic is just over here." He hopped over a fallen log as he led the way. "You know, you have to *want* this for it to work. If you're unsure, nothing will happen."

"I need to be able to protect myself, it isn't about wanting." She sighed.

"Then you need to convince yourself you want it. There's a thousand ways to protect yourself, kid. If you don't talk to the island seriously, it won't take you seriously either. What I'm trying to say is you have a choice to make, kid." Doc glanced at her over his shoulder. "That this path is *yours* to walk, nobody else's. Mordred's not here to force anything on you. Neither is Grinn. You get to pick."

She nodded. That was both a relief and a pain in the ass. She hated being jerked around by Mordred and Grinn. But at the same point in time, it took the pressure off her own choices. *Welcome to being an adult, I guess.*

Doc stopped on the edge of the forest, right as it turned into a field. Just on the edge of the long grass was a boulder that about reached up to her shoulder. "Here we are."

"What?" She looked around. "Seriously? This is it? This is the heart of Avalon's magic?"

He shrugged. "What were you expecting?"

"I don't know, like... something epic. A cave, a pool of

glowing blood or something—I don't know." She scratched the back of her neck. "It's just a rock. Not an even terribly big one either."

Doc smiled at her as if she were a three-year-old who had just tried to tell him how the world worked. "Magic isn't always about pomp and circumstance. Especially not when Avalon is involved."

Walking up to the rock, she poked it. Yep, felt just like a rock. A normal rock. "What do I do now?"

"That's up for you to figure out." Doc turned and began walking away. "I'll be back in a few hours. See if you haven't blown up or melted yet. C'mon, dog. Let's go find something to eat."

"Wait—hold on—you're going to just *leave* me here?" She couldn't believe it. "I don't know what to do!"

"That's the whole point, kid—you need to figure it out for yourself. Have fun! Try not to die!" He whistled. Eod jogged up beside him, tail wagging, eager to hunt whatever it was that Doc was going after.

Her shoulders slumped as she realized that... yeah. Doc had just fucked off. And left her there. Alone. Entirely alone.

To try to figure out how to tap into the island's magic.

"God, I fucking hate this place sometimes." She put her head in her hands and let out a long, ragged sigh. Throwing up her hands a moment later in frustration, she sat down on the grass with her back to the boulder.

"I guess I'd better get started. Doing..." She gestured to the forest, not knowing to whom she was talking. It probably didn't matter. "Something."

Nobody answered, which was probably a good thing. Shutting her eyes, she leaned her head back against the boulder. "Avalon? Are you there?"

Now she felt like a goddamn moron.

Silence.

"Hello?" she asked nobody.

Silence.

I am so seriously sick of taking shit from this goddamn island. Now it won't even pick up the proverbial fucking phone.

* * *

"You are a fool."

Mordred couldn't help but hold back a smile at Galahad's insult. "That is quite well established, thank you."

"You are a madman and a fool." Galahad shook his head. "Why would you do such a thing—to place your life in danger? Are you so grief-stricken from Gwendolyn's departure that you no longer wish to keep living? If so, I would rather you not involve the rest of us in this scheme."

Mordred sighed. "I do not wish to die, Galahad."

"Then you are not properly explaining how this does not instantly accomplish that end."

Mordred paced back and forth along the edge of his tent. He was used to sleeping in the leather and fabric structure almost more than he was accustomed to sleeping in a bed in his keep. He had spent most of his life in the fields of war, listening to the sounds of armies on the move, after all. "The demon is a coward and will keep himself hidden until I am vulnerable. Only then will he strike—when his victory is certain."

"And you plan to make yourself vulnerable to draw him out. Yes, you've said this." Galahad had to sit in the tent to keep from having to keep his head crooked at an uncomfortable angle. Mordred was tall, yes—but Galahad was sometimes problematically so. "You will put your head on the executioner's block in hopes that the axe does *not* drop."

"This is precisely why I am speaking to you, Galahad." He rolled his eyes. "And why I wish to entrust the Gossamer Lady with the proverbial axe itself."

"You do not think she will take the opportunity to rid the world of you?" The Knight in Gold arched his gray eyebrow. "Your death grants me my freedom. And therefore, our future together. Do you not think she would be tempted?"

"Tempted? Yes. Most certainly. And it is that logic in her choice that I am counting on Grinn to believe in." Mordred kept pacing back and forth as his mind tried to process all the possible outcomes. It was possible that Zoe would use the opportunity to end his life. But he did not think it would come to pass. "Your love understands the danger that Grinn poses. She will see the wisdom in this ploy."

"Perhaps. Perhaps she will not care for what will come." Galahad shook his head, letting out a heavy breath. "But that is not like her, you are correct."

"Grinn only believes in the shallow desires of those around him—that all of us are driven by the same base need for revenge that he is. Zoe is the only elemental I would entrust to see past her own selfish needs." Mordred ran a hand over his hair. "Though it remains risky."

"It is a clever ploy. But the odds are not good that it will end in your favor. There is a risk that you will lose it all."

"Yes. I am aware. There are no other cards for me to play—nothing that Grinn desires deeply enough to venture out of his hole. He loves no one but himself and his hatred." Mordred poured himself a mug of wine before taking a deep gulp of it. He did not like the idea any more than Galahad did. But there were meager few options in front of him.

"I will send for a messenger." Galahad pushed up from the chair, the wooden legs creaking under his weight. "Shall we tell the others?"

"No. Leave the rest of the knights out of this. I do not need Percival's sycophantic whining cluttering up my thoughts."

Galahad huffed a single laugh. "So be it." He turned to

leave the tent before pausing. "For what it is worth, Mordred—I do not wish your death."

Mordred turned his attention to the other man. To say that his relationship with the fae knight was complicated, would be to put it mildly. Even after so many centuries, Galahad remained guarded with his emotions. It was odd to hear such an admission. Odd, but not unwelcome. Bowing his head to the Knight in Gold, he took it as graciously as he could. "When Grinn is dead..."

"No, when Grinn is dead, there will be the elementals to contend with." Galahad smiled thinly. "I fear I am bound to your service until the grave. I am in no need of such false hope."

Damn Galahad for always being right.

And damn himself for being such a cretin. "I wish to find a way to reunite you with your love. Permanently." The pervasive grief he had felt over the past few days dug its talons into his heart and squeezed. "You have lost too much time together. I find myself more recently sympathetic."

Galahad's smile turned wistful if a little forlorn. "Yes. But I have one thing that you do not."

"Oh?"

Galahad left the tent on one final word. And it crushed what remained of Mordred's mood. "Hope."

* * *

"This *suuuuuuuucks!*" Gwen stretched out on the grass, glaring at the blue sky up above. It'd been a long time since Doc left, though she had no way of knowing exactly how much time had passed. However long it had taken her to pace around the rock, looking for any kind of magical inscription or clue, then to wander around in a circle some more, then to throw pebbles at the rock, then to lie down in the grass.

Now she was exceedingly bored.

Flopping her arms out at her sides like she was going to make a snow angel, she let out a long, ragged sigh. "Do something!"

Silence.

"Anything!"

Nothing.

She growled and put her hands over her eyes. "Okay, think, Gwen. Think. *Think*. What did Doc say? That I had to commune with the island?" She tried to replay all their conversations in her head, searching for clues. How did someone commune with an island? Okay, without an epic amount of drugs, anyway.

Tapping her hands into the grass, she thought it through.

Maybe she needed a reason. Wasn't that how these mythological things worked in the stories? Doing her best to remember all the history classes she'd taken, she tried to think. What if she made a wish?

That raised an important next question. What did she want? What did she honestly *want*, and why?

She wanted to be able to protect herself.

That meant that she wanted power.

But everybody wanted power. What made her so special? Why would Avalon grant her such a thing, and nobody else?

Shutting her eyes, she tried to focus on that. She wanted power not just to protect herself, though—she wanted power to protect others. To protect Mordred and even Grinn from themselves and their stupid, terrible war. To protect the elementals from going back into the Crystal. Even total shitheads like Lady Thorn.

But it was more than that.

There were thousands upon thousands of *people* who lived on the island. Villagers—some normal, some magical—some human and some very not. There were woods filled with creatures the likes of which she had only dreamed of. Sure, most of them wanted to eat her, but that wasn't entirely their fault.

They didn't deserve to die, caught up in the middle of a three-way epic showdown between a bunch of power-mad assholes.

Avalon needed protecting, Mordred was right about that. But he was going about it the wrong way. *When all you have is a hammer, everything looks like a nail.* She hated that phrase when her dad used to throw it around, but now it made so much more sense. Mordred only had one means of protecting the island at his disposal—magic-defeating iron—so that was going to be what he used.

There had to be another way.

There *had* to be. She refused to accept otherwise.

"You kept me here for a reason, Avalon," she whispered. "I want to help you. I want to help everyone. I want to see this place thrive without the risk of war. Grinn and Mordred will kill each other. And then the elementals will just go back to doing what they do best—being warlord assholes who kill everyone in their way. And if either Grinn or Mordred survive, it'll be war against the elementals, and *then* the elementals go back to rampaging around the island. I want to fix it. I don't know how, but right now it doesn't matter because I *can't*. Help me."

Silence.

Tears stung her eyes. "I love him. I can't just leave him to die."

More silence. She let out a sigh. "Please. I'll give you anything you want."

A dark shadow passed over her. Blinking her eyes open, she expected to see Doc looming over her, mocking her for her idiotic plea.

But it wasn't Doc.

It wasn't even a person or an animal that had made the sun go dark.

It was a black and terrible cloud, swirling high above the trees.

And getting closer.

It was a tornado.

"Oh fuck!"

She scrambled up as fast as she could to try to run away. But it was too little, too late.

Her feet left the ground as the sudden wind yanked her upside down as the world around her went black.

Gwen screamed.

* * *

Mordred stepped into the glade that the Gossamer Lady called home, her small, thatched cottage by the treeline as quaint as it ever had been. The pond in the center was shimmering in the afternoon sunlight. It was, by all accounts, a serene and beautiful place.

He vanished his armor as he approached—even dismissing his gauntlets. It struck him as interesting that it took active focus now for him to appear truly human. He had become so accustomed to his metal hands that it was an effort to keep them flesh and bone.

But he had not come to threaten Zoe. He had come to broker a bargain with the elemental. And anything that could be construed as a weapon, he wished to discard.

He had ridden through the night and most of the day to arrive at her home, leaving behind his army and all his knights. He would not have the looming presence of his forces influencing her either.

"Hello, prince." Zoe shimmered into existence, hovering over the small pond, her butterfly wings spread. "Have you come to punish me for my involvement with Lancelot's uprising?"

"No, Gossamer Lady. I have not."

A thin dark eyebrow arched up in disbelief.

He shook his head. "I know how I am perceived. I expected there to be backlash after the Crystal shattered and you were all freed. I do not blame you for thinking I am a tyrant."

She hummed thoughtfully. "Then why have you come, and done so alone?"

"I have a favor to ask of you." He braced himself for her laughter and quick dismissal. But instead, she studied him silently, waiting for him to explain. "I seek the destruction of the demon, Grinn."

"Yes. I know this." Her sheer clothing floated in the air around her as though caught in a drifting stream. "You wish for me to stand against him at your side?"

"Not quite." He took in a breath and left it out in a huff. This was the point of no return. It was beyond dangerous to put his life in her hands. But there was no other way. "He is hiding. Waiting for the chance to strike when I am weakened or vulnerable. I must be near death. I wish to force his hand and allow him to believe I am so without it being true. And I will need your help to accomplish this task."

"Interesting." She tapped her chin thoughtfully. "An illusion will not work. He is clever and will see through such a ruse."

"Precisely. Which is why the danger must be real—or at least perceived to be real." He straightened his shoulders. "I... wish to place my life in your hands, Gossamer Lady."

Her magenta eyes flew wide. She stared at him in shock.

"The magic that binds your love to me—I wish to replicate it. I will create a crystal that allows you to tap into the spell that I will embed into my own flesh." He clenched his fists and relaxed it. "Using the smaller crystal, you will be able to harm me however you wish."

Zoe floated to the shore, her bare feet touching the grass as she landed and folded her wings at her back. "Why would you do this, when you know I desire nothing more than to have my Galahad returned to me? Killing you would accomplish this."

"Because you know that Galahad would not go along with such a self-interested act." He smirked. "He is too damnably *good*."

She chuckled, nodding. "Yes. He would see such an act as dishonorable. You are quite right. Then—tell me, why should I interfere now? The demon has yet to do anything wrong."

"You know it is only a matter of time. You can see into the hearts of others. Tell me he does not still wish to burn this world to ashes, and I will stop my war." The weariness of his existence weighed on him suddenly, his shoulders drooping as if with a literal burden. "I wish nothing more than to spend my days alone and in peace, Gossamer Lady."

"With your Gwendolyn?" She tilted her head to the side slightly.

"I..." He took a breath, held it, and, through the exhale, finished his sentence. "Sent her back to Earth."

Zoe clicked her tongue in disappointment. "Mordred."

"Yes. I know. I am well aware. But without her elemental magic, she was mortal. I could not see her harmed by those who would seek to harm me. I—" What was the use in denying it? Zoe knew the truth, plain as day. "I love her."

"I know." She reached up her hand and placed her palm against his cheek, her touch soft and warm like the kiss of the morning sun. "You and Galahad are far too eager to sacrifice yourselves for those around you. It is frustrating."

He smiled gently. "Yes. I can imagine so."

"Tell me, prince—if I agree to help you..." The hope in her voice made her question an obvious one.

"I will release Galahad from my service." It would be a great loss, not having the knight at his side. But it had been too long for the cruelty to continue. And he could no longer pretend that he did not sympathize with the Knight in Gold's desire to be in the arms of the woman he loved.

She narrowed her eyes slightly. "It would put you at a great disadvantage in the wars to come."

"Perhaps he could be persuaded to take pity on an old fool and stand at my side—but only if he chooses to." Mordred took Zoe's hand in his, lifting it from his cheek. Her hand was so small, and delicate compared to his. It felt like the petal of a flower.

Zoe smiled wistfully. "I fear he loves you too much to see you suffer alone."

Mordred fought the instinct to scoff at the idea. But perhaps she was not wrong—perhaps Galahad did indeed care for him. Or, perhaps Zoe was lying, and only using the notion to further prompt Mordred to release Galahad.

Trust was hard for him. He knew this. He accepted it.

But that was what this moment was attempting to teach him —how to *trust*. He supposed he no longer cared for the outcome if he were betrayed. He had no desire to die. Yet he did not know how deeply he desired to continue to live alone.

Only his duty to his uncle and to Avalon remained to inspire him.

"Very well, prince." Zoe took a step away from him. "Perform your spell. I will do as you ask."

Nodding, he took another step away from her in return, and placed his hand on his chest, over his heart. Shutting his eyes, he focused. It was difficult to work the magic on himself, but it was not impossible. Iron twisted beneath his fingers, and he forced it into his flesh, the same he had done to the other knights so long ago. He snarled in pain as he felt the crystal begin to form, digging into his flesh and forcing itself into his body.

The agony of it took him down to one knee by the time he finished the enchantment, his head reeling. Taking a moment to steel himself, he focused on linking the new magic to an item. He would not give Zoe the power outright—no, it had to be tied to an object that he could take from her when the deed was done.

A necklace would do.

A talisman made of iron, hanging upon a delicate chain. The twisting knots of the delicate piece tangled around a glistening opalescent shard that pulsed with the beat of his heart.

When he was finished, sitting in his palm was the key to his life. The key to his continued existence. *This should have belonged to Gwendolyn. But that was not the path that fate took us.*

Forcing himself back to his feet with a grunt, he nearly toppled back over. It felt as though he had just gone through another boxing match with Galahad.

Zoe merely looked on; her expression curious but otherwise unreadable. It was impossible to know what she thought of the whole debacle, or his clear suffering. He held the necklace out to her, dangling it from his fingers. She took it, running her fingers over the shard of magic in the center. Donning the necklace, she fluttered her wings and took flight once more, hovering a few feet from the ground.

The Gossamer Lady's tone was grim. "It is time for us to get to work, Prince in Iron."

Yes. He supposed it was.

SIX

Gwen woke up. Or, really, honestly, she had already been awake—she just suddenly became *aware* of herself. It was like the lights had been turned off, and then suddenly, they were flicked back on.

The last thing she remembered was the tornado. And screaming at the top of her lungs as she got sucked up into the swirling vortex in the sky.

One moment it had only been a confusing and gut-wrenching mess of up-down-up-down, left-right-left-right. The next, she was... sitting in a field.

But it wasn't a normal field.

The grass that swayed in the breeze around her was almost translucent, as if made from stained glass. The field glittered in the pale rays of the moon like it was made from, well, crystal. It wasn't until she blinked and rubbed her eyes that she realized that the grass itself was *glowing*. Faintly, barely noticeably, but it was—a whitish opalescent color that seemed to shift as it moved.

The trees around the field were the same, the leaves white and shimmering with every color of the rainbow.

It was the same kind of glow that had come from the Iron Crystal—the glow of the magic of Avalon. Wherever she was, it *was* magic. Pushing herself to her feet, she brushed herself off and took in her surroundings. The sky overhead was one enormous band of galaxy, like seeing the Milky Way on a dark night.

Gwen had never seen anything so beautiful in her life. Yet it didn't... feel *real*. And it had nothing to do with the fact that everything was faintly glowing. She felt kind of detached, like the world around her was also an oil painting. Fuzzy, and indistinct when she wasn't looking directly at it.

Like a dream.

She was in a dream.

But whose?

Not hers, that was for sure.

"Hello?" she called out, but no one responded. Just the faint whisper of wind, and the rustle of grass and leaves.

Where *was* she? She had been yelling at Avalon, and then the tornado, and then here.

A dragonfly flitted past her, and it might have been made of stained glass. It rested on a long blade of grass next to her. She marveled at it for a moment before she couldn't help herself and reached out a finger to touch it. When she got close, it flew away before disappearing altogether.

It wasn't real.

More proof that this was a vision.

Shutting her eyes, she took a deep breath and let it out. She tried to... she didn't even know. *Sense* what was going on around her? She listened. And she waited.

And then she knew.

She didn't know *how* she knew. But it was like the world around her was whispering, and the moment she stopped to truly listen, there it was.

This wasn't just a dream of Avalon.

Avalon *was* a dream.

The whole island—all of it. That was why there were no natives that weren't animals. Even then, she got the sense that they were all borrowed from different worlds as well. The land, the trees, the mountains, the volcano—it was a *dream*. A dream of some enormous, otherworldly *thing* that she could feel there at the corners of her mind.

She was in the presence of a god. Or as close to it as she could imagine, she supposed. Keeping her eyes shut, she tried to focus on it some more—tried to glimpse the entity that had brought her here.

Shapes danced in front of her eyes in the absence of light, her mind desperately trying to come up with something in the nothingness.

The shapes were horrifying monsters—long-limbed with thin, terrifying claws that were as long as her whole body. The figures had gaping, empty eye sockets in misshapen, almost insectoid-looking skulls. They loomed around her, nightmarish, but strangely... beautiful.

She jolted, her eyes shooting open. Whatever this creature, or *creatures*, was, it wasn't some bearded old man, or any of the other possible options for deities. This was something else entirely.

But she didn't feel threatened. Whatever these things were, they were *watching* her. Waiting. Whispering. This island was their dream, and now she was a part of it.

But it didn't stop her from feeling extremely small and snack-sized. Shivering, she wrapped her arms around herself and tried to breathe. Her breath caught in her throat, and she felt her heart start pounding. She hadn't suffered a panic attack in weeks. But here it was, rearing its head again.

Was it Avalon's magic that calmed her nerves?

Or was it Mordred's presence?

She supposed it didn't matter which one it was. Or if it was a mix of the two. She went to shut her eyes again but thought better of it. She struggled to focus on her breathing and counting back slowly from ten. Just focus on the next number, on the next inhale and exhale, muttering the numbers to herself.

But her mind didn't latch onto the numbers.

Her mind latched onto *him*. Onto the memory of his arms around her. Of his kiss. Of the strength in his touch. Of his smile, of his laugh. Of his fury.

Of how much she loved him.

And how much she had come to love Avalon.

"I want to belong here," she whispered to the dream around her. "I want to belong on Avalon—for real. Not because I've borrowed someone's power. Not because I'm someone's pet human who got dragged here against my will either."

She took a deep breath, held it, and slowly let it out. The panic was slowly receding as she made her argument to the empty air that wasn't so empty. "I—I care about this place. About this island and the people on it. And I want to *help* them. Not just the elementals, but everybody." She remembered the scarecrow in the store named Bert. The villagers she had met—well, okay, the ones that hadn't tried to kill her. Tim and Maewenn. How many others were there, caught up in all the warring forces, who deserved to live a happy life?

"But I can't do that if I can't stand on my own. I can't stop the wars that are coming if I can't *defend* them. Or myself. I love Mordred—and—I know I shouldn't, but I care about that stupid demon." She chuckled and shrugged. "And Doc. And Tim. And Maewenn. And Galahad. And all the rest. And if someone doesn't stop all this from going down, they'll—who knows who won't make it out the other side?"

Silence.

But they were listening, whoever—whatever—they were. She could feel their attention on her. It made the hair on the back of her neck stand up.

"I know I'm nobody. I'm just a kid from Kansas. I grew up

raising *goats*, for fuck's sake." She chuckled. "But I'm here now. And I want to stay. Your dream is beautiful—it's—it's the most amazing thing I've ever seen. Let me help save it. Please. I don't know what else to do."

Nothing.

Then, a thought. A thought that wasn't hers. It wasn't words —it wasn't even a feeling. It was simply *knowing*.

God, that felt so weird.

There was a choice before her. Stay on Avalon forever or return to Earth. There would be no changing her mind. Once she made the decision, she could never, ever leave. Even her soul would be bound to the island.

There would be no reunion with her family. Not in this life, or the next. She could never see them, tell them that she loved them, tell them that she was okay. Her feet would never touch the ground of any other world but Avalon.

Choose.

Now.

She was trembling. She had never felt so little in all her life. Could she really say goodbye to Earth forever? To any chance she could ever go home, even just for a brief visit?

Her other option was leaving Avalon forever. Never coming back. Never seeing Mordred again. No hope of a reunion. Maewenn, Tim, Doc, Galahad—she would miss them all.

It was a goodbye to one part of her life or the other.

No takebacks.

No changing her mind.

No what-ifs. No bargains.

This was it.

Choose.

Now.

At home, she was just Gwendolyn Wright. A farmer's daughter with a panic attack problem. Normal. Boring. With a future that was just as flat as her past had been. Uninteresting—

but safe. She could raise a family if she wanted. But part of her would always be in Avalon.

On Avalon, Gwendolyn Wright meant something. Or at least she had the opportunity to mean something. She could go on adventures. See magical creatures and make strange friends. This was a world of magic. But it was also a world of death, of disaster, of danger.

Not to mention the man she loved. And all the friends she'd yet to meet.

Opening her eyes, she straightened her shoulders.

She made her choice.

"Yeah. Fuck it. Let's do this. Lay it on me."

The world went dark around her like the lights had switched off.

And the ground opened up beneath her feet, sending her careening down into the darkness.

"*Fuck!*"

Gwen was falling.

Again.

Gwen was *super* sick of falling.

She wondered if that was going to be her life now, just endlessly falling for the rest of her mortal life. How long would it take for her to get used to it? Or would she just end up dying from a heart attack?

Her answer came a few moments later when the darkness parted, and she was now falling... with scenery. She wasn't sure if that made it better or worse. She had tumbled out of a large, angry storm cloud, and was now hurtling toward the forest and the ground below.

Yep.

It was worse.

Definitely worse.

Now she had a new, fun, and interesting reason to scream her goddamn head off as she watched the ground grow slowly closer. She had never been skydiving before, and now she *really* had no interest in ever trying it.

She was going to die.

The island had decided that it wanted to turn her into a bug on a windshield. She was just going to splatter all over the landscape.

She managed to flail her limbs around enough to stabilize so she could hold steady. It gave her a much nicer view of her impending death. It was terrifying, but at least she didn't feel like she was going to puke the way she did when she was falling and spinning at the same time.

I'm going to die.

There was a sudden, strange sense of calm that overtook her, as the thought really sank in through the deafening rush of the wind as she hurtled downward. She was going to die—it was just that simple. There wasn't anything she could do about it. There wasn't anything she could do to stop it. It was just a fact.

She stopped screaming. There wasn't a point in it anymore.

Shutting her eyes, she just embraced the falling.

Spreading out her arms, she tried to trick herself into thinking she wasn't falling, that she was flying. Imagining the wings she had owned for a *hot second* but had never had a chance to really use, she pretended she could feel the air rushing against the leathery skin of her dragon's wings, helping her soar overhead—not falling out of control.

Wait.

Hold on.

She *could* feel her wings.

What the—

Opening her eyes, she couldn't believe what she saw. Her wings were back! She could fly!

There was only one problem with that.

Gwen didn't know how to fly.

Now she was gliding even faster at the quickly approaching

ground. Instead of holding her aloft, she was inadvertently diving. Screaming, she flapped, and desperately tried to change her trajectory. *Pull up, pull up!*

Half through panic, half through some desperate kind of instinct, she managed to slowly change direction, pulling up from the insane dive. She felt the strain on her wings, cringing from the ache as she overcorrected too quickly.

It was effective, however. She was slowing down. It was working! She was now headed downward at an angle, slower than before. But still far too fast for comfort.

Opting to try to change her path a little more gently, she found that it was actually pretty easy to glide. By the time the trees became detailed enough that she could make out their individual structures, she was *flying*. Really, actually *flying!*

Laughing, she spread her arms out wide as she soared. What had been the most terrifying moment of her life had now become one of the most joyful.

It felt incredible.

Truly amazing.

She was *flying*.

She flapped her wings experimentally, feeling the extra bit of lift from the movement pull her a few feet higher atop the treeline.

If she reached down her hand, she could touch the leaves as she went by. Every shade of green was below her.

Who cared if her wings were leathery and gross, and not feathered or pretty? They worked. And they made this possible. She had never felt so free in her life.

This was the most beautiful moment she had ever experienced.

Right until she looked up.

And smashed into an evergreen that had grown much taller than all the rest.

The next few moments were a tangled mess of limbs, snapping branches, more snapping branches, even more tangled limbs. The world was spinning around her as she went through bough after bough. Sky, tree, branch, sky, branch, tree, sky, branch, tree, other tree, sky.

Ground.

She hit the forest floor with a *thud.*

Two things warred for supremacy in Gwen's mind—the urge to throw up and the pain of the impact. She groaned and experimentally moved her limbs. Okay, she could wiggle her toes and her fingers. Her wings were still there.

But goddamn it, that had fucking hurt.

Rolling onto her stomach, she shoved to her hands and knees. And then something was licking her face. "What the f—" She laughed and pushed the fluffy creature away. "Oh. Hello, Eod."

The dog sat down, tail thumping against the pine needles and underbrush, and barked. "*Hi!*"

She blinked. Wait. Had the dog just... talked? She didn't really hear it, not like she heard sound, but there had still been no mistaking it. The voice had been in her head.

"Great... I can talk to animals now. Or rather, I guess you can talk to me." That was something Doc could do. Did that mean she was a wizard now? She had her leathery dragon wings, in shades of red—like when she was an elemental.

But she hadn't been able to hear Eod before. "How'd you know where to find me?"

Eod tilted his head to the side slightly. "*Magic man. Said sit. Wait. Good boy. I sat. I wait. Good boy.*"

Magic man. She sighed. Doc. "Nice of him to ditch me. I'm glad he brought you here. And yes. You are a very good boy." She scratched Eod's head.

His tongue rolled out of his mouth in doggy bliss. "*Good boy!*"

Getting back to her feet, she brushed the pine needles

off herself, picking at some that were stuck with sap. She *hated* tree sap. Hopefully, she didn't have too much of it in her hair. Which, what the hell— Her hair was wild shades of red and orange again. Holding out her hand, she focused, and watched as her hand turned to fire, just like before.

She had fire again! That was great. She had just started to get used to it, and even enjoy it, when Grinn took it back. But the "speaking to animals" thing was *bizarre*. She wondered what the island had really done to her.

I wish Doc was here. Man, what a weird impulse. But the wizard had left her to her own devices. Either because she needed to be or because he got bored again and wandered off.

Sighing, she wrapped her wings around her shoulders and looked off into the woods. She had no idea where she was. "I guess we just head in the direction of a town? I don't know what else to do. But standing out here isn't going to help."

Eod stood and began sniffing the air. *"Food this way."* He began trotting off into the brush before stopping and looking back at her. He barked. *"Follow!"*

"Sure, sure." She supposed the fact that she could under-stand the dog wasn't the weirdest part of her time in Avalon. Hell, it wasn't even the weirdest part of her *day*. Might as well accept it for what it was and start following him through the trees.

Humming a tune to herself, she watched the birds and insects flitting around her. It was weird to think they were all dreamed into existence. But she knew nothing about real deities and what they were capable of—she wasn't sure why she was at all surprised.

She was starting to get used to her life of hiking in circles, thinking about her choices. Avalon had given her elemental power, at least as far as she could tell. Mordred and Grinn were probably still steamrolling forward into an inevitable clash. And after that? Whoever was left standing would be the target of the elementals.

At least before the elementals turned on each other.

Either way, it was going to be a messy, bloody, deadly clusterfuck.

Avalon was the dream of gods.

And they had chosen her to help save it from itself.

Now I just need to figure out how.

No pressure.

* * *

Mordred stood with his knights—his *remaining* knights, as Lancelot's absence was still palpable—around a table that had been set up in his war tent. It bore a map of Avalon, this one smaller and paper rather than the large metal one in his keep.

"There were no fires, save for those that came from chimneys," Bors said as he shook his head. "There was no sign of the demon."

Mordred let out a breath. That made little sense. Grinn was known to ignite anything that grew close to him simply by his presence alone. He would set a forest ablaze simply by traveling through it. "Nothing?"

"Nothing," Gawain confirmed.

Mordred tapped the tip of his pointer finger claw on the table as he studied the map. Avalon was mostly covered in forests and wildlands. "And the lava field to the north?" The section of molten runoff from the center mountain was the only area that was rocky enough for Grinn to cause no damage.

"Tristan and I saw no signs of him there." Percival's expression was grim as he watched Mordred. "We spoke to Ignir. He has no love for Grinn. He has not seen him, and we have no reason to disbelieve his word."

Mordred snorted. "I am surprised the dragon did not burn

you to a crisp for daring to speak with him."

"We spoke to him from a distance." Tristan smiled faintly, though it did not last long.

Mordred continued to tap his claw against the table with a repetitive *tick, tick, tick*. It helped him think. For even if his thoughts were at a standstill, the noise somehow urged them forward.

Where could the demon have gone?

Where could he hide if it was not the lava fields?

It hit him then. Shutting his eyes, he groaned.

"What is it?" The tone of the Knight in Gold was both curious and filled with dread.

"He has gone into the caves." Mordred straightened his back, rolling his shoulders. The muscles were none too pleased about it. "He is inside the volcano." Reaching down, he picked up the little iron figurine of the demon and placed it in the center of the map.

The mountain that dominated the center of Avalon was a *mostly* dormant volcano—the lava that flowed ambiently into the ocean to the north was the only expression of its true nature. It had not erupted, as far as Mordred was aware, in the history of the island. Or at least for as long as it had held sentient creatures.

"If he has gone below ground, we will never be able to find him." Percival grimaced. "There are too many entrances and exits—and there are only so many of us. Even if we cut off every *known* exit, the odds that he would wriggle his way out of a new crevice is far too likely."

Fate was closing in around Mordred. This was too convenient. Perhaps the island was finally fixing its error from so long ago. "We cannot surround the mountain. Nor can we storm in to find him. You are right—he would simply flee. No, we will need to draw him out. We will need to bait a trap." Mordred very much hated when he was right.

He hated it very, very much.

"And what in the *literal* hell could we use to bait him?" Percival snorted. "There is nothing he wishes for more than the destruction of all of Avalon. There is nothing we have to bargain with."

"You are nearly correct." Mordred smirked. "There is one thing he wishes for more than the death of us all."

"Oh?" Galahad arched an eyebrow. "And what would that be?"

"To see me suffer." Mordred turned from the table. He had work to do. "Galahad, with me. We must speak."

"Yes, my prince." Ever the loyal servant, Galahad followed.

Loyal, for now.

Until he was free.

Without his strongest knight, and if he were left vulnerable from the spell he cast for Zoe, Mordred would make a tempting piece of bait, indeed. Grinn's hatred consumed him—and his desire to twist the knife in Mordred's side was his only weakness.

But the danger would be real.

Mordred would be left exposed.

Someone would seek to capitalize on the moment, he was certain. Too many of his so-called allies would see the chance to end him and seize it. Would it be Galahad who ended him? Or Percival? Or perhaps the doe-eyed Tristan would surprise him in the end.

It might be the Gossamer Lady herself.

Or any other number of elementals who loathed him.

Mordred would see Grinn wiped from the face of Avalon.

But he suspected he would be shortly at the demon's heels into the great beyond.

Mordred hated when he was right.

And he was suspicious it was about to happen again.

SEVEN

Gwen glanced up at the sky as she followed Eod through the woods. It was starting to get dark. "Hey buddy, we should probably make camp. How far is the town?"

"Food still far." Eod sniffed the air and wagged his tail half-heartedly in agreement.

It was bizarre to "hear" the dog in her head. It was like a thought that wasn't her own. He didn't even really have a voice per se. The thoughts were just there. But it was oddly comforting all the same. "There's a river that way," she said as she pointed through the glade to the left. "I can catch some fish."

"Food!" Eod wagged faster. *"Food food food"*—he kept repeating the thought as he ran toward the river. Damn it all if his excitement wasn't just a little contagious. Honestly, it was probably the only thing keeping her from having another panic attack.

Or maybe it was her new magic.

One or the other. Or both.

But either way, she was smiling to herself as she followed the dog to the river. Seeing as she didn't have a tent, or a bedroll, or any supplies at all, she searched for a comfortably grassy spot, somewhere sleeping on the ground wouldn't totally suck.

But at least she was alive. And she had her dog. Well—Eod wasn't *literally* her dog, technically he was Mordred's. But for all intents and purposes? Eod was hers now. She looked down into the river and let out a breath.

The last time she had gone fishing for dinner was with Grinn. It felt like such a long time ago, but it couldn't have been more than a few weeks at most. Eod was happily gathering sticks, piling them up in the center of the clearing. It took her a second to realize why—a campfire.

"You're such a good boy." She smiled at him.

"*Food! Food food food—*"

Right. He was being a good boy. But he also wanted dinner. That tracked. Chuckling, she stripped off her clothes to wade into the river. She didn't want to burn them off accidentally or get soaked. She'd already wandered into a village butt-ass naked *once* in her life. She didn't need to do that again.

Once she was up to her waist, she put her hands just below the surface and focused on summoning her fire. Sure enough, the water began to heat up around her. Steam slowly curled from the surface until, just like before, the poor fish caught in the really-had-no-business-nearly-boiling river bobbed up to the top.

She felt kind of bad for them, but... To quote Eod, *food*.

She chucked the dead fish to the side of the river as they bobbed up in front of her. It was a relief to have her fire back—it was funny, how she had hated it at first, but how terrible it had felt to have it taken away from her.

Or taken back, really.

Once she had a decent pile of fish for the two of them, she waded back to shore. She was still dripping wet, but a few seconds with her whole body turned into fire fixed that issue *real* fast. She pulled her dress back on—struggling to navigate her damn wings—but pretty soon, she had a fire going and was sitting there with her pile of trout.

It was exactly at that point that she realized she had no way to clean the fish. And while Eod would probably be happy to just gobble the damn things down whole, she didn't want him to get a bone stuck in his system.

She didn't want to go at them with her bare hands either. But she didn't know what else to do.

"*Magic?*"

She blinked and looked up at Eod. That thought had been his. He was lying there next to her, his head on his paws, watching her every move with the fish. Furrowing her brow, she shook her head. "What do you mean?"

"*Magic.*" He thumped his tail on the ground, clearly proud of himself for coming up with such a solid plan. Despite the fact that she had *no idea* what he was talking about. To be fair, he was a dog, and he was trying his best.

Letting out a breath, she thought through that one word. Magic.

It was about then that she realized this was the first time since coming to Avalon that she was alone, not counting Eod. She always had someone telling her things. Doc would tell her what was going on. Mordred would tell her what to do. And Grinn would tell her off. Her chuckle ended in a sad sigh.

Now she had nobody to tell her anything.

And she got the serious suspicion that was by design. Why else would Doc have abandoned her? He had brought Eod to where he knew she was going to crash-land, and then up and left her.

No, this was about her figuring out things on her own.

Magic.

Why would Eod have suggested that one word? What could he sense that she didn't? Did she have magic now? What if she wasn't just an elemental anymore?

What did that even mean if it were true? Was she some weird... elemental–wizard hybrid? And how the hell was she even supposed to figure that out? Or use it?

Too many questions she couldn't answer. Not without trying to do something, at any rate.

But do what?

Frowning down at the pile of fish, she knew she needed a knife to clean them. Maybe she could try to... create a knife?

There wasn't any harm in trying, she supposed.

She shut her eyes and held her hand out in front of her, palm open and up. "I would like a knife."

Nothing. Not like she was expecting otherwise.

"Knife."

Nothing. Maybe she needed to say it harder.

"*Kniiiiiiiiiiiiiiiiife.*"

Nothing. Maybe she needed to be polite?

"Knife. Please."

Nope.

Dropping her hand into her lap, she took a moment to think it over. Maybe it was like when Mordred taught her to control her power. She had to not just think about it, had to *feel* it.

Picking up her hand again, she did just that. She focused on what it would feel like to have an iron knife in her hand. She pictured one of Mordred's dinner knives, hand-forged with a twisted handle. What it would feel like in her hand, the weight of it, the slight cold of the touch of iron.

Her thoughts wandered to the touch of Mordred's iron gauntlets, the sharp points of his claws as they grazed her skin.

Her hand went cold.

Eyes flying open, she shrieked and jumped back, waving her hand as if to try to get a spider off it. But there was no getting this off her hand—it *was* her hand!

Her hand was made out of iron!

"Fuck! Fuck fuck fuck—" She waved her hand again, whining, before giving up at trying to simply flick the material off. Taking a deep breath, she held it, and slowly let it out. Her hand was made out of iron.

Like when it was made from fire, but—metal.

Chewing her lip, she focused on the sensation. Tried to turn it into something, the same way she did when she made little fireballs or the like. And sure enough, she watched as metal seemed to form from her palm and begin to mesh into a kitchen knife.

"I really don't understand this, but okay." She focused on making her hand normal again. The metal slowly receded but the knife remained. "At least this means we can eat dinner without hacking up bones."

"*Food!*" Eod's tail whumped on the ground.

Dogs.

"Eat, then sleep. I feel like I've been hit by a truck. Or, y'know, a tree." Smiling half-heartedly, she went to work. Dinner was peaceful, sitting by the fire on the ground with Eod who happily gobbled up whatever she gave him. The fishy remains were put into the river, and she settled down on a grassy spot, using Eod's flank for a pillow. He didn't seem to mind.

Sleep was slow to come—there was always a rock pressing into her in some weird way. It seemed like every time she moved one, she discovered another. But she was exhausted, and her need for rest slowly won over her uncomfortable situation.

Just as she began to nod off, a horrible thought crept into her mind, too late to keep her awake. Controlling iron on Avalon was a *big* fucking deal.

What will Mordred do when he finds out he isn't the only one who can control iron?

* * *

Mordred was dreaming of a happier time.

Sitting around a fire on whatever boxes and logs they could drag around to make it more comfortable, he raised his mug in salute to the men across from him. Galahad. Bors. Gawain. Tristan. Percival. Lancelot. Himself.

And Arthur.

His king and leader was leaning up against a crate, sitting on the ground, laughing at Gawain's dramatic retelling of some mishap on a battlefield where the knight had become stuck in the mud and had to hack at his opponents like a fool.

They were mortal men—all save for Galahad, with his longer lifespan and magical lineage.

Mordred missed those days. They were simpler. They were full of *hope*. Mordred had counted these men as his family and would never have once believed that they might turn their backs on him.

How naive he had been.

Someone sat down at his side. Someone who did not belong in the dream. He shut his eyes. Her hand found his, intertwining their fingers. He was without his gauntlets—for this was long before the notion of becoming an elemental had even entered his mind.

"Is that... him?"

"Yes."

"He's not as old as I thought he'd be. He's also kinda skinny."

"Trust me, he is as formidable as any of us." He chuckled, turning his attention to Gwendolyn. In his dreams, she appeared as she had as an elemental, not a human. Interesting that his mind gave her that appearance, or she unconsciously chose it herself. Her hair had returned to the fiery shades of red that he had adored so very much. Her wings had also returned.

Curious.

Reaching out his other hand, he stroked it over her hair. He knew it was truly her in his dreams—he had known the moment she had spoken in their previous encounter. The magic he embedded inside her before she left must be strong enough to bridge the gap between their worlds.

They sat in silence for a moment before she smiled sadly at him. "Are you all right?"

"I am on the warpath. So... no. Though there is comfort in it. This is where I belong." He gestured at the encampment around him. "Stationary life within a keep has always felt odd to me. As though I were wasting my time somehow."

"Not a guy built for retirement. Noted." She leaned up against his arm, resting her cheek against his bicep. She watched the knights as they continued to replay memories before them both.

"Will you ever forgive me for sending you away?"

"Yeah. I understand why. I don't *like* it, but I understand. I am—was—a weakness. People would try to use me against you." She sighed.

"I fear we were doomed from the start." Turning, he scooped her up and placed her onto his lap, sitting sideways. He wrapped his arms around her, wishing to hold her, careful to avoid crushing her wings.

She snuggled into him, tucking her head against his neck. Though they were never to meet again in the waking world, they would have their dreams. He could be at peace with that.

For as long as it lasted before he died.

"I'm sorry, Mordred. For not telling you about me and Grinn. I just didn't know what to do. I haven't felt like I could control anything since I showed up here."

"You were right to be wary of me. The need for revenge—the hatred that he and I share for each other—it is a force that is hard to overcome. You were trapped betwixt us—caught in a centuries-old war you had no stake in." He kissed the top of her head. She smelled like the campfire. Welcoming and warm.

"I do have a stake in it, though." She sighed. "I don't want you to die. And to be honest, I don't want him to die either."

"One of us is going to die. Very soon."

"I know, I know. And I know he probably deserves it. But..."

"You are compassionate by nature."

"Yeah, but also—like, some part of me still holds onto the fact that he was my cat for ten years. I took care of him. Fed him. Talked to him for a decade. All of my young life, he was there, being the asshole that he is." She chuckled, and he joined her. Letting out another disheartened breath, she continued. "But he was still there. I know he hates me. I just can't hate him back."

"It is part of what I adore about you, Gwendolyn Wright. That in your heart, you always hope for the best in those around you. Even an unforgivable tyrant, alone, with only usurpers and traitors around him." He tilted her head up to him with the crook of a finger.

"You aren't alone. You have people who care about you. Galahad. Maewenn. Me."

"One who has returned to Earth. And two others. In sixteen hundred years." He managed to smile, if weakly. "Yes, I have done so well for myself."

She laughed. "Yeah, but you do this shit to yourself."

"I have come to think there may be wisdom in that." He turned his attention to the men around the fire, who were oblivious to her existence in the dream. "I have decided to release Galahad."

"Really?" She blinked, surprised.

"He should be with his love. They have sacrificed enough time for my foolishness. But it will be a heavy loss when he leaves my side." That would, technically, only leave him with Maewenn for anything resembling a friend. The other knights loathed him, and his soldiers were forced to follow him. He truly was a sorry bastard.

"What about the others?"

"Should I survive the ordeal with Grinn, the other elementals will surely come for me. Without any other knights to aid me, I would fall to their numbers." He shook his head. "And they would not stand willingly beside me. Of this, I am certain."

"Maybe. I don't know the others. I barely had a chance to meet any of them. Except Percival. He can go get wrecked." She glanced around the group again before her attention settled once more on Arthur. "He has a nice smile."

"He led by inspiration and loyalty. It was a lesson that I was never capable of learning. You would have adored him—and he you. You share a penchant for kindness." He combed his fingers through her hair, loving the silky sensation against his fingers. "He likely would have swept you away for himself."

"Too skinny for me. I like guys I can climb like a tree, apparently." She snickered. "Where's Merlin?"

He had to laugh at her obsession with the old wizard. "He was wont to come and go as he pleased. He was not always at the king's side. Next time, I will have to try to summon a memory with him, so you can placate this silly fascination of yours."

She turned her attention back to him. She touched his cheek, then played with a strand of his blond hair. "You look so weird as a normal human."

"Why, thank you for your flattery."

Chuckling, she kissed him. Slowly, but not without its passion. "You know what I mean."

He held her closer, returning the kiss, deciding he was not finished with it just yet. Shutting his eyes, he leaned his forehead against hers. "I will cherish these moments, Gwendolyn. I meant my words to you, though they were spoken in a dream. I love you. And I always shall."

"Damn it, don't make me cry." She sniffled and wiped her

eye with her hand. "I'm so sick of crying." She nuzzled into him. "I love you, Mordred."

"And I love you, Gwendolyn Wright. No matter where you may be."

* * *

Mordred thought she was on Earth. He had no clue that she was still on Avalon. She was worried her appearance, and her dragon wings, might have given it away. But he seemed to write it off as just a figment of the dream.

Gwen was, once more, withholding information from him. She couldn't tell him the truth, no matter how much she wanted to.

I'm still on Avalon, and now I'm a... something. Apparently, I'm supposed to protect the island from everyone, and I have no idea how. Remember how you're the only one who can control iron, and all the other elementals hate you for it? Yeah, about that. I can do it too! Surprise! Yeah, that'd go over like a lead balloon.

What would he do when he found out? It was only a matter of time. She couldn't hide from him forever. But she wasn't ready yet. She needed to figure out how to control her power. If she didn't, it might have disastrous consequences. *Watch—it'd just be my luck that every time I sneezed, I'd blow up a tree or something.*

No, she needed some kind of mastery over herself before she told Mordred the truth. While she was pretty certain he wasn't going to kill her because she had become a new threat to the island—she honestly didn't know what he *would* do. Try to cast some sort of magic on her, to keep her under control, like he had his knights?

Maybe he'd just let her be free. Maybe he'd trust her to not turn on him.

Yeah. Right. Because I have such a great record for telling him the truth.

The most likely outcome was that he would use her power to kill Grinn, whether she liked it or not. Because she wouldn't blame him if he did. But she was just repeating the same pattern with him, again and again. And it felt so very wrong.

I'll tell him in a few days. Once I get my feet under me. Once I figure out what's going on. He can't be that mad if it's only a few days. He'll understand. Right?

That might give her enough time to find Grinn and convince him to declare peace. She wasn't an idiot—she knew it probably wouldn't work. But she needed to try.

It was her job now. To protect the island and everyone on it.

Even if it meant trying to protect them from themselves.

She kissed Mordred one last time as she felt the dream begin to fade.

She didn't know how she'd pull it off. But she'd fix this. Somehow. Someway.

She *had* to.

EIGHT

Gwen spent the better part of the morning walking before they finally came to the edges of a decently sized town. Chewing her lip, she thought about what her plan was going to be. She knew from experience that the non-elemental, somewhat-magical villagers in Avalon did *not* take kindly to elementals. Not like she blamed them. They really did just rampage around like they owned the place.

So, marching into the middle of town with dragon wings was going to be a great recipe for getting shot. Again. She focused on them, and it took some effort—but she managed to get them to shimmer out of existence, leaving her only with her fire-colored hair. That involved a little more work than the wings, but she at least got it to be a consistent shade of red.

"Good enough for government work." She smiled, just a little proud of herself.

All right—she looked vaguely not-elemental-y. Now what? She didn't have any money or supplies. She only had the clothes on her back and a dog that was currently intent on sniffing the grass and shrubs for rabbits.

Maybe she should start at the tavern, though she really

hoped this one had better food than the last place. The tavern was always a good place for information and stuff, right? She could offer to wait tables or something for food and a spot to sleep in the back. She just needed a day or two to get her feet under her and figure out what she should do about Grinn and Mordred.

Seemed like a good enough plan.

Now, she just had to focus on not getting shot. She really hated getting shot.

"C'mon, doggo." She patted her thigh as she headed into the town. Eod jogged to catch up before walking alongside her happily.

Oh, to be a dog without a care in the world. Well, except food. And finding critters to murder.

She got a few odd looks from folks as she made her way through the town. She knew it wasn't because she looked weird —hell, half the people glancing at her had horns or tails. No, she was probably getting looks because she was a stranger, and it was a small place. But nobody screamed, "Guards" or "Quick, kill her!" so she'd call it a win.

It wasn't long before she found the tavern. She assumed it was a tavern, anyway—but she had a pretty good clue. Hanging from a post over the door, from weathered and fraying ropes, was a wooden carved sign that looked like it had seen better days. The paint that had been slapped into the grooves showed a mug of beer and a turkey leg, but no writing. She supposed that made sense, if most of the people in the town couldn't read.

Letting out a breath, she braced herself. Glancing down at Eod, she patted him. "Be good, okay? You have one rule—don't embarrass me."

Those big, almost human eyes looked up at her curiously as he cocked his head to the side. *"What im-bare-ass?"*

Chuckling, she shook her head. "Never mind. Man, I hope this doesn't end poorly." Pushing open the door, the smell of woodsmoke and roasting food hit her almost immediately. The main room of the tavern was dark, the wood posts and floors worn smooth from time, and stained in deep, muddled amber tones.

A man stood behind the bar, wiping down the surface. He was tall and broad, but with friendly features buried underneath a thick graying beard.

Eod, tail wagging, ran right up to the counter and hopped up, placing his two front paws on the bar like he was a customer. "*Hi!*"

"Hah!" The man laughed. "Sorry, boy, I don't think you drink alcohol." He reached out and scratched Eod on the head. The dog was still happily wagging his tail, just glad of the attention.

"Sorry about that." Gwen smiled sheepishly as she walked up to the bar. "He's friendly and well behaved. Mostly. Except for the paws on the bar."

"I can see that." The man was still smiling, the wrinkles by his eyes creasing. "It's quite all right. I have a few of my own at home."

Eod hopped down a moment later, deciding it was now more interesting to sniff around on the floor, likely smelling some spilled food from meals gone by.

"How can I help you, miss?" The man turned his attention to her, smile unwavering.

"Well..." Gwen braced herself for what was going to happen next. It could go one of two ways. "It's complicated, but I'm afraid I don't have any money or anything. I was hoping you might be willing to trade labor for a meal and a place to stay while I figure out where to go next."

The man hummed. "Someone throw you out, did they?"

She tried not to snort. "You could put it that way."

"Damn fool." He reached his hand over the bar to her. "Walter."

"Gwen." She took his hand and shook it. It was rough and just as broad as the rest of him. It reminded her of her uncle, who had grown up working on a farm.

"Well, Gwen. I think you have a very reasonable deal. Do you know how to clean tables? I'm always in need of help during the busy times." Walter went back to wiping down the bar.

"I do." That was such a relief. Not having to sleep in the woods tonight would be wonderful, while she tried to figure out her next steps. She had to discover where Grinn was hiding and try to head Mordred off at the pass.

But she'd have a real meal and a bed. Or meal and bed-*ish*, at any rate. She didn't really have high hopes for a medieval-style tavern, but beggars and choosers and all that jazz. And this place seemed different. Nicer. Homier. Cozy, even. She instantly liked it.

"We have an empty room upstairs for you tonight, and we'll make sure your stomach is full—you and the pup." Walter smiled. "Though I expect he'll be plenty full after begging for scraps tonight."

"I hope you don't mind him wandering around. I'm sure he'd go outside or upstairs if you prefer." Gwen scratched Eod's rump as the large dog leaned up against her.

"Nah. Places like this always feel better with a pup around." Walter reached under the bar and grabbed a rag. He tossed it to her. "Bucket's in back and the well's in the town center."

"Get a bucket of water and start wiping down tables. Got it." Tucking the rag into the belt she was wearing over her dress, she headed into the back to get said bucket.

The next few hours of "work" felt... wonderfully normal. Mundane. She found herself faintly smiling as she wiped down the tables in preparation for customers to come in. Eod was having a grand old time, "helping" Walter. Really, it was obvious that the tavern owner had a soft spot for dogs and was altogether too happy to spoil the animal.

Things picked up when the patrons started coming in. A few at a time, but before long the place was bustling with every kind of person and monster she could imagine. A minotaur sitting next to a woman who looked like Medusa—but at least her gaze didn't turn anyone to stone.

A woman with wings and cloven hooves was chatting up someone who looked human enough, until his eyes blinked like those of a lizard. But not a single one of them was an elemental, or at least not that she could tell. These were just the "normal" people of Avalon. And they were all laughing, drinking, and enjoying the food.

They were all having a nice evening.

And so was she.

It was such a different experience compared to her life lately, that she didn't even mind bussing tables and taking orders for folks. It was kind of entertaining, really—as it was something to occupy her mind that wasn't "impending war" or "imminent death."

Imagine that.

So it caught her entirely by surprise when she walked up to a table of newcomers and recognized one of the people there. She blinked.

It seemed the recognition was mutual.

A rusted metal pumpkin with a jagged jack o'lantern face on the front of it, perched atop the body of a straw-stuffed scare-crow, swiveled to look at her. "Gwendolyn?"

"I—But—" She stammered uselessly for a moment before shaking her head and trying again. "Bert? From that store, right?" It felt like an eon ago that the rusted metal jack o'lantern had started talking to her from the shelf of the general store. Mordred had taken her to see one of the nearby cities. And Bert had instantly glommed onto her, insisting that she was their savior.

This was going to be trouble, wasn't it?

"You got it." He laughed and slapped his padded leather glove for a hand on his leg. "The gods must be with us, sending you here! Our savior, who shattered the—"

"*Sshh!*" She waved at him to stop talking. "Don't talk so loud."

"Why not? Everyone should know you're the one who—" Bert clearly didn't get the memo.

His friend sitting next to him, who had one eye like a cyclops, smacked him upside the head, jostling the metal pumpkin on the wooden broom handle he had for a neck. "Shut it, tin can. Can't you see she's spying on the enemy?"

"Spying on the..." Gwen furrowed her brow. "What in the hell are you talking about? And what enemy?"

"You're spying on the elementals, clearly." The cyclops grinned. "Though why you're doing it here, in a town with only us villagers, I don't know. I won't question your secret plan."

Oh, right. Bert had blathered something about a revolution. Sighing, she ran a hand down over her face. "Sure. Whatever. Just—I don't want anybody to freak out and try to murder me. I'm pretending to be normal right now. The last time I walked into a village as a"—she glanced around to make sure no one was listening—"elemental, someone tried to shoot me. And that was after someone else successfully *did*."

"Well, we aren't going to look a gift-savior in the mouth," a woman sitting across from Bert chimed in. She smiled, and her teeth were all extremely pointy. "Especially when there's so much work to be done. We're on a mission."

"Right. Whatever. What do you want to eat?" Gwen wished she had a little notepad like waitresses tended to carry, but honestly the choices on the menu were so limited, it didn't really matter.

"You... don't want to hear about our mission?" The woman frowned. "I thought you were our sav—"

"Stop." Gwen shut her eyes. "Just stop. I'm not your savior. I'm not anybody. I didn't even break the Crystal, Mordred did."

"But because you got him to do it," Bert added. "I heard the story from one of the guards."

"Whatever." She sighed. "I've got my own nonsense to deal with, I'm sorry. I'm trying to keep him and Grinn from murdering each other and the whole island while they're at it."

The woman grinned again, flashing those pointy teeth. "Funny you should say that—that's our mission too."

Gwen stammered again uselessly for a second before forcing herself to stop and take a breath. "Fine. But can we talk about this later? I have a job to do."

"You want to stop talking about saving the world so you can wait tables?" Bert tilted his metal head to the side slightly.

"Walter's being nice to me. The owner. So, yes. I said I was going to do a thing, so I'm going to do the thing." She smiled. Honestly, she didn't want the only moment of simplicity she'd had in weeks to end so quickly. "What do you want to eat?"

Bert's two companions ordered their food and drink. Bert didn't order anything, on account of being a magical metal pumpkin on a prop body stuffed with hay. She walked back to the bar, shaking her head, to get the two beers Bert's people had ordered.

"Friends of yours?" Walter asked, arching a thick eyebrow.

"Acquaintances." She shrugged. "They were surprised to see me here." That was the truth. Just not the whole of it. That was slowly getting easier over time, she supposed. "And vice versa."

"Well, steer clear of them if you can." Walter huffed and shook his head as he poured the beer for Bert's table. "They're troublemakers, that lot—rabble-rousers."

"That sounds accurate, from what little I know of them."

She chuckled and took the two mugs. "I'll be careful." She headed back to the table in question and put them down in front of Bert's two able-to-drink-liquid friends.

"Tomorrow morning, on the edge of town," Bert whispered to her loudly, like he was some sort of secret agent. A really bad one. "We'll talk."

"Fine, sure." She wouldn't turn down the opportunity to get a little help in finding Grinn and stopping his war. But she knew the pack at the table likely meant trouble, and she had plenty of her own to go around.

The hour passed quietly, and for a little while Gwen honestly believed she might get through the night unscathed. Unfortunately, she wasn't so lucky. It was about half an hour before closing that the trouble began while she was bussing a table.

"Hey, cute thing—come sit on my lap, will you?" A drunken man with the horns of a young deer grinned at her lopsidedly over the rim of his mug of beer. He was seated at a table with four other men, who all laughed at their friend's antics and joined in leering at her. "There's a pretty silver coin in it for you."

Sighing, she ignored the man, going about her business of stacking plates and mugs.

"C'mon now. I'm not askin' for much. Just sit on my lap. Join us. We'd love to talk to you." He pulled a silver coin out of his pocket and held it up between his fingers. "All yours. Jus' for a little company."

"Sure." Picking up one of the plates on the table, she glared at him. "If I get to shove this plate up your ass, first."

The table of men laughed, but it was clear her threat didn't dissuade the deer-horned man. "I like the feisty ones! C'mon, pretty thing—Walter can spare you for half an hour."

"Oh? That's how little time it'd take? How charming—" Gwen grimaced. And it was then that she noticed the smell of something burning. Looking down, she watched as smoke curled from the wooden plate she held—from under her fingers.

She was burning the plate.

Swearing under her breath, she quickly put it out with the rag at her belt, praying nobody had noticed. "Leave me alone." Without another look at the table or anything around her, she hurried into the back, carrying the wooden plate under the rag.

Once she reached privacy, she unfolded the rag to look at what she had done. Sure enough, burned into the plate was a handprint. Her thumb on the top, and her fingers on the bottom. She had charred it black, but luckily hadn't actually set it on fire. "Shit. *Shit.*" Maybe she could get rid of the plate before Walter noticed and figured out she was a—

"I sent them away." Walter walked into the back room, frowning at her. "Sorry you had to put up with that. He's a louse." He glanced down at the plate.

Gwen fought the urge to hide it behind her back like she was a child. It was too late. She felt tears sting her eyes. "I'm sorry I didn't say anything, I was afraid you'd—you'd—"

"What, learn you were a bit clumsy and burned a plate on a candle?" He smiled knowingly and took the plate from her before promptly tossing it into the bin of garbage. "It's just a plate. Nothing to worry over. Once you're done cleaning those tables, you can stop for the night. But be careful, will you? The last thing I need is this place burning down." He walked from the kitchen, a faint smile still on his face.

He knew what she was. He *knew.* And... he was letting it slide. Wiping her eyes, she let out a wavering breath, trying to calm down after the rush of adrenaline. She liked the innkeeper, and she had really enjoyed her day. The last thing she wanted was for him to turn on her once he learned she was an elemental. Or a wizard. Or whatever she was now.

Heading back out to the floor, she did as he had instructed, focusing on cleaning the tables and mopping up the floor. Eod was lounging in front of the fireplace, watching her movements. Her protector, as always.

The rest of the night went without incident, and she bid Walter goodnight as she headed up to the room he had lent her for the night, Eod happily following her.

"*Nice man. Food!*" Eod "said" to her, blissfully unaware of their near brush with disaster. Or at least chaos.

"He's a very nice man, you're right." She walked into the room and shut the door behind her, throwing the latch. Eod wasted no time in jumping onto the bed, turning around a few times, and flopping down with a heavy contented sigh.

Stripping off her dress until she was just in her shift, she climbed into bed under the heavy comforter, happily sinking into the soft mattress. It'd been a long time since she worked a day on her feet, and she had that ache that came after a trip to the gym.

Rolling onto her back, she thought over what she could do to thank Walter. Her fire power wasn't going to do anything that wasn't disastrous. And he had his fair share of metal knives. Then, it occurred to her. If she could summon iron and fire— why not try other elements?

She'd have to be careful not to blow the place up. She'd have to focus.

Holding her hand up, she closed her fingers into a fist and, shutting her eyes, imagined what it would feel like to hold a gold coin in her palm. She imagined the ridges of the carved face and back, the weight of it, the chill of the metal.

It took a few moments of focus.

But then it was there. No longer her imagination, but *real*. Opening her eyes, she held up the coin and watched the moonlight glint off its surface through the window. Laughing quietly, she turned it over. "Fire, iron, *and* gold. I wonder what else I can do?"

"*Magic*," Eod reminded her, clearly trying to be helpful.

Placing the gold coin on the dresser, she snuggled into the pillow and fell asleep with a smile on her face. She didn't know if a single gold piece covered the cost of the room—but she figured it couldn't hurt.

For the first time in a long time, she was too tired to dream, and her night went undisturbed by visitors. And her aching body was grateful for it.

Even if she did miss the chance to see Mordred.

* * *

Mordred sat atop his iron horse. His army was once more on the move. It felt odd, the strange presence embedded in his chest—the crystal shard that now could end his life, should Zoe feel so inclined.

It was a risk. A terrible risk. But one he had no choice but to gamble upon.

At least he could take solace in the company of Gwendolyn in his dreams. At least he could hold her, and tell her how much he loved her, and beg every night for forgiveness for having sent her away. It was not the same as holding her in the real world and was indeed a pale shadow of what could have been. But in an empty home, a ghost was welcome company.

He would, quite simply, take what he could get. And be happy with it.

The regular plod of his horse and the sound of the army behind him set a familiar tempo to his thoughts. A scheme had been set with Zoe—an engineered confrontation between Mordred and the Gossamer Lady. It would leave him weakened, hopefully enough for Grinn to come from the shadows and show himself.

Unfortunately, the plot was predicated on a few variables that he could not control. The first was quite simply alerting Grinn to his vulnerable state. If the demon was not watching him carefully, there was no point to the misadventure. But if Mordred knew his opponent at all, he knew the demon was keeping a close eye on Mordred's army and their movements.

The second variable was the other elementals. Would they swoop in before Grinn reared his ugly head? Lady Thorn was not one to give up on revenge without payment in full. The vultures would be circling him, it was just a matter of whether or not they dove in to finish him off.

Or if his knights would work to protect him.

They could not act overtly to hurt him—but would they save his life, if it came to it? No. He suspected they very much would not. Save for perhaps Galahad. Even then, he could not be certain whether the Knight in Gold would defend him.

Mordred's death meant freedom. For him, for the other knights—for all of Avalon.

Turning his attention up to the sky, he watched the white clouds lazily drift overhead. A blue sky that had been missing from the world for so very long. All due to his actions—all due to his pathetic attempt to protect the island.

All due to a vow he made to his dying uncle. That he would seek to protect Avalon at all costs. Even from itself. Someday, he wondered if his thoughts would ever be allowed to drift elsewhere. Likely it would be the day he died.

He could only pray that his final thoughts were of the woman he loved.

One of his scouts rode back toward him. "My liege!" The iron soldier who hailed him was not riding a horse—instead, he was part of his horse. Mordred had taken his inspiration from old depictions of a centaur. It made the scout fast and nimble, if somewhat nightmarish, with the twisted details and asymmetrical design of his armor.

"Speak." Mordred did not slow his horse or the legions behind him as the scout pulled around to walk beside him.

"There are elementals ahead. Ten of them. They wish to parley with you."

Ten elementals. Hardly enough to stand against him and his army. Whatever could they be after? They knew the Iron Crystal had been remade as it lumbered behind him. It was hardly subtle. Violence could not be on their minds—it was suicidal if so.

Intrigued, he kicked the side of his horse and commanded it to gallop.

Perhaps they had come to aid him in his war against the demon.

Or perhaps Zoe had already betrayed him.

He supposed there was only one way to find out.

NINE

Gwen slipped the gold coin underneath Walter's door as she snuck out that morning. It wasn't exactly "early" but then again, the tavern was open late. She didn't want to have to explain to the kind innkeeper exactly the kind of mess she was about to get herself into, and she really didn't want to keep lying to him either. So she tiptoed down the stairs, with Eod being far less careful not to make a racket as he headed toward the front door.

She hadn't thought to ask which "edge of town" Bert and his friends wanted to meet her at, but she supposed it didn't matter. Eod would be able to sniff them out, she was sure. But she had one thing to do first—now that she'd figured out she could summon money, she wanted to buy herself a decent cloak. Luckily, the one store in town seemed to sell a little bit of everything, and it was already open.

"Stay." She patted Eod on the head. "I'll get you some bread and cheese or something."

"Food? Okay, stay for food." Eod lay down by the door with a grunt, those large, doleful eyes watching her.

"You're the best doggo." She smiled down at him and headed inside. The bell over the door chimed as she walked in.

"Mornin', lass!" a woman greeted her cheerfully from behind the counter. She had short, curly blonde hair and a round, inviting face with rosy cheeks and freckles. Gwen instantly liked her. The store smelled like baked goods and like woodsmoke.

"Good morning." She smiled. "I was hoping to buy a cloak and some food for the road."

"Of course, of course." The woman walked out from behind the counter, humming to herself as she went about gathering up a basket of goods. "And some meat for that hound you have, eh?"

"He'll gnaw my leg off if I don't." Gwen chuckled. "Truth be told, he's a sweetheart. Unless you're a rabbit." Well, except for that one guy that Eod attacked after she had been shot through with an arrow—but she figured that counted vaguely as self-defense.

"Reminds me of the Prince in Iron's dogs. Fearsome things, those beasts—yours seems like a gentle giant."

"Yeah." She smiled, hoping her nervousness didn't show.

Luckily, the woman wasn't really paying much attention to her, still pulling down various goods from the shelves before heading to the back. "Afraid I don't have much in the way of cloaks that'd fit you, but I do have one I think you'd like." She returned with a folded-up piece of gray wool. She unfurled it and, sure enough, it looked like a moderately thick wool cloak with a hood. It'd be perfect to hide Gwen's fire-colored hair, should it get out of control.

Smiling again, Gwen took it and tried it on. It just barely reached her ankles. It was the perfect length, and it was wonderfully comfortable. "I love it."

"Fantastic. Ten shillings for the lot." The woman walked back behind the counter.

Summoning another gold coin into her hand without

revealing where it came from, Gwen placed it down on the counter. "Will this do?"

Judging by the look on the woman's face, yes—yes, it would very much do.

"Are—are you sure, lass?" the woman stammered.

"I am." Gwen smiled gently. "I don't have much use for it." She picked up the handle of the wicker basket. "Mind if I take this too?"

"Of—of course." The storekeeper chuckled. "For this, you could have the whole damn shop if you wanted it." The woman picked up the gold coin and tossed it in her palm, testing the weight. "And I mean the building."

Oh. Huh. Well, all right then. She must have given Walter a lot more than she had figured. He deserved it. And so did the lovely shopkeeper. "Thank you. Well, have a wonderful day." She headed for the door.

"You—you too." The woman laughed again in disbelief, as if it were her lucky day. And maybe it was. Gwen had never even so much as won five dollars on a scratch ticket. She couldn't imagine what it'd be like for who-knows-how-much to just land in her lap like that.

Gwen felt a little bit like a fairy godmother as she walked out of the store and looked down at Eod. "Don't worry, I got you some snacks."

"Food! Food food food food—" Eod was up and sniffing the basket, tail wagging excitedly.

Gwen laughed and had to pick the basket up to keep the dog from just grabbing an entire cured sausage and eating it whole. "Easy there!" She ripped off a chunk of bread and fed it to him. "All right. We'll save the rest for later."

"But I want it noooooooooow—" the dog whined.

She sighed and gave him a chunk of the sausage. "Fine. But that's it. We need to find Bert and his friends.

"Metal straw man?" Eod tilted his head.

"Yeah, him."

Eod sniffed the ground. *"This way!"* He took off jogging to the right down the dirt street, confirming Gwen's suspicion that the dog would be able to help her find them.

She came across them just a few minutes later. They had a cart hitched to a horse. Bert was in the driver's seat, and his two friends—the cyclops and the pointy-toothed lady—were sitting on the back.

"There's our hero!" Bert waved at her, his leather glove for a hand was overstuffed with straw.

"I'm not—" She sighed. It wasn't worth arguing about. She figured she'd lose that battle every single time she tried to wage it. "Hi." She smiled faintly at Bert's two friends. "I'm Gwen. Nice to meet you."

"We've heard all about you," the woman said with a smirk. She blinked—and she blinked like an alligator. There was a film that came up over her eyes. It was a little... unsettling, but sure. Whatever. Gwen had seen a lot scarier things in Avalon than a crocodile woman. It made her pointy teeth make a lot more sense, she supposed. "I'm Lina. This is Mirkon." She jabbed a thumb toward the cyclops. "And you already know Bert."

Eod jumped up onto the cart without any hesitation. *"I'M DOG!"*

Gwen couldn't help but laugh as Eod licked Lina's face, his tail wagging furiously. "And this is Eod. He would like you all to know that he's a dog."

"I hadn't noticed." Lina laughed. She didn't seem to mind, as she reached up and started petting Eod. "Hello, friend." Lina grunted as Eod sat on her lap with all his weight. "Oh, all right then. Make yourself right at home."

"He does that, sorry." Gwen smiled, placing the basket of food on the back of the cart.

"I might lose feeling in my feet, but I don't mind. Reminds

me of the pup I grew up with. Never knew his own size." Lina kept scratching Eod's neck, much to the dog's delight.

"Can we get to the matter at hand?" Bert shook his rusted pumpkin for a head. "We have business to attend to." He swiveled in his seat to turn toward the back of the cart. "And a world to save."

"I have one goal—to stop this war between Grinn and Mordred. I can't let them kill each other. I just can't." Gwen sighed. "I've been trying to figure out where Grinn's gone to, but I have no clue where to start looking."

"Well, it's a good thing we know exactly where he is," Mirkon said with a prideful grin.

"Uh huh." Gwen arched an eyebrow. "I don't want to sound skeptical, but I'm skeptical. How?"

"I run a network of spies." Bert almost sounded smug before his tone turned serious. "The fact of the matter is—if those two idiots set fire to this world or put all the magic of the world back into an Iron Crystal, we *all* suffer. We—the normal folk of Avalon—are getting really tired of being subject to the power-hungry whims of elementals."

"Normal. Says a man with a pumpkin for a head. Who has a cyclops and a crocodile lady for friends."

"Alligator," Lina corrected her, laughing. "And we're perfectly normal. You're the newcomer, remember."

Gwen supposed that was fair. "All right, Bert-the-pumpkin-headed-scarecrow-who-runs-a-revolutionary-spy-ring. Where is Grinn, then?"

"Holed up in the mountain in the center of the island, deep in the caves. It's a dormant volcano, and word on the street is he's trying to make it a lot less dormant."

She shut her eyes. Yeah, that sounded a lot like Grinn. "Great."

"Hop on. We'll take you there."

She supposed she couldn't argue with the help. She climbed

onto the cart and sat next to Lina, Eod flopping between the two of them. She frowned down at her lap as Bert flicked the reins, and the horse began to walk, pulling the cart behind it.

"What is it?" Mirkon asked.

"I don't know what I'm going to do when I get there. When I find Grinn and Mordred, if I'm not too late. I don't think I can convince them to stop."

"Nobody believed that the Iron Crystal would ever be broken," Bert said from the front of the cart. "Everyone believed that the magic of Avalon would be trapped forever. But you proved that wrong. You'll fix this. I know it."

"I wish I had half your confidence." Gwen smiled, if half-heartedly.

"You'll see. I'm never wrong."

Lina leaned over toward her. "He's often wrong," she whispered loudly.

"I heard that," Bert retorted.

"But, okay, sure—follow this to its logical conclusion. If I manage to stop either Mordred or Grinn, one of them probably... doesn't walk away from this. I don't know how else this gets resolved." Gwen cringed. She couldn't stand the idea of either of them dying, for very different reasons.

She loved Mordred.

And part of her cared deeply about her grumpy old cat, even if he did turn out to be an asshole demon. All right, she always knew he was an asshole. The demon part was the new troublesome bit.

"Okay, and?" Mirkon blinked his one eye. "What's the problem with that?"

"It's complicated. Anyway—"

"Ah." Lina leaned back on the railing of the cart. "I see."

"What?" Gwen turned her attention to the alligator woman. "You see what?"

"You have a thing for the demon."

"No!" She made a face. "I do *not* have a thing for the demon!"

Lina cackled. "Then it's Mordred, huh? You go for the tall, dark, and gloomy type. Well, everyone has their flaws." She crossed her feet at the ankles in front of her. "Can't hold that against you. I married an overweight cyclops."

"I am *not* overweight." Mirkon huffed. "I'm just a little fluffy. And you *like* it."

"Way more than I need to know." Gwen put her hands over her face. "And fine. I won't deny I have feelings for Mordred. No point in lying about it."

"No one's perfect." Lina shrugged. "So, the demon dies. What's the problem?"

Gwen stared off into the woods for a long moment, debating how to explain it. With a sad sigh, she decided to just tell them the whole story, from the very beginning. Her finding the poor, sick stray cat when she was young. Taking care of it for a decade only for it to drag her through a portal and make her believe her home had burned to the ground. Her fall into Avalon as a false elemental. Her fall into love with Mordred. The destruction of the Crystal, Lancelot's death—her being human again, and then now a wizard.

"Witch," Lina corrected again.

"I'm sorry, what?" Gwen blinked.

"In Avalon, magic users who are men are called wizards. Women are witches. And no, they're not all crones and hags like the stories of old. You're a witch now." Lina smiled. "And that means we have a chance of winning." Her expression fell. "Not that I'm not sorry about all you've been through."

Mirkon was watching her with a deeper sense of sympathy. "Sounds like you have your own problems without us heaping our nonsense on top."

"What's been done to you all isn't fair either." Gwen pulled her legs under her as she shifted forward to scratch Eod between the ears. "Caught in the middle of a bunch of asshole elementals waging war on each other for no good reason. That isn't right. I just don't know how to fix it. I don't agree with Mordred, or what he did, but... I see why he resorted to it in the end."

The cart was silent for a moment, save for the plod of the horse's hooves and the creak of the wooden cartwheels on the dense dirt road. It wasn't exactly the smoothest ride in the world, but she'd take it over having to walk the whole way. Flying would require, one, her figuring out how to actually *do* that without crashing into shit—and two, it would mean leaving Eod behind, and she wouldn't ever do that if she could help it.

So, cart it was.

They rode in silence for a moment before Lina broke it again. "I'm sorry. You shouldn't have to put up with any of this."

"Thanks. But... I guess, I wished for something interesting to happen to me. I should've been more specific."

Lina snorted. The woman seemed a bit sarcastic and maybe a little bitey—no pun intended—but Gwen liked her. "So, what're you going to do?"

"Make it up as I go and do my best, I suppose. I don't know what other option I have."

"Sometimes, that's all we can do. Do our best and hope for the best." Mirkon reached out and patted her on the calf. "Try not to think too much about how you're our only hope."

"*Mirk,*" Lina snapped.

Gwen laughed. For some reason, it was extremely comical to her that she was suddenly the savior of the "normal" folk of Avalon. Comical, ridiculous, tragic, and extremely funny. Letting out a long, ragged sigh, she smiled. "We're screwed, you know."

"I've been trying to tell these two idiots that for years before the Iron Crystal sent us into hiding. Shame they don't listen."

Lina playfully nudged her shoulder. "They just keep pushing us along, one foot in front of the other."

"One foot in front of the other." Gwen let out a breath. All this time since coming to Avalon, she had been trying to come up with a *plan*. And it never got her anywhere except into deeper shit. Maybe she should just go along with the flow, for once. Maybe it was all right not to have a scheme or an idea—just to throw herself into the fray with an agenda and nothing more.

She had to save this world from war.

Somehow.

One way or the other.

TEN

Mordred slowed his horse to a walk as he approached the elementals standing in the center of the road. To say that he was surprised to see who it was, in particular, was to put it mildly.

When he grew close, he stopped his steed. "Greetings, Lady Thorn. I hope this day finds you well." Though he did his best to keep his voice even, he knew his sarcasm was leaking through.

The woman in question was eyeing him warily. Her cadre of other elementals, he did not know by name. He recognized a few from the failed siege of his keep, however. Thorn grimaced and looked away as if her next words caused her physical pain. "We wish to talk."

He laughed. He did not need to elaborate further.

Thorn continued to look utterly disgusted. "We have no desire to be imprisoned again."

"I did not suppose you would." He was glad he still wore his helm. She did not need to see the roll of his eyes. "Do you have anything of use to say to me?"

"Nor do we wish to see the world burn at the hands of the Ash King." Thorn clenched her fists as she shifted her weight from one bare foot to the other. She looked, as she always did, as though she had recently just crawled out from under a garbage heap.

"That comes as a surprise to me, seeing as you were standing beside him at the failed attack of my home." Mordred was curious as to where this conversation was leading. Wherever it was, it was against Thorn's better judgment. Or, perhaps, the elemental felt as though she had no better choice. Either way, it was at least interesting.

"The enemy of my enemy." Thorn sneered. "This world cannot suffer both of you."

"You would be surprised to find that I agree. I march against the demon—not the elementals. You may do as you wish. But if you threaten my campaign to see that bastard rid from this world, you will find yourself in the Iron Crystal once more." He was not one to make idle threats. And he suspected Thorn knew it.

She spat on the ground at the mention of the Iron Crystal. A flash of fear—of some great horror—flickered across her features. "You cannot imagine what it is like to suffer that fate. You cannot fathom what you have done to me—to my people. To *your* people."

"If you were all not so keen on terrorizing Avalon, perhaps it would not have been necessary. I hope to avoid it a second time." He tightened his gauntlet on the horse's reins. "But know that I will not hesitate."

"Nor did I believe for a second you would." Thorn shot him a vicious glare. "You have no heart—no ounce of sympathy in your soul for the suffering you inflict on others."

"That is neither here nor there, Lady Thorn. If you have merely come to scold me like a child, I will be on my way." He began to turn his iron stallion, knowing that would motivate her to speak. And he was not wrong.

"Wait."

He turned his horse back to her. The creature was annoyed at the change of direction and snorted, pawing at the dirt and leaving a heavy gouge on the surface, despite how heavily packed it was.

Thorn took a breath, held it, and let it out in a rough sigh. "We have come to make a deal with you."

That inspired him to laugh again. He was, to be frank, honestly surprised.

Thorn did not take his laughter well. She bared her teeth at him like a feral animal. "If you will not listen, so be it!"

"I am still here, am I not? Speak, Lady Thorn. I will hear your proposal."

Thorn hesitated before speaking. "We will assist you in killing the demon Grinn. We know where he is."

It was his turn to sit in silence for a moment. He had his suspicions—but it was only just that. Suspicion. Proof would be valuable. If it was trustworthy. "And what do you ask for in exchange?" Ten elementals on his side against the demon would help—not simply because it would aid in his search, but when it was time to do battle against the bastard, they could at least provide a significant distraction.

But he knew it would not come free.

The question now was simply the cost involved.

"You surrender to us when he is dead." Thorn lifted her chin in defiance. "You should stand trial for what you did to us —to Avalon."

"A trial you are very well aware I will lose, and promptly lose my life shortly after. That is your end goal here, is it not, Lady Thorn?" And, if he were to reverse their roles, perhaps he would not blame her so very much.

She shrugged. "I have made my feelings for you well known."

Shutting his eyes behind his helm, he let out a weary breath. Grinn's life for his life. Thorn would see them both dead. What did he have to lose? What of value was left to him, once Grinn was dead?

Perhaps Percival is right. Perhaps I have grown weak and tired of this game. Perhaps I do secretly wish to seek a permanent end to it.

Gwendolyn was gone.

He had sent away the woman he loved.

Caliburn had been destroyed in the name of protecting her —an act that had set forth this new turn of events. The sword that had been entrusted to him by King Arthur, he had cast aside and allowed to be destroyed.

He had already broken his oath to his uncle a thousand times over. What else did he have to gain? An eternity of being despised, of being alone? Of recapturing all the magic of Avalon and imprisoning it—and the elementals—into the new Iron Crystal? Or he would be left constantly guessing at the shadows, wondering if an elemental assassin had come to end his life.

He had vowed to free Galahad, the only one of his knights who could even pretend to have for him any semblance of empathy or camaraderie. He found himself asking one simple question, over and over again—

What was the point in it all?

What good had he truly done in all his years?

None.

The villagers he sought to protect despised him. The elementals who he sought to protect them from found him equally loathsome. Perhaps, if he had not known love, he could have tolerated it all for a thousand years more.

But now... without Gwendolyn at his side? Without her smile, her laugh, her touch?

Even in their dreams, it was a poor facsimile. And he knew her well enough that she would "save" herself for him and ignore all other suitors in an attempt to stay honorable toward their love. It was unkind. Deeply unkind. He had banished her for her safety.

And now, he had to die for her happiness.

Thorn and the others watched him, curious but patient. Letting him think through his decision. All that mattered—all that was left—was the death of the demon. Grinn had to die.

After that?

After that, he could rest.

His jaw twitched as he committed to his decision. "Very well. I accept your bargain, Lady Thorn. Where is he?"

She grinned. "He has taken to the network of caves at the foot of the mountain. But he is avoiding the volcanic areas—likely thinking you would search there first. The entrance he is using is on the northwest side. My commander Inthoti saw him there, not a day ago." She jerked a thumb behind her in the direction of a creature whose gender was long since lost to time, worn away like the limestone that made up their body.

"I will meet you there. Go ahead of the army, ensure you track his movements if he leaves. Stay discreet—we do not wish to alert him before it is necessary."

"First—you do not *order* me about." She bared her teeth again, her hands closing into tight fists. "And second, do you not think the approach of your army will give it away?"

Perhaps she was right. A smaller force—his knights, plus Thorn and her elementals—would be enough to end the demon. If Mordred split his troops, he could have a legion at every exit of the caverns. Zoe's control over him would be tempting enough bait to lure the rat out of its den. Then they would strike.

It was a good plan. A very good plan. But there was only one problem with it.

What would stop Lady Thorn from turning on him, the moment he was weakened? "And what is my guarantee of your honesty?"

"I do not think you get to have one." She tilted her head to the side slightly, a mild look of insanity in her eyes. "I am not the one who has committed terrible crimes—who has tortured every elemental on this island for three centuries. What guarantee do I have that you will not betray *my* trust and place me in the Crystal the moment the demon is dead?"

That was a fair point. "It seems we are simply left to... trust each other."

"I dislike it just as much as you. Do not worry much over that." She huffed. "But I am sick of the pointless bloodshed. I wish a quick end to you both. With as little damage to the others as possible."

That was intriguing. "You were one of the bloodiest of the warlords before the Crystal."

"Yes." She winced. "And I find myself sick of screams."

Perhaps there was hope for the island, after all.

After his death, there might be peace.

And that was a sacrifice he knew his uncle would approve of.

Not that it would not be far too little and far too late. "I will meet you at the caverns with my knights. My armies will divide and cover a perimeter. We will smoke him out." He paused. "No pun intended."

She snorted, but not at his poor joke. "And how will you do that?"

"You will see." He turned his stallion. Without another word, he kicked the creature's sides and set it off in a gallop back toward his legions. There was work to do.

It was a strange feeling, to be certain of his impending death. He expected to fear it, even after all the centuries he had spent alive. Even after all the narrowly avoided moments of catastrophe in all his battles and wars. But that was the difference, was it not? All of those moments came with the *chance* of death.

This was *knowing* his death was coming. Like an old man, told of a growth that would take his life. He did not know how long he had, but he knew it was not very much. And there was an odd... peace was the wrong word.

Consolation.

Simplicity.

That was it. His death was *simple.* It was *known.* It was *inevitable.* And there was a simplicity to be found in the surrendering of chance. Of hope.

He would not tell Gwendolyn. It would grieve her too much. He would not say goodbye to her a second time. He would spend his dreams with her while he could. He would savor every moment by her side, even as a ghost. And the knowledge of their last kiss would be his burden to bear alone.

There was enough that he had forced upon her in such a short time.

She was mortal and back with her family. Young suitors would come calling for her—especially with her newfound courage. She should be with her own kind. She should love, and be loved, a mortal boy who would give her happiness and a family.

Not him.

Not a doomed soul, destined for tragedy.

Percival believed that Mordred had become tired and weak. That Gwendolyn was inspiring him to abandon all desire to live. No. That was not true. It was her absence that had done it. The ride back to the encampment did not take long at all. When he stormed into his tent, he summoned Galahad. The Knight in Gold ducked under the entrance to his tent a few moments later.

"Yes, my prince?"

Mordred sank into a chair by a table, staring down at a map of Avalon. Picking up a small iron statue of Grinn, he placed it at the foot of the mountain, where the main entrance to the caverns was located. "You will be freed within the week."

The Knight in Gold sounded doubtful but did not argue. "What are my orders?"

Good man. He knew not to ask for the details, as they did not matter. "Gather the other knights. Prepare them for a march on horseback. We cannot take our dragons, as we cannot alert the bastard. I will split my forces. They will block the other exits so he cannot retreat."

"Will the six of us suffice?"

"Sixteen. Lady Thorn has decided to join us. For a price."

The stretch of silence between them told Mordred all he needed to know. Galahad understood the price that Lady Thorn must have asked for. And it seemed he did not wish to pry further. "Shall I send Zoe a message to meet us there?"

"Yes."

Galahad hesitated for a moment but said nothing else before he departed from the tent. Mordred shut his eyes, and let the reality of it all slowly sink in. He was going to die. But so would the bastard Grinn.

And he could rest well with that knowledge.

One thought would not leave him, would not stop troubling him. He was more and more certain that he had done the right thing by sending his firebird away. Her suffering would be lessened if she did not know his fate. It was cruel, yes—but the less cruel of the two options.

Such was the way of his existence.

Always performing the lesser of two evils.

Forgive me, Gwendolyn.

ELEVEN

Even with the constant jostling of the cart and the creak of the wheels, Gwen nodded off. She'd hoped her nap would be peaceful. Normal.

Nope.

But it wasn't Mordred's dreams she found herself in. Wherever she had suddenly found herself—it wasn't Avalon. Not because the landscape was any weirder than anything she had seen on the island, but because the sky was *entirely wrong*.

Because it was purple.

Solid purple.

With black clouds.

To say that it was a little fucked up would be to put it mildly.

That was before she considered the fact that the trees weren't trees at all, but enormous, glowing mushrooms. They stretched a hundred feet above her like evergreens. *This must be how Alice would have felt. Jeez.* She didn't like how small it made her feel, even if the rest of the strange, jungle-like environment was exactly how she would have expected it. Ferns, vines, other smaller trees and shrubs. Just purple sky, black clouds, and enormous goddamn super-mushrooms.

"Where the hell *am* I?"

Something told her that was exactly where she was, however. Hell. She wasn't sure *how* she knew. She just *did*. Probably because if she was in someone else's dreams, she knew because they knew.

And if she was in hell?

There was only one person who could be responsible for this.

Letting out a heavy sigh, she started walking down a trail through the overgrowth. The air was filled with chirps and animal cries that she didn't recognize. She supposed this was better than fields of lava with screaming, tortured souls—or some sort of Martian wasteland. She hadn't really thought too much about what hell must look like.

Rounding a corner, she heard voices. She ducked close to the tree, not wanting to be seen yet. What she saw was even more surprising and strange than the giant mushrooms and purple-black sky.

It was Grinn.

Though she almost didn't recognize him.

It was his voice that gave him away. He was sitting in the middle of a clearing, talking with someone outside of her line of sight. He looked... healthy. She couldn't count his ribs or the ridges of his spine. His eyes were both there, as were his horns and his fangs. He didn't look like a half-starved, mangy, demonic alley cat. He still was very much a monster, but a healthy one. His ribs weren't showing, and his coat was shiny and clean.

And if she wasn't mistaken, whoever he was talking to, he was *smiling* at. That was even weirder than the purple sky. She crept closer, peering around the tree to see who it was.

It was another demon, one that looked similar to Grinn, at

least in species. But this one was smaller in frame and didn't have horns. The voice was decidedly feminine, and she was lying on the edge of the clearing, telling Grinn some sort of story about hunting the wildlife. They were laughing about it, though Gwen was too far away to really make out the details.

That must be his wife.

It was a second later when there was a rustle in the bushes behind Grinn. His ear turned to listen to it, but he ignored it. A pair of small, glowing red eyes appeared in the long grass. A smaller demon jumped from the underbrush, snarling, and tackled Grinn's flicking tail. He roared in fake pain, and fell over, tussling with the smaller creature.

Another creature bounded from the grass, joining in their sibling's game with Grinn.

It was his whole family.

It reminded her of watching a pride of lions at the zoo.

Her heart broke. Absolutely shattered in her chest. This was why he hated Avalon so much—this was why he wanted the whole place to burn. Because this was what they took away from him.

Grinn sniffed the air, his ears going flat. He snarled, low in his throat.

Uh oh.

Those red eyes focused directly on her.

Oh, shit.

She backed away, hoping maybe he'd—

"*You!*" he bellowed.

Nope.

She shrieked as he ran toward her, the world fading away as he did. The phantoms of his family disappeared with the landscape. And as he ran, his body changed back to the version she recognized. The world was suddenly a dark cave, barely lit by faintly glowing moss along the walls.

"I'm sorry!" She threw her arms up over her head, not

wanting to learn what would happen if he mauled her in their sleep. "I didn't mean to—"

"I thought I was finally *rid* of you!" he snarled, pacing around in front of her, clearly furious.

Lowering her arms, she took a step away from him. "I wasn't trying to—I don't know why or how I'm here. I'm sorry. I really didn't want to intrude."

"The only thing I thought I had left was the sanctity of my own mind. And here I am, robbed even of that." He huffed, dark smoke curling from his nostrils. The cracks in his horns were glowing red, as if the insides of them were made of molten rock. Maybe they were. "Leave me be, you insipid child, and stop haunting me!"

"I—I don't want—I don't know how—I didn't do this on purpose."

He stalked away from her, his tail swishing angrily behind him. He sat by the edge of the wall, sulking. "If you even think of mocking me, I will tear your limbs off, and we shall see what kind of permanent damage I can impart on you, dreams or no."

"I... why do you think I was going to mock you?"

"Why do you think?" He rolled his one good eye.

His family? She frowned. "Having people you love and miss doesn't make you weak, Grinn."

"It has been well over a thousand years since they have gone. Yes. It does."

She wanted to hug him. But she knew that really would get her limbs ripped off. She leaned against the wall and wrapped her arms around herself instead. "No, it doesn't. They were the only things in Avalon you cared about, and they were brutally taken away from you. I don't blame you for hating everybody."

"Finally, she speaks sense."

"But I still don't think you should murder everybody."

"It was nice while it lasted." He lay down with a grunt. "If you have come to entreat me to act with *kindness* and *forgive-*

ness"—the spite in those words was almost comically thick—"then you are wasting your time. Begone."

"Mordred will be coming for you."

"Speaking of, I thought he would send you away. Why are you still here? And why do you look like a fire elemental?" He tilted his head to the side slightly. "What have you been scheming at, girl?"

She really hated being called a girl. But there were a lot worse things that Grinn had called her, so she guessed she'd put up with it. "He tried. Galahad told the boat to send me home. It turned around and dropped me back in Avalon."

Grinn snorted. "Then my suspicions are true—the island itself is an idiot." He lowered his head onto his paws, shutting his one good eye. "And the rest?"

"I... uh... I don't know. I asked the island for help, and now I think I'm a wizard? Or a witch. Whatever. I still have weird elemental powers, but I don't really understand them."

She expected a lot of things. But hysterical laughter wasn't on the list. Grinn rolled onto his side, he was laughing so hard that he wheezed at the end as he struggled to breathe.

"It isn't funny!" She put her hands on her hips.

"Oh, trust me—it very much is." He kept having to stop talking to laugh before he finally managed to calm down his snickering. "You're a new witch of Avalon? By the pits, this place truly is doomed. I should burn it all down as a matter of mercy."

"Look, asshole—" She shook a finger at him. "I'm doing my fucking best."

"I know, and that is part of the reason this is so terribly funny."

Sighing, she slumped against the wall, crossing her arms over her chest again. "Whatever."

"Mordred doesn't know."

It wasn't a question; it was a statement. She shook her head. "How'd you guess?"

"If he did, I suspect you would be trapped in the Crystal or enslaved to him with one of those charms he uses to control his knights. You are too powerful now to be allowed to run amok." He huffed, another curl of black smoke rising from his nostrils. "He will only ever allow one soul to reign supreme around here —himself."

"You're wrong. He wouldn't do that." Glaring down at the rocks, she would like to think that was true, but no, she wasn't totally certain. Mordred *might* try to embed a crystal in her to control her—a safety kill switch. Especially if he was the one holding the key to the button.

She was also just mad that Grinn saw it all so plainly. *Shit*.

"Mm-hm." Grinn put his head back down on his paws. "We could join forces. Torch this place ourselves."

"No."

"Had to try." He shut his one good eye. "Now, go away, *witch*." He snickered at the word.

She sighed. "What are you doing in here, anyway?"

"Like I would tell you."

"I want to stop this war, Grinn. I don't want you and Mordred killing each other."

"Our rivalry and our path to mutual destruction started long before you were here. Do not be so egotistical as to think you're important enough to intervene." His tail thumped against the stone. "Human hubris knows no bounds."

"I'm trying to *help* you, you piece of shit." She rubbed her hands over her face. "Why can't you see that?"

"Because you have no reason to help me."

"Except the fact that I—" She sighed. "Never mind. You know what? Never mind. I'm going to stop this war, whether you like it or not."

"There are only two ways to stop me from destroying

Avalon, Gwendolyn. Either kill me or imprison me in the Crystal. And the latter is a fate worse than death. I found a way to escape once—I will do it again." He grimaced, baring his one good fang.

Yeah. She knew all that. And that was the problem. "And there's no way to convince you otherwise?"

"No."

"I don't want you to die, Grinn."

"I believe you are the only person with that opinion. You may wish to reconsider it." He shut his eye. "Now *go away*."

Maybe he was right. Maybe there wasn't any hope, and she was just being naive. Maybe she was just remembering the asshole cat that she grew too fond of.

She walked away.

And really regretted having taken a nap at all.

I hate this. I hate all of this.

* * *

Gwen woke up as the cart lurched heavily to one side. She blinked a few times, rubbing at her eyes, trying to clear the sleep from them. Lina and Mirkon were also curled up on their sides, napping. Lina was using Eod as a pillow. Gwen smiled and tried not to feel a little jealous.

Bert was still driving the cart. The sun was starting to set, revealing that she had slept for a lot longer than she had thought. Carefully standing up, she stepped over the folks in the cart to sit down next to the scarecrow. "You must be tired."

"Nope. I don't sleep. Don't need to."

"Really?" Gwen frowned. She didn't know why that made her sad. "So you don't dream?"

"I have plenty of dreams. But not like you do." He chuckled, shrugging his stuffed shoulders. He was wearing a thick wool shirt, with bits of straw poking out of random places. "I don't sleep, but sometimes I go away—I just lose track of time, and then sometimes years could pass. Like when I was in that damn store. When I drift off like that, I think interesting thoughts. It's hard to explain."

That was close enough to dreaming, she figured. "I think I get it. Kind of like meditating."

"Sure. Whatever that is." The rusted pumpkin head swiveled to look at her. "Are you all right? You look upset."

"Bad dream." She frowned down at her lap. "I don't know how to stop Grinn. And I don't want him to die."

"Some people can't be helped. And for someone like you, that's the worst thing to hear." Bert reached out and wrapped an arm around her before hugging her into his side. He smelled like the hay loft of her parents' barn. It brought tears to her eyes unexpectedly. She didn't miss her old life, but she missed feeling safe. Feeling like she had, well, a home. "You want to fix everything and make everyone happy."

"And I keep fucking it up, everywhere I go."

"I wouldn't say that. You convinced Mordred to destroy the Crystal, didn't you? And because of that, my friends are free. And so is the magic that fuels the world."

"Right. But now a bunch of jackass elementals are going to ruin it again, if Grinn and Mordred don't rip it apart first." She sighed.

"I have faith in you. You're our savior, after all. You'll find a way."

Gwen wished she had half of Bert's confidence. Just half. Maybe even a third. "Maybe I need to stop letting the elementals push me around. Grinn and Mordred both."

"That's the spirit! Show those bastards who's boss." Bert laughed. "Stand up to them. What's the worst that happens?"

"Gee, I don't know." She smirked half-heartedly. "Death, torture, imprisonment—or all three and not in that order."

"Bah." The scarecrow shrugged. "What's living without a

little risk? The other option is you continue like you have been —at their mercy, like the rest of us. Grinn manipulated and used you. Mordred wants to control you because he can't *help* it. And when he sees what you've become now? A witch of Avalon? That'll only get worse."

She would like to think Mordred wouldn't try to imprison her, but... he'd already done it a few times before. She loved him, but there was no fooling herself over who he was and what he was capable of. He'd seek to "protect her" from others, or herself, or both. A golden cage was still a cage.

Or a hole in the ground.

Or burned to cinders because of Grinn.

No biggie.

TWELVE

Mordred found himself longing for sleep. That was not wholly uncommon for him—he did suffer from insomnia, after all. But this was a distinctly different kind of longing that he found himself with. No, this longing was because sleep meant the possibility of *her*. For only in his dreams would he ever hold her again.

Though he could not say how many nights remained where he would even have that opportunity. *You are the one who sent her away. You are the one who made it so.*

He knew it had been the only way to save her life. To protect her. But it still did not spare him the needles of doubt that jabbed at his mind from time to time. It was simply another reason on the list to despise himself.

At least when I am dead, I will not loathe my own nature. Unless there is a realm of suffering waiting for us. No, he doubted there was an afterlife waiting for him—good or bad. It was his suspicion that the island itself simply collected those who had passed on, but he had no proof of that but his own feelings.

How many days until he died? Two weeks? Two months?

He could not imagine that once Grinn was dead that the elementals would linger long in their decision to kill him. For that, he was almost grateful.

How many nights did he have left with Gwendolyn? Perhaps fourteen. Perhaps sixty. He would not tell her what was coming for him—she was on Earth, safe, with her own kind. There was nothing she could do to stop his imminent death. He did not want her to grieve for him. He would tell her that the magic was simply fading away—that Avalon was too far to let it last for long. That would explain his absence.

It was important that she believe she was never going to see him again. Or else, she might spend the rest of her days waiting for the man in her dreams to come again—committing herself to a lonely life.

No, he would not have that. She deserved more.

When sleep did finally come for him, and the magic he had embedded in her linked them together once more, he found himself in her world for a change. The sun was high, illuminating a few puffy white clouds amid an otherwise clear blue sky. He was...

He could not precisely say where he was.

A field, that much he knew. It was huge, the grass cut low, with embankments on two sides. He saw cornstalks growing that stretched as far as he could see in three directions, and a large building on the fourth that he could not identify. It was boxy and strange.

There were children running about, playing some kind of game. Sitting on wooden benches was a small crowd of adults.

One of the children in the field wielded a blunted weapon of wood. He swung it at a ball being hurled by another child. *Thwack!* The sound of the impact echoed off the building.

The ball went flying, and the child ran toward a small white square on the dirt. The crowd cheered. Whatever the goal was, it seemed the child had been successful.

He let out a quiet *huh*.

"Holy *shit*." Someone laughed. Someone whose voice he would never not recognize. Turning, he smiled faintly at Gwendolyn. She did not look human, despite this clearly being Earth. Her hair was once again shades of fire, and a pair of red wings were folded at her back. She was lounging in the grass, leaning back on her hands, her legs crossed at the ankles. The smile on her face was one of amusement and adoration both. "You look *so* fucking funny here."

"You have dragon wings."

She snickered. "Yeah, but you look like you got lost on the way to a Halloween contest." She looked down at herself. "All right, fine. I guess we both do."

"Where are we?"

"A happy memory. My dad used to coach Little League Baseball. I think he was always sad that he didn't have a boy, so he did this instead." Gwen patted the grass next to her. "I used to come to watch. Mostly because there was soft serve."

"Soft serve?" He arched an eyebrow.

"Ice cream."

He did not know what that was either. A food item, he assumed. He shrugged, turning his attention back to the children running about. There was a man on the field, clapping and shouting encouragement. He vaguely resembled Gwendolyn. Mordred could only presume it was her father.

In another world, I would ask him for permission to marry her. He had never considered the idea of marriage—not *once*. And yet, here he was, finding another lost moment to mourn.

"I just realized you've probably never had ice cream. Or hot dogs. Or a hamburger." Gwen leaned back on her elbows, kicking her feet out in front of her. "I suppose it wouldn't do you any good to eat it in a dream. Probably wouldn't taste like much."

"No. Very likely not."

She frowned, clearly saddened by that.

It was that expression that finally inspired him to sit down at her side. Reaching out, he slid the points of his fingers through her hair, combing through the strands and brushing against her scalp. She shuffled closer to him and leaned against him.

"Are you home?" He kissed the top of her head.

"I'm home."

"Are you safe?"

"As much as anybody ever is, yeah."

He could not imagine how scared and confused her family must be. He did not ask. "And the dog?"

"Eod is great. Making friends. Currently asleep on my legs cutting off the circulation, probably."

He smiled sadly. How he wished to be there with her. What precious few nights they had left to share together. "I would expect no less."

"Are *you* okay?" She lifted her head to look up at him.

"I am fine." He vanished one of his gauntlets, wishing to feel her skin against his fingers as he brushed the pad of his thumb over her cheekbone, even if it was a phantom of a memory in a dream. "Do not worry over me."

"You're going to war. With Grinn. Of course I'm worried."

He let a small, wicked smile creep over his features. "I could ease those worries of yours..."

"Ew! Dude, my dad's like—*right there*—" She pointed.

"He is only a figment."

"I'm not taking that chance." She smacked his chest.

Laughing at the moment, his laughter stilled when she frowned. She poked at the shard in his chest. Ah. Yes. Right. *That.*

"What the—" She pulled the collar of his shirt aside, revealing the gem that was embedded in his chest. "Mordred? What—"

"It is nothing for you to be concerned over. I am fine." He tugged the fabric over the shard, hiding it once more.

"Nothing to—but that's—how—*why?*" She shook her head. "Who did that to you?"

"I did. Please, do not trouble yourself over it."

It was clear that his attempts to dissuade her did nothing. She straddled his lap—a distracting movement. He might have been tempted to follow through on that distraction if it were not for how she was glaring at him. "Don't tell me not to 'trouble myself.' What do you *mean*, you did that to yourself? Why?"

He sighed. Leaning back on his elbows, mimicking her pose from before, he watched her idly. He would have to give her something. At least she could not meddle in his affairs from Earth. He knew she would stop at nothing to do so, were that not the case. "I must draw Grinn out from the caves in which he hides. I need to put bait in the trap."

"And you made yourself bait?" She shook her head. "But I don't get it."

"The magic that fuels this shard in my chest is of two parts. Half my elemental gift, and half that which my mother imparted upon me. That half is not subject to my control over it once the power is spun. In other words, I may have made the lock, but I no longer own the key."

"Who has the key?"

"The Gossamer Lady." At Gwen's blank expression, he continued, idly shrugging a shoulder. "She is one of the few with which I would trust my life. Not for my sake, mind you. But she will not break her promise and kill me, if only to spare her love the dishonor."

Letting out a sigh, she covered her eyes with her hand. "This is so fucking dumb, Mordred. What does Galahad think about all this?"

"He despises every second of everything that has transpired as of late. It is how I know that it is a plan worth doing. Or at least in keeping with my character." He chuckled and lay flat on his back. He had to admit that the idle sounds of the game being played were somehow comforting. Coupled with the warmth of the sun, it was quite pleasant.

"Can you undo it?" She tentatively touched the gem through his clothes.

"Yes. When the time comes." He likely could not undo the magic fast enough if Zoe were to weaponize it against him— well, truly weaponize it—but he would not share that information with Gwendolyn. She did not need to know about the details.

"This is fucking dumb."

"So you have said." He urged her to lower herself down to him so that he could kiss her. She let him pull her close. But just as he was about to kiss her, she pulled her head back and fixed him with a glare. He blinked. "What?"

"Don't get out of this conversation with cuddles."

"I was not intending on cuddling you."

She rolled her eyes.

He chuckled. "Very well."

Frowning, she touched the gem through his clothes again, carefully running her fingers along its ridges. "Does it hurt?"

"No, my firefly." He placed his hand over the back of hers.

Tears welled in her eyes suddenly. "I'm not your firefly anymore. I'm not a fire elemental."

"You will always be my firefly." He smiled faintly. Tonight, he would simply enjoy her presence. It was clear she was not in the mood for anything more.

She flopped down into the grass beside him, snuggling close to his side. "Can't you just... not go to war with Grinn?" She rested her forehead against his neck.

"And allow him to regain his strength, only to wage destruction upon Avalon? No. You know I must stop him."

"I know." She sighed. "There's just one of him, though, and you have a whole army."

"You have not seen the magnitude of what he is capable of. I am glad you will be spared such a sight." He kissed the top of her head.

After a silence, she let out a quiet "Yeah." She paused again. "I'm just worried."

"I know you are. But none of this is your concern any longer."

"That's not fair. You know I love you. Even if—even if we're not together, it doesn't mean I don't *care*." She lifted her head to shoot him a look. "Don't be dismissive."

"Forgive me." He traced his fingers over her cheek. "I simply wish to spare you the strife."

Her expression softened. "I know. You sent me away to protect me. I get it. It doesn't mean I like it."

"Welcome to being in my presence." He smirked. "I believe you just defined my entire reign as the Prince in Iron."

"Well, maybe if you weren't such an asshole about it." She poked him in the center of his chest. "You don't have to lean in."

"Where would the fun in that be?" He chuckled. "If I am to be despised by an entire realm, I might as well 'lean in,' wouldn't you say?"

She rolled her eyes. He caught her in a kiss before she could give him some other playful but embittered response. When he broke away, her eyes were shut. "I love you, my firefly."

Her voice was soft and unsure. "Why is it... every time you say that it feels like a goodbye?"

For a long moment, he was not sure how to respond. He wished to tell her the truth. But he wished to protect her. "Because someday, it might be true."

Wincing, she ducked her head onto his shoulder again. She didn't deny his words.

Wrapping his arms around her, he held her. Simply held

her, in that intimate embrace, and took comfort in her presence. In her companionship.

Because someday soon, it would be gone from him forever.

* * *

When Gwen woke up in the back of the cart, she was in a fucking *mood*. At least Bert and the rest seemed content to leave her in silence as she stared at the road ahead of them. Grinn was in the caves in the center of the isle. Mordred knew he was there—he had specifically referenced the caves.

That meant she was in a race to get to Grinn first.

Not like she'd have any goddamn chance of talking the demon out of torching the world. But she had to try. She had to see if she could dissuade the two men from their collision course. This was complicated by the fact that Mordred had given Zoe the ability to hurt him—even kill him, maybe.

Gwen frowned down at her lap. After petting Eod for a moment, she climbed up to the front seat and sat down next to the scarecrow. "What do you know about the Gossamer Lady?"

"Hm?" Bert shrugged. "I have no love for any of the elementals. She talks about wanting to maintain peace and balance— but she has done nothing to help. She's usually passive to the point where I swear she enjoys the chaos other people cause, she just doesn't want to get her hands dirty."

Great. More politics. Leaning her elbows on her knees, Gwen propped her head up in her hands. "Can she be trusted?"

"I couldn't honestly tell you. I've never met her."

"She seemed nice, the few times I met her, but... I don't know." She sighed. "I don't know who to trust." Even Mordred. There was no telling what he'd do when he found out about Gwen's newfound witch-ness.

"Well, first, you can trust me." Bert patted her on the back. "You're going to save us all, so I'm here to help you."

"Right. Sure." She smirked. "Ever consider I might not be *able* to save Avalon?"

"Well, if you can't, we're all screwed—so. I have nobody better lined up."

Gwen glared at him.

He laughed. "Oh come on, I'm teasing."

Grumbling to herself, she stared back at the road ahead of them.

"I have faith in you. Even if you don't have faith in yourself. And that counts for something, doesn't it? And why're you asking about the Gossamer Lady, anyway?"

"I think she's going to have a big part to play in all of this, and I just... don't know her well enough to figure out if I can trust her or not."

"Then I would assume you can't."

"I think that's how Mordred wound up the way he is." She straightened up and stretched. They had been riding in the cart nonstop for at least a day, and she was starting to get a little antsy. "Never being willing to trust anybody."

"For someone his age, and with all he's been through, I can't say I blame him." Bert shook his rusted pumpkin head. "Not that I agree with anything he does because of it. I can understand him, but that doesn't mean I have to *like* him."

Gwen smiled. "That's fair. I can't say he hasn't earned his mistrust of people. I certainly haven't been helping him. I've betrayed his trust twice so far. Soon to be three times." She ran her hands through her hair, cringing at the thought of what Mordred was going to say to her when he saw her again. "I don't know why he hasn't just stabbed me yet."

"Because he loves you."

"How—" She blinked. "How do you know that?"

The scarecrow snorted. "I wasn't born *yesterday*. It's *obvious*. You got him to shatter the Crystal and yet you're still running around with your head attached to your shoulders? A man like him only does that for one reason."

Gwen's shoulders fell. "I guess I'm the only idiot who didn't notice."

"It's hard to see when you're in the middle of it. And once you've been around a few hundred years, you'll get the hang of it."

"A few hundred years." She stared down at her hands. "I can't even comprehend living that long."

"Well, you better start. Don't go doing anything stupid, though—just because you don't age, doesn't mean you can't die. Lancelot proved that point well enough."

She shut her eyes. "Poor Lancelot..."

"No, no 'poor Lancelot.' That moron got exactly what was coming to him. He decided he wanted to make some idiotic noble last stand—but he was only out for revenge. When hate consumes a person, there's only one way it ends. In a grave."

"Like Grinn and Mordred."

"Grinn's doomed, as far as I can tell." Bert let out a sigh and wrapped his straw-stuffed arm around her shoulders in a hug. "But Mordred has more in his heart than hatred. I wouldn't give up on him so soon."

"Would you be able to forgive him for what he's done? Would anybody? I don't see how the people of Avalon would just... let him live peacefully after this." Wiping her eyes, she sniffled. She really hated how much she'd been crying lately.

"We villagers just want to live our lives and be left alone, without fear of rampaging power-mad elementals and their foolish wars. We want a chance to be free and happy. If that means he lurks in his keep somewhere, or takes up farming, we don't care. We just want him to *stop*."

"I think he would. I think he wants the same thing. Peace."

"Then it's the others I'm more concerned about, not him.

Besides, I have a woman on the inside now—you're our secret weapon."

She chuckled at that. She certainly didn't feel like a secret weapon. "Thanks, Bert. For everything."

"Anytime. That's what friends're for, after all. You're not in this alone. Just remember that."

Glancing back at the rest of the cart, she smiled. Lina was petting Eod, talking to him quietly in that dorky voice that people only managed to pull off when talking to animals. And Mirkon was reading a book, a contented smile on his face.

She had friends.

And he was right. That was enough for her for now.

"I'll do everything I can to fix things, Bert. For you and for everyone."

"That's all I need to hear." Bert patted her again on the shoulder before taking the reins in both hands again. "We'll be at the mountain very soon. Then it's up to you to find Grinn in the caves before it's too late."

Yeah. Stop a demon. With the power of *friendship*.

She could hear Grinn laughing at her in her head already.

* * *

Mordred sat on a small boulder in the camp he had set up for the night. He had chosen Galahad to accompany him and no one else. The other knights would spread out and travel separately. They were not to alert the demon before they were all in place. Mordred had to look weak—the bait in the trap—before he could snap it shut around the bastard.

Staring into the flames, however, he could not help but wish his firefly were there with him. The loneliness clawed at him in a way that he could not have anticipated. It was troublesome in more than one way, however. Not only was he facing his own grief, but he was also burdened with a newfound guilt for the grief he had caused his closest excuse for a friend. There had always been regret and sympathy in his heart for denying Galahad his love—but now he knew its sting firsthand.

Shutting his eyes, he knew what he had to do. His jaw twitched. The rational side of his mind screamed at him that it was foolish; that it would place him at a significant disadvantage. But his honor, his dignity, demanded otherwise.

Standing from the rock, he walked to where Galahad was sitting upon a stump. "On your feet, knight."

The other man arched a gray eyebrow up at him. "What have I done?"

"Get up, will you?" Mordred rolled his eyes.

"As you wish." With a slight shrug, the Knight in Gold stood, brushing himself off. He waited with a quizzical expression.

Mordred was not accustomed to looking *up* at people. He was immensely tall himself, and yet he always felt like a child standing next to the Knight in Gold. Also, upon reflection, that might be for more reasons than simply the height difference between them.

It was neither here nor there.

Holding out his hand, he hovered his palm over the crystal shard that was embedded in Galahad's chest.

Galahad blinked. "I—"

"Quiet. I need to focus." Mordred shut his eyes. It was true —he did not wish to be distracted. Pulling the magic from Galahad's body, especially after so many years of it being there, was troublesome. But like pin bones in a fish, once he knew how to search for them and pull them away, they came without difficulty.

Soon, all that was left was the shard itself. Part magic, part iron, he had to thread both out of the man's flesh to keep it from murdering him. *That would truly be my luck, would it not? In an attempt to do something noble, I destroy the man entirely.*

He tried not to laugh.

Finally, the shard was freed. He simply vanished the iron from whence it came, into the ether. The magic followed suit with nothing to hold it in the physical world.

Galahad let out a breath. He scratched his chest over the linen tunic he wore. "That... I do not... I do not understand, prince."

"I am no longer your prince." Mordred shook his head and walked away, slumping down onto the boulder he had been sitting on previously. Exhaustion hit him like a falling tree.

"Why?"

Mordred shut his eyes again. "I bargained with the Gossamer Lady. And, moreover, I find myself tired of pretending that you are my friend. If you wish to see the demon felled, I would have you stand by my side of your volition. Not mine." He paused. "And I can no longer suffer my own hypocrisy, I suppose."

Galahad let out a rush of air, and sat down on the stump, still scratching at his chest. "I... do not know what to say. Or what to do."

"You wish to be with your love. Go. You are free."

"But I swore an oath to you, all those years ago."

"An oath that was broken long ago, when you joined the others in betraying me." Mordred did not intend to let so much bitterness seep into his voice. He thought he was accustomed to being alone—he thought he was accustomed to the emptiness of betrayal. Or at least certainly he should no longer care about the events of the far-distant past. Yet here he was. Wrong on all counts. "And do not act as though this was some manner of kindness on my part—it was a bargain, as I said."

"Perhaps." Galahad sighed. "You tend to find a way to blame your kindness upon rational choices. I do not think you made this deal with Zoe simply for your own ends. I think you needed an excuse."

It was Mordred's turn to be surprised, if a little annoyed. "Read into this act what you will. I have kept you imprisoned to my service against your will for centuries."

"Yes. You have. A punishment that I do not believe fully suited the crime if I am to be honest." Galahad smirked.

"You have no longer any reason to spare me your opinions in full."

Galahad shook his head. "I never did any such thing."

"And that is another reason for why I have freed you." Mordred felt the crushing exhaustion bear down on him even harder. "For you are the closest thing to a friend that I have, as pathetic as that may be. I tire of not knowing who to trust. And with my own death fast approaching, I find myself with no patience for it."

The creases at the edges of Galahad's eyes deepened as he frowned at Mordred. "I still do not know why you agreed to stand trial."

"Because there is no other way. Because it is the *honorable* thing to do." Mordred pushed up from the rock with greater effort than before, grunting as he did. "I need to rest. If you are there when I face the demon, I will be grateful. If you are not, I will understand."

Galahad sat there in silence, watching Mordred in equal parts confusion, happiness, and grief. "I..."

"At the very least, go see her, will you?" Mordred walked into his tent. "You know where I am bound."

Galahad did not respond. Mordred suspected that was for the best. He knew the Knight in Gold would be gone when he awoke in the morning. The simple question would be—would he return?

Was the Knight in Gold truly his friend? Or was his loyalty only to Zoe? Mordred did not know if his shaky alliance with the Gossamer Lady would hold. And if it did not...

Mordred knew who Galahad would choose.

For he would do precisely the same.

Vanishing his armor and stripping off his clothing, save for his britches, he collapsed onto the cot. Sleep would come for him quickly—that was the one small benefit to expending his power in such a way.

And with sleep, perchance, would come Gwendolyn and the peace of her embrace.

Even if he could count on two hands the times they had left to share together.

Do not think of such things.

Be grateful for what you were given.

For there is only one thing that separates me from the demon Grinn.

And it is that I can still allow myself to love.

THIRTEEN

"Are you all right?"

Gwen knew it was a stupid question, even before she asked it.

They were standing in the ruins of Camelot. Though, they were no longer ruins. And she suspected this was before it wound up on Avalon.

The castle was humbler than she would have expected. It reminded her a great deal of Mordred's keep, although less... *spooky* was probably the right word for it. Mordred had an aesthetic that didn't exactly make the place inviting, to say the least.

But Camelot felt warm—like a home. There was a table in the center of the great hall with eight seats, all made of wood, and all fairly similar. She knew who they were for because they were all seated. All save Mordred, who was watching the scene, his bladed fingers fidgeting.

Lancelot, Galahad, Percival, Bors, Gawain, Tristan, and Arthur himself. They were all human—save for Galahad, of course. And they were playing a game of dice. Wooden disks were being used for currency, much like a game of poker.

They were all chatting and laughing. Lancelot reached over and slapped Galahad on the back, and the tall, older fae merely shook his head and chuckled.

"I was always the outsider." Mordred's voice was so quiet, she almost didn't hear him. She walked up beside him and hugged his arm, not minding the chill of his armor. She was used to its sharp pointy bits and the texture of the engravings. "Even as a mortal man, I was never truly welcome."

"Arthur believed in you."

Mordred snorted. "And look what happened."

"I dunno. I think you did the best you could, given everything you had to work with." She rested her cheek against his upper arm. "I think he'd understand."

"If I were cleverer, like him—if I could lead, command the respect and loyalty the way he did?" Mordred shut his eyes and shook his head. "No, Gwendolyn. I was a poor choice. He should have chosen Lancelot or Galahad. Not me."

"Maybe it's because you're secretly his kid," she teased. "Nepotism!" She was trying to cheer him up. All she got was a slight and temporary smirk. Sighing, she took his hand and wove her fingers through his. The metal of his gauntlet was no longer strange or foreign to her. It was weirdly comforting. "Can we go somewhere cheerier? Take me to a happier memory."

"This is a happy memory." He grimaced. "Bah. When did I become so *morose?*" He shook his head. "Forgive me. I am acting like a child." But there was a strange grief in his voice.

"You don't... expect to survive this, do you?" She frowned up at him. "You're planning on dying."

"I am not planning on anything. I am merely accepting that it is—" He stopped himself.

"Say it. Don't lie to me."

"Yes, because you are a paragon of truth." He rolled his eyes. His shoulders drooped a little. "I did not mean to lash out."

"You're not wrong." She rested her cheek against his arm again. "I keep hiding things from you." *I still am.*

"I leave you little choice in the matter." He shifted to wrap his arm around her and pull her close. After a long pause, he finally finished his thought from before. "I am merely accepting that my death is inevitable."

"Why?"

"A band of other elementals wish to place me on trial after Grinn is defeated. In exchange, they will aid me in my quest to see the monster finally felled." His jaw ticked. It was clear he wasn't thrilled with the idea. "Caliburn is lost. And I do not have the allies I would need to end him. I see no other way forward."

"That doesn't mean there isn't one." She leaned back a bit to watch his expression. "You agreed to this? You know they're going to find you guilty."

"Yes. Of course they will. I held them imprisoned for three hundred years in a hell of my design. I did all that I could to fulfill my vow to Arthur that I would keep Avalon safe. And I will fall, knowing that I saved this isle from Grinn at least."

Resting her forehead against his breastplate, she sighed. Why did he have to be so weirdly tyrannical and yet noble at the same time? Couldn't he just cackle and laugh like a *normal* villain? Why did he have to be so... *good* about it?

The air around her changed. It was no longer warm and filled with the smell of burning wood and the sound of laughter. It was cold. And silent.

She turned. When she saw where she was, she tried not to laugh. "I said cheery, Mordred."

"I fear this is the best I can manage."

It was a crypt. Not just any crypt, however. The sarcoph-agus in front of her was made of white marble, polished and untouched by the weather. Every detail on it was as crisp as the day it had been carved. The figure lying atop it was of King

Arthur in repose, hands across his chest and holding the hilt of a marble Caliburn.

Nudging away from Mordred, she stepped up to it to examine it. For some reason, it felt more significant than the memories of the man that the Prince in Iron had shown her. But it wasn't the only sarcophagus in the room. There were six more, arranged in a circle, around the main dais. One for each of Arthur's knights, depicting them all, and made of the elemental metal that represented them.

Except one was missing.

Iron.

She furrowed her brow.

As if reading her thoughts, Mordred shook his head. "I do not deserve to be buried here."

"Mordred..."

"You are one of the few in this world to hold a high opinion of me, Gwendolyn. For that, I am grateful. But you must understand." He gestured with a clawed gauntlet at the monuments around them. "Arthur suffered mortal wounds. Merlin, in his *great wisdom*"—the sarcasm was as subtle as a train—"brought Camelot here in an attempt to save his life. In hopes that the magic of this place might recognize the greatness in Arthur. And magic did arrive that night. And magic gifted all of his knights with elemental powers of honor and dignity. And it gave to *me* the gift of iron—a gift that should not be. A gift that gave me power that was meant to be his. Arthur, upon seeing this, gave me Caliburn and made me swear an oath to protect this place. To protect those who could not help themselves."

She listened. She had heard this all before, but there was something about this retelling of it that felt... raw. That felt final.

His hands clenched into fists. "He was not yet dead before the knights turned upon me. They thought that if I died, perhaps the magic would try again. That it would rightly choose

Arthur. That it had picked me *by mistake*. Like lightning finding the incorrect path to ground. And there was some part of me that believed them." He sneered. "But the other part of me was greedy. I wish I could say that it was simply my desire to continue living that bade me to strike them all down. But it was not. I saw the chance for the throne ahead of me—to rule the magic of Avalon—and I wished to take it. I wished to exit the shadow of my uncle and become something of myself. To prove that I was not simply his *lesser*."

Gwen held perfectly still, rapt in his words, as Mordred walked up to the dais, his boots heavy on the marble floor, his steps echoing off the stone walls in the dreary crypt.

"I sought to save this world in the only way I knew how. With the only tool at my disposal. I tried compassion. I tried diplomacy. But the death and the chaos that the elementals rained upon the populace of Avalon could *not* be tolerated." He shook his head.

The leather of his gauntlets creaked as he clenched his fists somehow tighter. "Now, I shall make my last stand. I shall lay down my life to protect Avalon from the demon—to do that which no one else is willing to do. And I shall do it, not because I despise the demon—but because my honor shall not allow me to do otherwise."

Finally, he reached the side of Arthur's sarcophagus, molten, rusted, iron eyes focusing on the features of the dead king's representation. "I hated him for most of my life, Gwendolyn. And no small part of me still does. I was never my own self. I was never *Mordred*. I was his nephew. The usurper. The shadow that haunted him. The unwanted. The prince who would never be *king*. Every waking moment of my life has been judged in comparison to him."

"Not by me."

Her voice sounded so small in the chamber. And for a moment, she didn't even realize she had said the words out loud.

She hadn't really meant to. It had just happened. Her eyes stung with tears she blinked back.

Mordred smiled, if mournfully. "I love you, Gwendolyn." He opened his arms to her. She hugged him, which still felt like hugging a Buick, but whatever. He held her, kissing the top of her head. "And I shall go to my grave, grateful to fate that it saw fit to deliver me you, even if I could not keep you for long."

"What if..." She wanted to say, *What if I'm not really gone? What if I'm really on the island, and I'm now some sort of witchthing, and we can be together, if we can just get Grinn to agree to stop being an asshole? Which, okay, is like asking the sun not to shine, but you did that once before, so—*

She held it all back. While Mordred sounded defeated and resigned, she knew better, deep down. If he realized there was another player on the board that he might be able to use to win, he wouldn't hesitate. He was, above all, a warlord, and a military general. He wanted to win. And he wanted to win by the largest, safest margin possible. Wouldn't she, in his situation?

Yeah. Yeah, she would.

She'd also be scratching at the walls trying to find a way out of whatever shady deal he had made with the elementals to stand trial. But she knew that no small part of his acceptance of death was the fact that he believed she was on Earth.

Which she wasn't.

Which made her feel like a total shit-heel.

But she didn't know what else to do.

"What if there's another way?" She held onto him a little tighter.

"I have made my deal with Lady Thorn. I am not one to go back on my word."

Oh great. Her. "I don't like her. At all."

"Have you met?" He crooked a clawed finger under her chin to tilt her head toward him.

Fuck. "Uh—no. I mean, I just don't like the sound of her."

She kicked herself internally for nearly screwing that up and then coming up with the worst cover line ever.

"Hm." He shrugged. "She does what she feels she must. She has lived an unkind life. And I have made it worse, I fear."

"I don't want you to die, Mordred."

"I know. And for that, again, I am grateful beyond words. But if I must join the demon in the grave to see the threat he poses removed from Avalon, so be it. It is something I should have done a long time ago." He smiled faintly.

"But you have a whole army. You're Mordred. You have *iron*. Why do you need more help against Grinn?"

He chuckled. "You do not know the extent of that mad creature's power. Or the lengths that he will go to for victory. I do not wish to scorch the world to save it—he owns no such restraint. To make matters worse, the caves in which he hides are like a spider's web of connecting tunnels that link to a dormant volcano. If I do not have the means to smoke him out and ensure that I can strike quickly, he will retreat, and likely do the unthinkable. Armies are capable of a great many things, but swift attacks are not one of them."

She hated how much sense that made. And that he'd already predicted Grinn's plan to blow up the volcano. "So... you get Zoe to hurt you and bait the trap. Then Lady Thorn and her crew jump in to help take Grinn out?"

"Precisely."

"Fuck." It was a good plan. Grunting, she shut her eyes. "I hate this. I hate this so much."

"I wished to spare this from you. I wish we could have continued in our dreams as if nothing was wrong. I would have quietly vanished one night, and you would have been left to think that the magic that bound us simply faded. But you ask too many questions."

"What *is* the magic that's binding us, anyway?"

"Case in point." He chuckled.

She shot him a look. "I'm not trying to change the subject—I just don't understand."

He placed his palm over her collarbone by her shoulder. "I fear I could not say goodbye to you, though I sent you away. I... linked us."

"You—how?" She furrowed a brow. Then it hit her. "Oh God, you didn't."

"It is not the same kind of magic that bound my knights to me, do not be concerned." He chuckled again. "It is simply a thread to connect us. That is all."

"Jerk!" She slapped his chest, and immediately regretted it. Plate mail. "*Ow.*"

That got him laughing. He scooped her up, and the world around them melted and changed to the balcony of his keep. It was a starry night, the same as they had shared before the battle of his home. "Will you forgive me? I fear I was once more being selfish. I did not wish to give away what was mine." He sat her down on the railing and moved to step between her knees. It gave her a few inches of height and made the disparity between them a little less awkward.

"I'm not—" She sighed. She couldn't really hold it against him. One, she didn't blame him. And two, she was kind of grateful they still had some time together. "I forgive you."

"Thank you." He kissed her—slow and gentle, savoring it.

As if he were saying goodbye.

Again.

As if every moment with her was potentially his last.

Because it was.

Unless she did something to stop it.

But what?

FOURTEEN

Mordred was alone the next morning when he walked out of his tent. Galahad and all of his things were gone. He sighed, shaking his head. Disappointed? Yes. Surprised? Hardly. Mordred could not blame the Knight in Gold.

But one thing did strike him as strange. Mordred had always considered himself *alone*. In his convictions, in his actions, in his decisions—his knights served him simply because they had no choice. His iron amalgams were the same—his creations, forced to bow to him as they had no option to do otherwise.

Yet, as he packed up his tent and rolled up his things to place onto the back of his horse... Mordred found himself feeling distinctly alone in a way that he had not before. Cracking his neck from one side to the other, he mounted his steed and kicked the sides of the iron animal. The mountain was close—it was almost time to set the trap with its bait and wait to see if it would snap shut or if the wolf would be too wise to trigger it.

It was not a problem he could solve at the moment. That was a question for the future. And one that he had done his best to plan for—but he had been forced to place his fate in the hands of others. The Gossamer Lady. Lady Thorn. The Knight in Gold.

He despised every single second of it.

He was the Prince in Iron.

He was meant to have this all under *control*.

And when he asked the question of how it all happened, how everything all fell apart—the answer led him down the road to one person. One individual.

Gwendolyn.

It made him laugh, honestly, that Percival had been proved right in the end. The girl had been his undoing. But if he had been given a choice to avoid the chaos, and his own inevitable end, but in exchange never had known her? Never had the chance to love her, and *be loved by her* in return?

He did not know if he would take it.

If he could defeat the demon, he would die with pride. He could face his end knowing that he did all he could to save Avalon, even from itself.

And now, he could die knowing that he had—even for a brief moment—earned the real love of another. He did not regret sending her away. It was the only way to ensure that she remained safe. But how he longed to hold her—how he longed to kiss her. And not simply in their shared dreams, a pallid representation of the truth.

But that was not to be.

For she was gone, never to return.

He spurred his horse faster.

He wished all this business concluded.

* * *

Gwen sighed as she stared up at the rocky face of the mountain in front of her. A dark crevice in its face revealed the cave she was meant to go into, about a ten-foot climb up some rocks.

Somewhere in that mountain was an angry demon trying to blow up the world.

Bert placed his hands on his hips as he turned his rusty pumpkin head up toward the cave. "'Fraid this is as far as we can take you."

"That's fine. You're—uh—extremely flammable." She chuckled. "And Grinn is an asshole."

"Two very true things. Lina and Mirkon won't fare much better. We'll have to stay out here and try to stay out of the blast radius."

She shook her head. "Better you leave for the coast, honestly —the odds I talk Grinn out of this are slim to none. And the odds that Mordred kills Grinn before the demon detonates the volcano are slightly better, but still too risky. If that sucker goes off, you should be as far away as possible."

"I'm afraid there won't be anywhere for us to hide if you're right." Bert patted her on the shoulder. "But we'll stay out of the range of any battles, that's for certain."

Eod was sniffing around in the grass.

She frowned, watching the dog happily hunt for critters. "I think you should take Eod with you. I don't want him to get hurt."

"*What? No! Dog stay. Dog protect!*" Eod looked up to her, his ears drooped, obviously insulted that she'd make him leave her side.

Kneeling down on the ground, she opened her arms to the animal. He walked over, licking her face, tail wagging in that way that was both hopeful and sad.

"I just don't want you to get hurt. I love you too much to let that bastard do anything to you." She scratched him between the ears.

"*No hurt. Dog stay.*" Eod sat in front of her and let out a sad whine. "*Dog protect. Dog made promise.*"

Hugging the animal, she shut her eyes. There was no point in trying to deny that didn't break her heart. "Fine, fine…"

"*Yay!*" Eod happily thumped his tail on the ground.

"But you have to guard the entrance to the cave. To make sure nobody sneaks in after me. Okay?" She hoped that worked. She had once threatened to maim Grinn if he ever hurt Eod, but she didn't exactly consider the demon to be particularly predictable.

"*Okay! Protect cave.*" His tongue drooped out of his mouth sideways, making him look far more goofy than fearsome. She'd have it no other way.

Standing up, she took a breath and let it out. "All right. I guess I'm going in."

"We'll see you soon. And… good luck. We're all counting on you." Bert stuck out his leather glove for a hand, the straw poking out of it at odd angles.

She shook it and couldn't help but smile. "I know, I know. Quit reminding me."

Bert chuckled and headed off into the woods to where he had left the cart. "I have faith in you!" he called over his shoulder as he left. She had already said her goodbyes to Lina and Mirkon. Hopefully, she'd see them again soon.

"At least somebody does," she muttered to herself as she started climbing up the rocks toward the mouth of the cave. "Stay put, Eod—I'll be back soon."

"*Protect! Protect!*"

She chuckled. She loved that dog more than words could describe. When she made it to the entrance, she peered into the darkness. Nothing greeted her except silence. "Great. Cool," she grumbled to herself. "Find a demon in a network of caves. And not get super lost or fall into a hole and get stuck and die."

Holding her hand up, she set it on fire, using herself as a makeshift torch as she walked inside. How was she going to find Grinn?

"This is a bad idea. A very, very bad idea." But it was the only idea she had. The cave entrance was at least decently sized —she didn't have to squeeze through any small rocks. She'd try to take comfort in the fact that Grinn was huge, so therefore unlikely to hide down any tiny corridors—but he could also change into a cat. So. That small glimmer of hope was also thrown right the fuck out with the rest of it.

The cave was rather unremarkable, as caves go—the walls were made of rock. And the floor. And the ceiling. And the stalactites. Or were they stalagmites? She could never remember which one was which. She hadn't remembered in school, and she certainly didn't remember now. *Sorry, Mr. Bonover, I failed you.*

The cave was also remarkably dry at least—it wasn't moist or humid, and the air had that basement smell to it, but didn't smell like mold. That's all she'd need, trying to talk to Grinn and having an epic sneezing fit while she was at it.

It seemed like any old cave.

Right until a rock *moved.*

Not like, *rolled* because she had kicked it. But it—there was only one word for it.

The rock scampered.

It literally just took off in a direction like a rodent, only it was entirely rock-shaped. It ran away from her like a mouse might.

She stopped.

And stared.

"A scampering rock. Great. Just fuckin' great." Shaking her head, she continued on, working her way through the winding paths. She had another realization, about half an hour in.

How the *hell* was she going to get back out?

She stopped and slapped a hand over her face. "I should've been marking the walls. God, I'm such an *idiot*." Better late than never, she supposed. She summoned a piece of iron into her hand and scratched an arrow onto the wall, pointing back in the direction she had come. She did that every fifty feet or so, making sure that she carefully marked any splits in the path.

It might not get her all the way back to the entrance, but it'd get her closer than... well, wherever she was now.

The walking gave her time to think, as she wove her way deeper and deeper into the mountain, picking paths at random, having no way of knowing if she was heading closer to Grinn or farther away.

There had to be some way to track him. Some way of knowing where he was. She was a witch, right? A witch with the ability to summon a little of any element. But what *else* could she do? Was that it? Mordred had magic on top of his elemental powers, but that had come from his mother, he had said.

Could she do real magic?

Stopping, she figured it didn't hurt to give it a try. Nobody was around to make fun of her for muttering uselessly to herself in the dark, after all. She extinguished her fire, plunging her back into complete darkness. She took a deep breath. Maybe it was just like using her elemental gifts. Maybe it just took focus and intent.

She tried to listen, in the deafening silence of the caves. In the complete absence of light, shapes seemed to appear around her—twisted, strange monsters. Claws and talons, skulls with gaping eyes and distorted proportions watching her.

Taking another slow, careful breath, she tried to steady her heartbeat and ignore the monsters her mind—or the island—were conjuring for her. Avalon was made of magic. It had to be there, somewhere in the darkness—in the silence.

Reaching out her hand in front of her, into the emptiness, she pretended she was reaching out for a strand of yarn. She didn't know why she picked that. But she let her instincts guide her. *Show me the way to Grinn*, she grasped the thread in her hand. *Guide me to him.*

The thread in front of her began to shimmer and glow— barely there, but she could *see* it! It flickered like dew caught on a spider's web. But it stretched off into the darkness of the cave.

Maybe she was going insane. Or maybe, just maybe, the island was listening to her. Maybe her magic was real.

Or maybe she was completely hallucinating and was going to step off a cliff into a forty-foot drop and shatter both her legs.

Place your bets, kids. She started walking, following the strange glowing line that wove its way through the nothingness of the cave. When she didn't smash into a wall or fall to her death for the first hundred feet, she began to feel far more confident that the glowing thread was real.

It took her a few moments to realize that the thread was starting to fade—but only because there was light creeping in to replace it. It was a deep, eerie orange-red, and began to reveal the craggy surfaces of the rock.

The air quickly became thick and hot, and she wrinkled her nose at the smell of sulfur. It was about fifty feet later that she took another left turn, and found the area illuminated by fire. Specifically, *lava*. There were holes in the floor that stretched down below to another chamber that was boiling with it. The glow of the molten rock cast the room in bizarre and unsettling up-light. It made the whole situation somehow worse.

But that wasn't the only unsettling thing. There was writing on the walls—or at least she assumed it was writing. It was in a jagged, slashing language that she couldn't understand—something that was designed to be made with sharp objects. It covered the walls on both sides, and the writing was glowing red. Just a little. But enough.

Walking up to the wall, she reached out and touched her fingertips to the writing, and instantly regretted it. It... *tasted* bad. She didn't know how, but touching it gave her a taste in her mouth like licking a battery. Sour and bitter, and gross. She took a step back, and decided she really didn't like the writing—whatever it was. It made the hair on the back of her neck stand up. It must be magic.

But it felt *wrong*. This wasn't Avalon's magic. This was something else. Something that didn't belong there.

Grinn had to have something to do with it. She kept walking through the chamber, following the writing now, as it wound slowly deeper. The writing grew thicker and covered more and more of the walls as she went, until she finally found who she was looking for.

There he was. Grinn. The Ash King. Lying down on a rock that was glowing faintly with heat. He really was something terrifying when he was a full elemental—the cracks of his horns glowing, and smoke curling from his nostrils with every exhale. And around him, covering all the surfaces within his considerable reach, was more of the terrible writing.

It must be demonic magic.

He lifted his head upon hearing her, and his lips peeled back in a snarl. "*You*. Now what do you want? Go away, girl!"

"I—um—I'm sorry. But I couldn't—" She put out her hand and lowered it. "I just came to talk."

"I have had enough of listening to you yammer for a lifetime. I have nothing to say to you. I will do you the dignity of letting you live—now leave me be." He stood, shaking himself off like Eod might, the ash from his coat raining down to the rock beneath him. He prowled over to her. The air around him was even hotter.

"Please. I just want to—" She knew that if she wasn't a witchy-elemental-thingy-whatever, she'd probably be burning. Or unable to breathe. It was kind of painful even so. She winced and took a step back.

"I know what you want. It's obvious. You want me to declare *peeeeaacccee*—" He put his voice up an octave for that last word as he gestured in the air aimlessly before snorting in laughter. "Don't be a fool. Even if I were to accept such a ridiculous notion, do you honestly believe anyone here would let me live?" He sneered. "That bastard boyfriend of yours is already likely on his way here, hoping to lure me out, isn't he?"

"Um—" She panicked. "Uh—um—no. N—no, he isn't." She paused. "How did you know?"

"I didn't. But thank you for confirming my theory." He rolled his one good eye and turned around to walk away from her. "Go away, Gwendolyn. You have no business being in the middle of any of this. Be glad I do not kill you right here and now."

"But—" She really should have come up with an argument while she was traveling to the caves. Nothing had come to mind then, however, and nothing was coming to mind now.

Grinn sat back down on his rock. "It doesn't matter either way. Whether or not he's here, or hiding in his keep, him and this entire island is done for."

Maybe she could poke holes in his plan. Show him that he couldn't stand against Mordred, his iron army, *and* all the elementals. "What do you think will happen to the island if you succeed? That Avalon won't collect more people eventually, like it did before? Or do you want to be the only one on this island, with nobody else around?"

"Yes. I do." He laughed. In that dark, horrible way that told her that Grinn had a plan for that. And it wasn't going to be a plan she liked. He gestured a claw at the walls around him. "And if the powers that control this island are foolish enough to drag more victims here, I will simply murder them before their boats land on shore."

She cringed. Great, well, that was lovely. She looked over at the terrible writing on the walls. "You're using your demonic magic to reignite the volcano."

"Yes, indeed."

"But... this island has other fire elementals. And lava elementals. It won't do anything to them."

"Don't you fret, I've thought of that." The demon's smile was toothy and decidedly violent, clearly seeing the recognition on her face of what was coming. "The magic of my people will run deep in this place, making the explosion something that only a demon could survive. A shame there is only just the one of me, no?" The bastard had the balls to look gleeful as he finished his explanation. "And all of Avalon, and everyone on it —including you, and that iron bastard of yours—will be reduced to cinders and ash."

"But you can't." Gwen knew it was a stupid thing to say, but what the fuck else was she supposed to do when a demon threatened to destroy an entire island via a corrupted volcano? She wasn't even concerned for herself—not really. She didn't want to die, but if everybody else was dead too, she certainly wouldn't want to hang around with Grinn as her only company.

"Believe me, I very much can." Grinn yawned as if the conversation were boring to him. "Soon, this whole island will erupt in hellfire. So, congratulations on becoming a witch, or whatever it is this island turned you into. For as long as it lasts." He snorted and laid his head down on his folded paws. "Now, go away."

"But—" She shut her eyes. "I won't let you."

"And are you going to stop me? Precisely how? Are you planning on fighting me? Standing alongside Mordred?" He huffed. "Please. I've seen you fight. I am from the realm of Astaroth, the Archduke of *Wrath*. I have been in more battles than you've had seconds of life. Don't make me laugh."

No, she wasn't going to fight him. He was right, it was point-less. He'd mop the floor with her, and she'd just end up with her head ripped off for her trouble. "I don't want anybody to get hurt. That includes you."

"How sweet."

The sarcasm made her want to throw a rock at his head. She clenched her fists. "Why? Why do you have to do this?"

"Because I watched my family *die*, you fool." He lifted his head to glower at her. "Because I have been hated and despised for centuries. Because, for the simple fact that I am a *demon*, they hunt me."

"Right. And the fact that you're a genocidal maniac has nothing to do with it." It was her turn to snort in laughter. "You're totally above reproach in all of this. There is no way that's really what you believe. Don't lie to me."

"I do not care what you think, girl, first of all. Second of all —do not forget I have been on this isle, away from my family, for nearly fifteen hundred years. I began my time here attempting to find a way to coexist. I have long since given up."

"Away from—I thought they were dead?" She blinked.

"Demon souls return to hell to be reborn when we die." He laid his head down on his paws again. "My wife and my children live—and have spent countless years—without me." The weight of the words took the usual sarcasm out of his voice.

She blinked. "So... if you die, you'll just go home?"

"No. I have been too corrupted by Avalon's magic." He sneered, but turned his head away from her, again miming like he was going to just curl up and go to sleep. "My soul is too perverted by the elemental power. Avalon keeps what it takes. It wouldn't ever let me go. I will never see my family again. They are as good as dead to me."

Gwen stood there in silence for a long moment and didn't know what to say. Or do. But her anger and annoyance at him faltered and failed in the face of his tragedy. "I'm so sorry."

"I don't care."

Yep, there was the annoyance and anger back again. "I came here because I want to help you, Grinn—because I don't want to see you die. I'm trying to be your friend because I *do* care.

Because I've been here, trying to help you, since the moment we met!"

"You helped me because you have a pathetic need to be loved. You always came to me, whining and whimpering, complaining about some new tragedy in your pathetic mortal life. You wanted so *desperately* for your 'stray cat' to care about you." Grinn stepped closer to her, his lips pulling back in a grimace. "And I never have. Not once. Every second you spend in my presence I wish you nothing but suffering. I simply *needed* you. And I no longer do. Leave me be!"

Gwen was shaking with rage and hurt in equal measure. "Fine. I will find a way to stop you."

"You have no time. My preparations are nearly complete. I will detonate this island before the night falls tomorrow. So, unless you manage to summon the ability to undo demonic magic within the next thirty-six hours?" He sneered. "I think your time is better spent praying to whatever god you think will listen or sucking the cock of that idiot boyfriend of yours."

"Whatever." She turned on her heel and began walking away. "I'm done being insulted by you."

"Something tells me that isn't true."

She walked back into the darkness, no longer afraid she wouldn't be able to find her way out. "Fuck you, Grinn."

She listened to his laughter fade as she headed back toward the entrance of the cave.

And felt every ounce of hope she had for saving him fall away as she did.

* * *

Mordred stopped his horse as a familiar, yet unexpected figure was standing in the center of a clearing in front of him. He had left the main road and taken one of the thinner hunting trails that wound up to the entrance of the cave that Lady Thorn had directed him to. It had been Thorn he expected to meet here.

Not who he had instead found.

He narrowed his eyes. "Wizard? Why are you here?"

"Not getting involved, but also getting involved, but trying not to get involved." The other man shrugged. He scratched at the beard on his face that was stubble that had been allowed to get a few days out of control. "But getting involved, anyway."

"One of these days, it might behoove you to speak sense. Just once, perhaps. You might find that you enjoy it." Mordred disliked wasting time with the wizard, but it at least spared him from his own circular thoughts.

"I'm speaking perfect sense. You just choose not to understand me. That's your problem not mine." The mage shrugged. "Whatever. I'm going to just stand here and talk to you for a little while."

"Why?" Mordred arched his eyebrow.

The other man fished something out of the pocket of his faded blue robe. It looked like a pocket watch—one of the strange new devices that Mordred had seen on Earth before he had closed the gates. "Because I'm stalling for time."

"For... what, precisely?"

"To let them finish talking."

Mordred shut his eyes. He was always an inch away from throttling the eccentric magic-user. "Goodbye, wizard. I have business to attend." He nudged his horse to a walk, intending to simply go around the other man.

"No, no. Hey, hold on. Like—another minute. Maybe two. They're taking their sweet time." The wizard sniffed dismissively.

"If you do not tell me who we are waiting for, I am leaving." Mordred pulled his stallion to a stop again. The iron animal was displeased by the waiting, and he dug his hoof into the dirt angrily, kicking up a few rocks. "I will not bother to explain to you the importance of what I am here to do, since you already know."

"Great." It was clear the other man was not listening to him. He did not even bother to look up from his watch. Mordred shut his eyes, fighting the urge to smack the man. Or have his stallion trample him.

"Am I meant to simply stand here like a fool and wait, while you will not tell me why? I have tolerated your eccentricities on enough occasions. I demand that you—"

"Yeah, yeah." The other man waved his hand dismissively. "Just hold on a sec, will you?"

"No, I shall not 'just hold on a sec,' I—"

"Aaaaand—" The mage lifted his finger. "Here we go."

A barking from the woods caught Mordred's attention. He shifted in the saddle as a dog—a very familiar dog—ran from the woods.

It was not possible.

It was not possible at all.

Mordred dismounted his horse as Eod ran up to him, barking and eagerly jumping up in an attempt to lick his face. Distractedly, he greeted the animal. "But..."

"C'mon doggo, that's our cue to leave." The wizard started off into the woods, whistling for Eod, who ran over to the other man's side.

"Doc, what the *fuck* are you doing here? Get back here! Why'd you abandon me, you—" The all-too familiar female voice broke off abruptly.

And that was when he saw her.

Hair, the color of fire. Wings, the same. Beautiful. Perfect.

His firefly.

Had he lost his mind?

Had he truly gone mad?

How was it possible?

Her orange-yellow eyes went wide upon seeing him as she froze like a deer.

"C'mon, pup. Let's leave them to it," the wizard murmured as he walked away, taking Eod with him.

Mordred could simply do nothing but stare for the longest time. When he found his voice, he felt as though he were addressing a phantom. A spirit. An impossibility.

"Gwendolyn...?"

She smiled, nervous and shy. "Hi."

FIFTEEN

Mordred felt as though time had frozen around him.

It had to be an illusion of some kind—a trap. The wizard must have placed him under some manner of enchantment.

"Mordred, I—" The apparition of Gwendolyn spoke, her voice quiet and unsure. Frightened. The sound of his name on her lips cinched a vise around his heart.

Stepping toward her, wondering if the mirage would shatter, he closed the distance between them. She was watching him with those eyes the shade of flames, flicking between his, clearly uncertain.

She was afraid of him. Or perhaps, of what he would do.

This was no illusion.

It was her. She was real. And she was *here*.

Questions ran rampant through his mind. How was she still on Avalon? Had Galahad betrayed him? How was she an elemental of fire once more? How had that possibly come to pass? And was she here to aid him, or to harm him?

For one moment—one short moment in time—he allowed himself not to care.

Gwendolyn squeaked as he picked her up by the waist, seeking his lips with hers. She wrapped her legs around his waist as he pressed her against a tree, his heart overfull and breaking at the same moment.

His Gwendolyn had returned to Avalon. Or perhaps, she had never left.

Threading his claws into her hair, he pulled, drawing a gasp from her. It allowed him to deepen the kiss. He wanted to never forget the feeling of her. Their shared dreams had been only a ghost of reality—a pale shadow of what the waking world could offer them.

She moaned against his lips, wrapping her arms around his neck to hold onto him. Her beautiful dragon's wings were unfurled.

He wanted her. No, he needed her.

When he finally allowed them both to breathe, her chest was heaving as she tried to fill her lungs with air. "Mordred, I..."

"Do not speak." He pressed a metal digit to her lips, silencing her. "For when you do, it means the end of it all."

The end of his plans. The end of his life. Perhaps, even the end of Avalon itself.

She shut her eyes, nodding once to say that she understood. He had planned to die for he had no reason to live. Until *now*.

But everything had been set in motion to save the world from Grinn. And it was too late to stop. There were no other options before him. No other path that he could walk.

Yet, it could all wait just a few more moments, could it not? He kissed her again, seeking shelter from the coming pain in the pleasure of her embrace. His body tightened in the need for her —the desperate wanting that filled him whenever she was near. He would love her, like the bastard that he was, up against a tree in the forest. And he would cherish it for however long he had left.

For this would be their last dance.

*   *   *

Gwen wanted to cry. She wanted to scream. She wanted to weep in Mordred's arms and beg him for forgiveness. But that was going to wait.

Because this was about *them*. About the strength he possessed. About the way he moved. About the taste of his lips on hers—tinged just slightly with metal. His claws dug into her skin, just enough to sting, as he peeled her dress from her with an almost frantic speed, throwing it aside.

His armor vanished a moment later. She felt his desire pressing against her, and she moaned as his claws scratched her as he hefted her farther up the tree. She didn't care how the bark rubbed her back. She'd deal with that later.

She needed him just as badly. Needed to feel him—to revel in his skin against hers. And a moment later, they both had what they were so desperate for. He pressed inside her, slowly at first, before sinking himself home to the hilt with one vicious snap of his hips.

She wailed against his lips, clinging to him in desperation.

The tempo he set was furious. Passion, need, perhaps some anger—and *love*. All expressed in one, wild moment that made her heart soar and her nerves light up with ecstasy. Damn it, he felt so good as he took her like the warlord that he was.

Her body, her soul, her heart—they belonged to him. She could only cling to him as he rutted her, sending her to the heights of bliss and back again. His thrusts became somehow rougher, the tempo becoming erratic as he rammed himself as far as he could go. Burying his head into her hair, he let out a muffled roar as his pleasure crested, the feeling of him surging inside her carrying her right alongside him.

When she could process reality again, they were lying in the grass, half atop her discarded dress. He was kissing her, tenderly now—softly—as if to say sorry for what he had just done. Like she hadn't enjoyed every goddamn second of it.

She kissed him back, running her fingers along his cheek, stroking the edge of his cheekbone and then his jaw. He was too handsome for words. And she wanted to burn this image of him into her mind.

When they had settled for long enough, she tugged her dress back on and began lacing up the front, still sitting beside him in the grass. He was watching her, his expression turning more and more serious by the moment.

It was fess-up time.

She sighed, her wings slumping a little. They reacted to her mood, which was pretty weird to notice. But now wasn't the time to be fascinated with her wings. Shutting her eyes, she decided to just let it all out in a rush. "Galahad told the skiff to 'take me home,' in those exact words. The skiff went through the mist, and brought me back to the shore, where Doc was waiting for me."

Mordred let out a huff of a laugh.

"I... knew I couldn't come back to you—you'd just send me to Earth with more specific instructions that time." She shook her head. "I couldn't leave. I just couldn't abandon you and everybody else. I just *couldn't*. So I begged Doc to teach me how to use magic. Something, anything, any way to protect myself and prove to you that I—that I'm not a liability."

He stayed silent, letting her finish. She didn't know if that was a good thing or a bad thing.

"He took me to a place where he said the magic was stronger. Said that it was up to me to figure out how to tap into it. A tornado came out of nowhere—sucked me up into the sky, and everything went dark. I... I saw some weird shit, and then I think I talked to the island. Like, Avalon. It told me that it would give me power to protect myself and others."

"And in exchange?"

"I can't ever leave the island. Ever."

"You struck a deal with an Ancient. How charming." Mordred let out a heavy sigh. "And so, what have you become?"

"I—well, technically I saw more than one of them, and—" She held up her hand and changed it from flesh to rock. "I think... I'm a witch."

Mordred stood, his armor reappearing over him like molten metal. He paced away, running a gauntleted hand over his face. "And why did you not tell me you were on Avalon?"

"You'd hunt me down. Send me back to Earth."

"And after you became this... witch? Why not then?" His voice was flat. Emotionless. And that scared her. That meant he was getting pissed.

She stood, smoothing out her dress, letting her hand change back to normal. "I... I don't know." She was cornered. Shutting her eyes, she told him the truth. "I was scared. I guess I didn't know what you'd do. If you'd—"

"Try to use you as a weapon."

She really wished he'd face her. "Y—yeah. I mean, I get it, but—I—I just—"

"You still do not trust me, Gwendolyn."

"I—I mean—"

He cracked his neck from one side to the other. "Perhaps you are right not to. I find myself backed into a corner. There is only one new advantage I find myself with. And that is you." He finally turned to face her, and now she wished he hadn't. His expression was ice cold. "Now I must ask, to whom are you loyal? The demon or me?"

She blinked. "You. I'm loyal to you. I love you, Mordred."

"And I you." He clenched his hands into fists at his sides.

"But that has not stopped you from betraying me in the past. Several times, I might add."

She swallowed the rock in her throat and stared down at the ground. "I'm sorry. I'm sorry for all of that. I don't know what to do, and I'm trying my best. I—I can't hate Grinn, even though I know I should. I came here to try to stop him, but he wouldn't listen to me, and—"

"You went to speak to him *alone?*"

She shrank back from his outburst. "I know I shouldn't have, but—"

"He knows you are here. He knows you are"—he gestured at her with a claw—"whatever it is you have become! He could have hurt you. Captured you. You are not invulnerable!" He paced away again, letting out a ragged sigh. "You must learn to see him for what he is. You took a terrible risk."

"I—I know—but he—he was—"

"*He has never been your friend!*" Mordred rounded on her. The sound of his holler sent the birds in the trees scattering. "Not now. Not ever. He only seeks to use you, as he does all those around him. Whatever reason he had for letting you walk free, it is to his benefit, not yours. And certainly not mine. Do you understand?"

"I—I—yeah—"

As Mordred walked toward her, slowly, she felt as though she were staring down some kind of inevitable force of nature. That nothing, certainly not her, would ever get in his way. Whatever defeated part of him that she had seen in their dreams was gone.

This was the warlord.

And he was not about to surrender.

"Will you stand beside me against the demon and the elementals?" His gaze pinned her to the spot. She felt like she was stuck like a butterfly to a board.

Flicking her eyes between his, she searched for some kind of compassion. Some kind of leniency. But there wasn't any to be found. Just cold determination. "I—I don't want to hurt anybody."

"That time has long since passed, Gwendolyn. I sought to send you home for my safety *and* yours. You chose to stay. Now, you must face the consequences of your actions. Do you stand with me, or do you stand against me?"

"W—with—" she stammered. She tried to take a step back from him, but he snapped his hand forward, grasping her by the back of the neck and dragging her back to him, his claws pricking her skin dangerously.

"Are you so sure?" He arched an eyebrow. "I will not tolerate a fourth betrayal, Gwendolyn. My love for you is endless—my patience is not."

This side of him was always so unexpected. He had shown her a gentler side of him before. The kindness, the laughter. Not... not this. Not the Prince in Iron. She wished she hated it more than she did—even if she really would rather prefer it not be pointed at her.

The truth of the matter was, she loved both halves of his personality. The angry, dour exterior, and the softer interior.

"I understand," she murmured.

"I have one final question for you, my firefly." He toyed with a strand of her long, fire-colored hair, twirling it around his fingers. "These gifts of yours. Can you command any element?"

"I don't know. I think so. I haven't gone through the list."

"And does this extend to iron?"

There it was. There was the question she was waiting for. Cringing, she stared at the center of his breastplate and said nothing for a long moment. Apparently too long. The hand at the back of her neck tightened just a little in warning.

"Y—yeah. I think it does." Her voice sounded as small as she felt.

Mordred laughed.

It wasn't a joyful laugh.

Leaning forward, he kissed her forehead. "Then perhaps there is a way out of this for us, yet. Come. Show me where the monster is hiding." He turned from her, storming off into the woods.

It left her standing there with only one question—

What have I done?

SIXTEEN

Grinn despised waiting.

He despised it more than almost anything else he was ever tasked with doing—part and parcel, he supposed, because he was asked to do it so damn much.

Three hundred years in the Iron Crystal, give or take.

Ten years stuck as a cat on Earth with the child.

And now?

Now he was waiting for his work to be complete with the volcano. Soon, it would be corrupted beyond repair—his demonic influence turning it to hellfire. Finally, *finally*, Avalon would be destroyed and all the sniveling idiots that filled it would be wiped from existence.

If the universe were kind, the act would draw the attention of those in hell, and perhaps they would come bring him home. He snorted, a curl of smoke rising from his nostrils as he lay on the stone floor of the cave. No. There was no going home. Avalon had sunk its claws too deep into him to part with him now.

This was not about freedom.

This was about *revenge*.

They would all pay for what they had done to him. And more than that, he planned to make the island itself pay. Once this place was nothing but ash and bone, he would ensure no one would ever set foot upon Avalon ever again. Whatever sentience lay behind the magic would suffer along with everyone else.

Mordred would be dead.

Thorn would be dead.

Gwendolyn.

He sighed. He found the girl irritating, but not insufferable. Perhaps that was simply a sign he had spent too much time in her presence over the past ten years. Her insistence that she *cared* would feel more legitimate if she did not *care* about every living thing she came across. Every stray animal had to be fed. Every insect trapped indoors had to be saved. It was sickening.

And now she was a damnable *witch*.

The thought made him laugh. He folded his paws under his head and rested his chin on them. The spells had been woven but, like an acid, they took time to leach their way into the stone. Until then, there was nothing he could do but sit. And wait.

And that was something he was very well accustomed to doing.

He would have stayed there until it was all finished, except for the distinct crackle of powerful magic that washed over him. Someone had released a spell—and a large one at that. It wasn't Gwendolyn, he was damn sure of it. She was too new to wield something like that.

So who?

And what were they up to?

He couldn't risk someone meddling in his plans. Growling, he pushed himself up to his feet and padded through the cave, tail flicking angrily behind him as he went to find the source of the disturbance.

Whoever it was would pay a heavy price for the interruption.

He crept to the edge of the opening as he heard voices. Voices he recognized. Voices he *loathed.*

They had come for him, but all he had to do was wait just a little longer, and it would not matter.

When the voices rose to shouts of anger, he was intrigued. But when he heard Modred holler in agony—he was unable to resist his curiosity. If the Prince in Iron was suffering, Grinn *had* to see it for himself.

He'd earned that much.

* * *

Gwen was out of breath by the time Modred stopped his march through the woods. He had long legs, and she had to jog just to keep up with him. Sitting on a rock by the entrance to the cave was Doc. Eod barked happily and ran up to Modred, tail wagging.

"You—" She stormed up to Doc. "How *dare* you!"

"What?" The wizard threw up his hands in a show of helplessness. "What'd I do?"

"You abandoned me! You left me all alone in the middle of nowhere—" Gwen fought the urge to smack him.

"I didn't do anything of the sort. You had Eod. And he took you to the village where you made new friends." Doc planted his hands on his hips. "You figured things out just fine on your own."

"But—you—" she growled, shutting her eyes and counting back from three to keep from screaming at the wizard. "You could have helped me. Explained to me what was happening. Or showed me how to use magic."

"That would have been meddling."

"But—"

"Enough squabbling. What's done is done." The Prince in Iron patted Eod on the head idly as he gazed at the entrance to the cave. His expression was dour. "I can sense it. It will not be long."

"Mmh, stinks like hell." Doc wrinkled his nose. "I expect you're right."

Mordred's jaw twitched. "Fantastic."

Gwen wished she had a plan—wished she had something, anything at all to say. But instead, all she could do was wring the sleeve of her dress in her hands. She couldn't stop Grinn from blowing up the volcano. She couldn't stop Mordred from trying to kill Grinn.

Despite the fact she was now a so-called witch, she felt helpless.

There was swirl of magic from the side of the clearing. Mordred placed his hand on the hilt of his sword at his side. A moment later, out stepped two figures she was both happy and nervous to see.

Galahad and Zoe.

The Knight in Gold stared at Gwen, his mouth agape.

Zoe chuckled. "You just are full of surprises, are you not?" She spread her wings, and flitted over to her, gliding through the air before landing in front of her. "Were these but happier times." She placed her palm on Gwen's cheek.

"Yeah. It's—it's good to see you both." She glanced over at Galahad. "And that you're back together."

"For as long as it lasts." Galahad sighed. "But I am grateful for it, regardless." He bowed his head to Mordred in thanks.

But the Prince in Iron hardly looked relieved. "Why have you come, Zoe?"

Right. That whole stupid game. Someone was probably watching—if not a lot of people. Gwen cringed and took a step back, folding her wings around her shoulders. Doc called her over with a jerk of his head, and she decided standing next to the other wizard was a good plan. Eod jogged over, licking her hand in greeting. Let the adults deal with their nonsense.

"I come with a plea, Mordred, Prince of Iron. Stand down from this war with the demon and submit yourself for judgment for your crimes." Zoe stayed hovering in the air, her wings lazily moving at her back. "And if you do not do so willingly, I will force the matter."

"The demon intends to destroy this world."

"And we will deal with him in time."

"Time? *Time?*" Mordred laughed cruelly. "That is one thing we do not have, Gossamer Lady."

"We shall see. Stand down, prince."

"No."

Galahad moved to stand beside his love, drawing his sword from his hip. When Mordred took a step forward, Galahad charged, beginning the fight. Gwen had seen the two fight before—but something about this felt... different. This wasn't an anger-fueled knock-out fight like she had seen the night before Mordred had tried to send her to Earth.

It wasn't choreographed either—it didn't seem fake. But it looked like something the two of them had done many, many times as sparring partners.

Doc leaned over to murmur something to her. "The trees have eyes."

"I figured," she whispered back. "So... are we all going to die?"

"I honestly don't know." He shrugged. "For once, this is all a big black box to me. I don't know how any of this is going to play out."

"Really?" She blinked.

"No, of course not." He snickered. "I know how everything plays out. But it's more fun if we pretend I don't."

She really wanted to slap him upside the head. "God, I hate you sometimes."

"Yeah, I know." He reached into thin air and pulled out a bucket of movie popcorn. When she sighed heavily at his antics, he cackled. "What? Want some?"

"No." She sat down on the rock next to him, listening to the sound of metal clashing with metal as the two enormous fighters sparred.

Galahad was fighting as hard as he could, now—grunting and sweating as he tried to knock Mordred off balance. But the Prince in Iron was just a little faster. Hit just a little harder. And seemed entirely unfazed. They knew each other like the backs of their own hands—and Mordred was willing to use that to his advantage.

It was only a few moments before Mordred knocked Galahad to the ground. He kicked the golden-hilted sword out of the knight's reach. Mordred stood over him, rusted, jagged sword raised. "Goodbye, old *friend*."

"Enough!" Zoe grasped the necklace she wore. Something flashed, and Mordred screamed in pain. His sword fell to the dirt with a thump.

Gwen shot up. That wasn't faked. That was real. She knew it was part of the shitty "plan" to draw Grinn out from hiding—but watching Mordred's expression twist into agony as he staggered and fell to his knees wasn't part of some stupid game. "Mordred!"

Zoe kept up with the magic until Mordred doubled over, holding himself up with one elbow, the clawed gauntlet of his other hand pressed to his chest over his heart.

Gwen ran to Mordred, kneeling beside him, placing a hand on his back. "Mordred—"

"You will pay for that, Gossamer Lady—" the Prince in Iron ground out through gritted teeth. "I will pluck your wings from your back f—" He screamed as the magic arced through him again.

"I think you will not." Galahad picked up his sword from

the grass. He stalked toward Mordred, clearly intending to kill him.

Standing, Gwen got in between the Knight in Gold and Mordred. "Stop." She spread her leathery dragon's wings. "Don't make me fight you, Galahad."

The older, taller man's eyebrows lifted just slightly. "You?"

"I—I didn't say I knew *how* to fight you—" she stammered. "But I'll try."

He chuckled, his expression turning warm, the creases at the corners of his eyes deepening just a little. "I do not wish to harm you, Lady Gwendolyn. Please stand aside."

"No. For the same reason you'd never stand aside if Zoe was in danger. I love him, Galahad—and I won't let you, or anyone else, hurt him." She clenched her fists at her sides. "Not while I'm still standing."

She didn't know if this screwed up their ploy or not. But it was an honest response to the situation, wasn't it? And... maybe Galahad and Zoe had changed their minds. Maybe they preferred that Mordred die. She didn't know who her friends really were, of those present. Except Eod, and *potentially* Doc.

Everything was confusing. Everything was terrible.

And it didn't seem like the plan to trick Grinn out of the caves was even going to work.

"If you harm her—" Mordred's voice was shaky. The pain he was in was very, very real. "I will never let you rest, Galahad —not in this world or the next. No god, no fairy magic, no veil of death, would save you from my wrath."

"We shall see, prince." Galahad took a step forward.

Gwen raised her hand, about to do... something. She didn't know what. Maybe a wall of ice? Or fire? Or trees? Something, anything, to slow down the Knight in Gold.

But she never had to make up her mind.

"Well, isn't *this* charming?"

The demon emerged from the cave, one good eye glowing,

smoke curling from his maw as he spoke. It was like he was made from lava on the inside, every crack and seam glowing with fire. She'd never forget the sight of him, like something out of a nightmare, for as long as she lived.

Even if that was about two hours.

"How romantic." Grinn sneered. "To have you all tearing yourselves apart on my doorstep." He took a step forward, the grass around his feet singeing and turning black as he stalked closer to them. "I just couldn't resist the chance to get a closer view."

Mordred was fighting his way back to his feet. But just as he stood vertical, Zoe touched the necklace around her throat, and he screamed and fell back to the dirt.

The sound of Grinn's laughter was sickening.

"Stop it! Stop it, all of you!" Gwen let tears run down her cheeks. She didn't care about hiding them anymore.

"I offer you a bargain, Ash King," Zoe began. "You may kill Mordred, if you spare the island."

Grinn thought it over for a moment. "You see... normally, that would be wonderfully tempting. But why would I sacrifice one goal when both are here within my reach?" He chuckled. "Now, Gossamer Lady—give me that necklace, and you may spend the next few hours in the arms of your lover."

"No." Zoe retreated a few feet. Galahad quickly moved to stand between her and the demon.

"I wish to ensure Mordred spends the last few moments of his life in agony—the barest hint of what he forced upon the rest of us." Grinn lowered his head, prowling like a panther as he stalked toward Galahad and Zoe. "I wish to watch him scream and writhe in pure torment until the world burns around him."

"Stop this, Grinn. Please, stop this—" Gwen begged. But she might as well have been saying nothing at all. No one was listening to her.

"Stay back, demon." Galahad stood firm. "I will not let you harm her."

"I do not intend to give you the option." Grinn laughed.

Gwen almost missed the shifting of the brambles at the edge of the clearing. The forest itself came alive, fencing off the clearing on all sides. The branches of the bushes were thicker than her forearm, and the thorns were the size of her hand. They twisted and gnarled around each other. There would be no getting through them. Likely, not even by fire, with how quickly they were growing.

Lady Thorn stepped from them, emerging from the mass of brambles.

Before Gwen could open her mouth—

All hell broke loose.

SEVENTEEN

Mordred managed to flick his cape over him and change the panels from fabric to iron just in time before the full weight of the demon came down, crushing him into the grass and dirt. The sound of his claws scraping on the metal set his teeth on edge.

The Gossamer Lady had stayed true to her word at least—the moment that Grinn attacked, the pain had ceased. He would have to thank her later if he survived.

If he lived to see the morning, he would be sore. An odd thought to have in the thick of battle. It was always amusing to him to see what his mind focused on when he was in combat. Never anything useful.

Grinn snarled, his weight shifting off from Mordred as he retreated a few steps. As Mordred stood, letting his cloak return to fabric, he quickly lifted his claw to summon iron from the ground and block the demon's retreat. The coward was already running for the entrance to the cave, sensing that he was now surrounded and outnumbered.

Grinn roared, seeing his path blockaded. Fire burst from his nostrils as he turned back to face them, realizing that there was no escape.

Zoe vanished into a glimmer of light, which was wise. Battle was no place for the Gossamer Lady. Doc and Eod had already exited as well. Gwendolyn, however, remained.

Armor covered Galahad just in time for Grinn to spew fire from his lungs like a dragon, igniting the grass and underbrush. Gwen squeaked, throwing up her arms and promptly bursting into flames herself—as though she were once more a fire elemental.

While that was no longer wholly true, she was far more than that, he did have to admit that he adored her in red. Fire suited her.

Focus on the enemy, you idiot. Not her.

Grinn moved to run and escape into the woods. Briars and thornbushes, thick enough to block light, grew to block his path. He set them ablaze, but he could not destroy them and guard his back at the same time. Mordred moved to stand in the center of the clearing.

"Face me, coward." Mordred held his sword tight in his hand. "We end this now, once and for all."

Galahad stood beside him.

Mordred would appreciate the man's loyalty another time. "Keep him in the clearing, knight. Keep him from escaping. This fight is mine."

Galahad simply nodded.

Grinn laughed, turning back to face Mordred. He grimaced, baring his one good fang. "You are too late. The magic has already corrupted the volcano. Even if you kill me now, it cannot be reversed."

"You are lying. And stalling for time." Mordred shook his head. "And if you are speaking truth? Then your death will hardly harm the situation."

"Only I can stop it." Grinn paced back and forth, sizing up

his competition. Mordred, Galahad, and Gwendolyn. Two would fight him. The third likely would not. Mordred did not think Gwendolyn would betray either party—her heart was too gentle.

He could only hope, at any rate.

"And is this you, trying to strike a bargain?" Mordred huffed a laugh. "Please do not insult my intelligence after all these years. You will do anything to live another day so that you may try again to kill us all. No, demon."

Grinn snarled and leaped forward.

Mordred met the attack with his own.

One of them would not leave this place alive.

And he could not have been happier about it.

* * *

Gwen didn't know what to do. Grinn and Mordred were in a fight to the death.

The clash of claws and iron was a horrifying sound, coupled with the roar of fire and the snarls of the demon as they waged a fight long in the making. With each swing of Mordred's sword or swipe of Grinn's claws, Gwen's stomach lurched. She wanted to jump into the fray—but what good would it do? None at all. She'd just get cut down for the trouble.

She was still crying, though now her tears were made of liquid fire as they hit the dirt at her feet and sizzled.

She didn't want either of them to die.

But she didn't think she got a say in the matter.

It felt wrong, simply standing there and doing nothing as claw and fang and fire met steel and iron and flesh. She occasionally had to dodge them as they fought, neither gaining ground, nor losing ground. She wanted to jump in between them, to physically break up the fight—but it was like watching two trains crash into each other head-on at full speed.

It was inevitable.

This had always *been* inevitable.

Grinn was bleeding from a cut on his arm, where Mordred had managed to strike him. Mordred was favoring his left leg. And like a shark smelling blood, Grinn began to focus on that point, trying to take the big warrior down.

Mordred managed to knock Grinn off balance, sending the demon stumbling into a tree that promptly caught on fire from the heat that was rolling off the monster in waves. Gwendolyn lifted her hand, putting out the flame before it could spread and cause more damage.

Great. She supposed she served a purpose, after all.

Fucking glorified fire extinguisher with legs. While she was watching the man she loved and—okay, she had no idea what she felt about Grinn, really, but she knew she didn't want him to die—beat the absolute shit out of each other.

"Please stop—" She didn't know why she bothered. They weren't listening to her. "Please—"

She couldn't tell if the fight went on for too long, or not long enough. She wanted them to stop, and... well, they did. But not in the way she had wanted. Mordred raked one of his claws over Grinn's face—shredding the demon's only eye.

That was it.

That was how it would end.

Blinded, Grinn howled in agony, reeling back, staggering and lashing out at thin air. "You *bastard!*" he roared.

Mordred moved in, ramming his sword through Grinn's back leg. The demon howled a sound that was unlike anything she had ever heard before he staggered and fell.

"Goodbye, demon." Mordred lifted his sword, ready to drive it through Grinn's throat and end it.

"No—no—please!" Gwen couldn't help it. She couldn't. Before she even knew what she was doing, her feet had moved and she was standing between Mordred and Grinn, holding her hands up to try to stop the Prince in Iron. "Please, you win—you win, he's defeated—stop!"

Mordred's chest was heaving with a desperate attempt to catch his breath as he stared down at her from behind the dark sockets of his helm. He looked like something from a nightmare as well. A demon and a dark lord, fighting to the death. There were no knights in shining armor here. There was no *good guy*.

Well, okay, but Galahad didn't count.

"Please—" she begged. "Please, don't kill him."

Grinn laughed from where he lay, half-collapsed behind her, one paw-like hand pressed over his face where his only good eye had been destroyed. "Foolish, naive child. Let him end it. I am sick of this. Sick of all of *you*."

"Get out of the way, Gwendolyn." Mordred shifted his grip on his sword. "The demon must die."

There had to be another way. There had to be. She shook her head no. "I won't let you do this. He's blinded now. He's harmless."

"Harmless? *Harmless?* He is not your cat, Gwendolyn! He is not your friend! He never has been!" Mordred pointed at Grinn. "Look at him—do you think he will stop? Do you think he will not seek to find a way to destroy us all? To destroy you, along with the rest of us?" Mordred's hand tightened into a fist. "Step aside. This ends now."

Grinn was laughing, low and sarcastic and mocking. It wasn't helping her case.

But it just felt wrong. Wrong down to her soul that Grinn was going to die. "No."

Mordred paced away, clearly irate. "I would think you were in league with him if I could not attribute this to your childishness. You have one last chance, Gwendolyn, to step aside of your own volition."

"Or what?" Now she was getting angry. "You'll make me?"

"Yes. If that is what it takes." He turned to face her, some ten feet away. "Step aside."

"Go away, stupid girl." Grinn lowered himself down to the ground, surrendering. "You can't win here."

"I don't care." She clenched her fists at her sides. "This isn't right. And I'm not a *child* or a *stupid girl*." She glared at Mordred. "I won't let you kill him."

"Very well." Mordred squared his shoulders. "I fear I must tell you a secret of my own, Gwendolyn. The magic I embedded in you? I only meant for it to bind us. However—" He lifted his clawed gauntlet. "It has other uses as well."

"Wh—" She never got the rest out.

Her mind went white as pain seared through her like she had been plugged into a live socket. She heard screaming, and it took her a second to realize it was her voice doing it. She fell to her knees, then to her elbows, as spots appeared in her vision.

When the pain finally let up, she could barely breathe. Everything ached and tingled. It was like she had been struck by lightning.

And Mordred had done that to her.

The shock of it was almost as bad as the pain.

Almost.

Grinn was laughing, defiant and mocking, as Mordred walked past her, his sword lifted.

"No—" She couldn't see straight. She could barely move. And she couldn't stop the Prince in Iron as he drove his blade deep into Grinn's chest.

The demon howled once, in agony.

Mordred wrenched the blade from the demon, blood the color of tar oozing from the wound. The *fatal* wound.

Grinn was dying.

"*No!*" Something in her took over. Something else. Through her grief, something in her simply snapped. Forcing herself back up to her feet, she felt power surge through her. She gestured at

Mordred, honestly unsure of what she was even doing, until columns of iron shot up from the ground and smashed into the prince, sending him flying.

Mordred hit the ground hard, grunting in pain as he rolled to a stop.

She could feel the magic in her now. Not just hers—but *his*. Placing her hand over where she could feel his presence inside her, she pulled. Hissing in pain, she ripped the iron crystal out of herself. It wasn't a large wound. She'd heal.

The arrow had been far, far worse.

Tossing the little piece of bloody metal to the grass, she stood between Mordred and the dying demon. "Are you happy now?"

Mordred was slow to get to his feet. It was clear she had just injured him. Well, she was too pissed to care. And he had shot first, after all. "The deed is done, Gwendolyn. Stand down. We will discuss this in private."

In private?

Oh.

Right. She'd forgotten about everyone else.

Standing at the edges of the clearing were other elementals. Lady Thorn, Galahad—and many others she didn't recognize, of every shape and size and type. They all blended into a weird menagerie. And they were all *staring* at her.

She clenched her fists again. "Go away. All of you."

"It is too late to save him," Zoe said gently from where she was floating.

"I could ask you to heal him, but I won't." Gwen shook her head. "You probably wouldn't, even if you could."

The Gossamer Lady's silence told Gwen that she was right.

"Go away. All of you. This isn't a fucking play being put on for your entertainment. Let him die in peace." She didn't know where she got the balls to boss them all around. But seeing as she had just chucked Mordred across the clearing, and could command all elements, she figured that gave her a little bit of a leg to stand on. "*Now!*"

One by one, they obeyed, disappearing into whatever mist or smoke or vines they used to travel. All of them left, until only Mordred remained. He took a step toward her.

"You too." She glowered at him. "Go away."

Mordred stopped. Nodding once, he turned and did just that. She figured she'd have to find him later, and they'd have a lovely fight about this. But now wasn't the time. Because there wasn't any time left.

In the silence left behind by everyone's exits, she could hear Grinn's ragged, labored breathing. Tears stung her eyes again as she turned to face him. He was lying down, his head on his paws. She walked over to his head and sat down beside him. "Were you lying? About the volcano?"

"Yes. The magic dies with me. He *wins*." It was clearly hard to speak. "Now shut up and let me die."

Shutting her eyes, she didn't bother fighting back her tears. She let them run down her cheeks, unchecked. She sat there beside him in silence for a moment. "I—I could try to help you. Maybe I can remove the magic of Avalon, so you can go home."

"Do not *dare* try. Let me die in peace, girl. I do not need you making matters worse."

They sat in silence for a long moment. "I... I hope you get back to hell. To see your family."

He didn't reply. She didn't expect him to.

"If—if you do, if you do go home, please... I don't know, send me a letter, or something." She wiped her nose with the back of her hand, sniffling. She knew she shouldn't care about him. She knew he was a genocidal, egotistical, hateful monster.

But she did care.

She cared a great deal.

"I know you hate me. But I'm still sorry," she whispered. "Sorry I wasn't—I don't know, a better friend. Or—or—" She didn't even know what she was trying to say. "I'm going to miss you. I guess that does make me a stupid girl."

She sniffled again, staring up at the blue sky, dotted with clouds. It was starting to get dark, and the clouds were tinged yellow and orange by the setting sun. It was beautiful. It felt wrong. Wasn't it supposed to be raining when things like this happened?

Grinn shifted.

Wordlessly, he placed his head in her lap.

She choked back a sob as she rested her cheek against the top of his head, and gently petted the fur of his neck.

And she listened to his breathing as it slowed.

And then it stopped.

Gwen let out a broken sound and wept as his body turned to ash and disappeared.

EIGHTEEN

Gwen was still wiping her eyes when she found Mordred and the others. It wasn't hard. All she had to do was follow the sound of the *shouting*.

She was so very much over everybody's bullshit. She needed a drink and a nap. And to not have to listen to people screaming at each other for a hot fucking second.

But something told her she wasn't going to get any of those things. Not quite yet, at any rate.

Walking into the clearing, she found Mordred and Lady Thorn were the current ones in a shouting match.

"You are going back on our deal? Coward—spineless *coward!*" Thorn spat on the ground. "You are no better than the demon."

Mordred huffed a laugh, pulling his helm from his head. His hair was matted with sweat and blood. He had taken a beating during the fight. "I see. I am the traitorous one? You hardly held up your end of the bargain."

"I led you to the demon, did I not?" Thorn folded her arms over her chest.

"That was hardly the extent of our arrangement. You were

meant to stand with me in the fight against him." He smirked. "Not stand there and *gawk*, waiting to see who would win."

"I kept him from fleeing, did I not?" Thorn sneered. "I thought perhaps you did not need my help in felling him yourself."

"A cursory attempt and an invalid excuse. Galahad could have done the same. No. The fact remains, Thorn, that you did not hold up your agreement." Mordred vanished his helm and, cringing, wiped a section of drying blood from the back of his neck.

Thorn grimaced. "Then this means war. We will no longer suffer the threat of you."

"Hm." Mordred looked to Zoe, who was floating by the edge of the clearing, clinging to Galahad's arm. "What do you think, Gossamer Lady? Will you join the army to fight me, even if I vow peace and return to my keep with my Crystal and leave you all be?"

Zoe frowned, a crease in her brow forming as she considered it. "The fighting between the elementals will begin again in time. You will simply find yourself where you started, so long ago."

"The fighting will resume whether or not I am imprisoned. I find I have lost my taste for coddling children. I wish to go home. I wish to be left alone." He turned his gaze to Gwen, and she could hear the silent statement in that one look. *Alone with her.*

Her cheeks went warm, despite her continuing anger and annoyance with him at the moment. "Can't we just all fucking get along? Seriously? Don't you all see the—the cost of these things? How everyone suffers?" She rubbed a hand over her face, trying to bite back the tears that kept threatening to break free. "I'm sick of all this bullshit, and I'm the new kid in town."

"Hear, hear." Doc raised a bottle of alcohol from where he was sitting on a rock by the edge of the clearing.

Eod jogged up to her, tail wagging, but ears down. He was worried, clearly seeing how upset she was.

Smiling, she knelt and let the dog lick her cheeks, as he tried to cheer her up. It worked. "Good boy," she murmured to him. "I'm okay. Well, I'll be okay."

"He imprisoned us for three centuries, and you expect us to let this go without repercussions?" Thorn snarled. "He speaks of justice and honor, and yet *this* is how he behaves!" She pointed at Mordred. "You are not the king in the mountain— you are nothing but a bastard child of a dead lineage."

"Do you think I do not know that?" He arched an eyebrow in response. "I have known that from the moment I was born, *Lady* Thorn. Spare me your grandstanding."

Thorn was pacing now, back and forth across the clearing. Gwen could see shapes of people standing amongst the trees— other elementals, hiding and watching. Close enough to hear, far enough away to run if things went sour. And the odds they went sour were pretty high.

Mordred was willing to lay down his life for honor when he felt he had nothing to live for.

But now he had something to hold onto.

Her.

Gwen sighed. "Let us just go back to the keep. We'll stay there, Thorn. We won't cause problems. Please."

"Do not speak, child." Thorn reeled toward her, fists clenched tight. "You are an abomination who should not exist!"

"Watch your tongue." Doc stood from the rock and wavered on his feet for a moment. It kind of blew the seriousness of his tone. "She was chosen by the island. Her gifts were given by the same forces that gave you *yours*. She has as much right to exist as any one of you."

"Except for the fact that she has been corrupted by his power. I saw the shard you ripped from your flesh—how do we know his magics have not worked deeper than that?" Thorn looked Gwen up and down with an expression of sheer disgust. "Not that he would need magic."

Gwen rolled her eyes. "Step off, bitch, seriously. I'm sick of this bullshit. I haven't done anything to you—literally *nothing*—and you've been trying to pick a fight from the moment we've met. Are you just, like, always a miserable waste of air or is this just a personal vendetta of yours?"

Doc snickered and muttered something under his breath that neither Gwen nor Thorn seemed to catch. That was probably for the best.

Thorn studied her for a moment, then shrugged. "You are his little pet. His pawn. You have yet to do a single thing to convince me otherwise."

"Do you... like... have a partner? Someone you love?" Gwen tilted her head to the side slightly. "Are you with somebody?"

Thorn blanched. "No."

Gwen gave Thorn a deadpan look. "This is my shocked face."

Doc snickered again. Even Mordred had to hide a grin behind a wipe of his hand.

Thorn huffed. "I did not come here to be insulted by a literal child. The fact of the matter remains. The Prince in Iron is a criminal and needs to stand trial for his actions against his fellow elementals. That is the simple truth of it."

"And I heartily disagree." Mordred cracked his neck loudly and sighed. "And I am leaving. I am done with all of you. I am going home." He turned and began to walk away. "You can attempt to stop me if you like—we all know how it will end."

Seeing that she was losing her leverage, Thorn let out a low growl. "Do you feel no shame for the suffering that we all endured? The guilty and the innocent alike? What harm in the world did the Gossamer Lady ever do to Avalon, and yet you imprisoned her with all the rest of us! *Why?*"

Mordred stopped, and stared up at the sky for a moment,

clearly begging for patience. "Because I believed that she could not be trusted."

"And has your opinion changed?" Galahad asked, speaking up for the first time.

After a long pause, Mordred nodded. "Yes. It has."

"Then let her decide whether or not you should stand trial," the Knight in Gold suggested.

Mordred cast Galahad a withering glare. "You believe that I should be put to death?"

"No, my prince." The Knight in Gold stepped forward. "I do not believe that in the slightest. But... there is truth in Thorn's insistence that justice should be served. That you should be given a chance to speak your case. No one is above the law of Avalon. Not even you."

Mordred shut his eyes and let out a long, heavy sigh. "You say you do not wish for me to die, old *friend*, yet here you stand with the hangman's noose all the same."

"I am speaking as someone who holds honor above all else, nothing more."

"Nothing?" Mordred glanced to Zoe.

"Nothing. Including those I care for deeply."

Mordred let out another dreary sigh. The metal claws of his gauntlet slid against each other as he thought through the proposition. "And what do you think, Gossamer Lady?"

"As someone who suffered firsthand the imprisonment of the Crystal, I..." She wrung her hands in front of her, that crease between her brows growing deeper as she stared down at the ground. "I cannot say that I believe you will not try again. I find it difficult to believe we could all return to life as we knew it before the catastrophe occurred."

"Catastrophe—" Mordred shook his head. "What *catastrophe?* The world knew three hundred years without senseless death and war—without your idiot kin setting cities to ruin without any care for the lives they destroyed!"

"And with no sun. No love," Galahad dutifully reminded the prince, not like it was really needed. "There was a cost, Mordred."

"*Do you think I do not know that?*" Mordred shouted; his patience had clearly snapped. "I am quite well aware of it! And I was aware of it every waking moment of every day—and all my sleepless nights—hearing the cries of those I sent within the Iron Crystal. But I did it to save this world from all of them!" He gestured at those waiting in the woods. "And I shall not stand trial amongst those who would see my head impaled upon a pike simply out of the petty need for revenge. What of all the lives they have taken and spent, all those who could not defend themselves from their onslaught? What of the *justice* for them?"

Mordred reeled toward Thorn, storming up to her. The literally prickly woman held her ground until the last few feet of approach before he finally called her bluff and she took a staggering step back. Mordred sneered. "You speak of honor. I imprisoned you all to protect the innocents who could not defend themselves. Where is the honor in the actions of my so-called jurors? No. No, is my answer. And *no* it shall remain. I shall not stand for such a farce."

"I... I regret to say," Zoe began, hesitantly, as she grasped the necklace she still wore. The one that bound Mordred—the twisted version of the same magic he had used on his knights and on her. "You do not have a choice in the matter."

Mordred shut his eyes, his shoulders dropping. "It seems my trust in you has been severely misplaced, Gossamer Lady."

"Perhaps." Her large, pink-magenta eyes were beginning to water. "I do not wish to do this. I do not wish to hurt you. I, too, seek peace. But I see no path ahead for it without this."

"Without my death, you mean." Mordred turned to face her. "Speak plainly, Gossamer Lady. Do not hide in flowery language. You are sending me to my death."

Zoe shut her eyes, a tear slipping loose and running down her cheek. "Yes. I know."

Gwen shook her head, not sure what she was even meant to do or say. "Zoe, please—take the exile route. Let him—let *us*—just go home. He means it. He's a man of his word."

Lady Thorn scoffed and opened her mouth.

Gwen pointed at Thorn. "You shut the *fuck up* or I swear I will shove your head so far up your own ass you have to cut holes in your nipples to see!"

Thorn blinked. Her brow furrowed for a moment as if she were trying to contemplate how that would actually work. Shaking her head, she didn't respond at least.

Doc cackled before realizing it was the wrong time to laugh and coughed into his sleeve.

Turning her attention back to Mordred, Gwen stepped up to his side and put her hand in his gauntleted one, weaving her fingers between his. "I will not stand by and let him die, Zoe. If you hurt him, I will have to—do—" And that was where her resolve fell apart. "I don't know, something."

Mordred chuckled quietly, his hand tightening around hers. "So reassuring," he muttered to her.

"Shut up," she muttered back. "I'm doing my best."

He leaned over and kissed the top of her head. "Forgive me for my actions today."

"I shouldn't be such a naive softy, and you shouldn't be such a hard-nosed asshole. I get it." She sighed. "We'll scream at each other after all this sorts itself out."

"Deal." Mordred squeezed her hand gently. He leaned toward her again, kissing her gently before whispering in her ear. "Do not fight them here. Do not stand against them now. You are unprepared, exhausted, and outmatched. Our chance will come later."

Gwen nodded, biting back a fresh wave of tears.

Mordred straightened up to his full height. "You will have to wield the magic of that necklace, Zoe. I will not go willingly."

The Gossamer Lady let out a breath and nodded. "Yes. I know." She touched the necklace at her throat.

Mordred screamed and fell to his knees.

All Gwen could do was hold him until he slipped unconscious. It was honestly a relief when the lines of agony etched onto his face went smooth. She could pretend he was just sleeping.

She kissed him, and held him close, until a hand fell on her shoulder. It was Galahad. Standing, she took a step back from Mordred and let the Knight in Gold deal with the Prince in Iron.

Zoe floated over to her as if to start a conversation.

"No—fuck you right now. No." Gwen turned her back to the scene. "I need a *fucking drink*. Doc. Let's go."

"Yes, ma'am." Doc stood and gestured to her to come over to him. When she did, she basically fell against him, desperate for something to lean on. Doc hugged her tight. "You did good, kid. You did good."

"It doesn't feel like it."

"I know. C'mon. Let's eat, drink, sleep—tomorrow is going to be worse than this."

It was her turn to let out a ragged sigh. "Is this place ever going to stop fucking with me?"

"Nope! That should be on our travel brochure." Doc snickered. "Welcome to Avalon: Prepare to get fucked. We hope you enjoy your stay."

Gwen took the bottle from Doc's hand and took a hard swallow from it, not caring what alcohol it contained. Whatever it was, it burned, and it would do its job.

Mordred was being hauled away by Galahad. The trial would be tomorrow. She didn't bother asking when or where. Doc would already know.

"Tell me it's going to be okay, Doc." She felt hollowed out—empty inside. Too much had happened all at once.

"You know I can't, hon." He rubbed her back.

She rolled her eyes. "Lie."

"It's all gonna be okay."

Shutting her eyes, she let out a breath. "Thanks." One more swallow from the bottle and she handed it back. "Let's go."

Today had been terrible.

And tomorrow would be worse.

Great.

NINETEEN

"Where're we going?" Gwen followed Doc as he walked through the woods. They had camped in a clearing. He had asked about sleeping in the caves instead, but it... just didn't feel right.

She had cried herself to sleep badly enough as it was without the reminder of Grinn's death being all around her. And with Mordred's situation weighing on her, she was in a *terrible* mood the next morning as she followed Doc along a deer trail.

"I found us a ride." Doc had his hands shoved in his robe pockets. Eod was running ahead of them, sniffing every shrub and occasionally barreling off into the underbrush after a squirrel or a chipmunk.

"A ride to where, exactly?" It wasn't like it really mattered, but she was curious. "Where is the trial being held?"

"Oh, Camelot of course."

She sighed. Yeah, of course. Why not? Why not put Mordred on trial in his uncle's old home? Why not completely add insult to injury, and let the haunting memory of King Arthur judge him as well? Rubbing her hand over her face, she really didn't want to deal with any of this. She wanted to crawl under a rock and sleep for two straight weeks. But nope. She had to go watch the trial of the man she loved which would *likely* result in him being sentenced to death, and the start of a new war against the elementals.

When the forest gave way to a field, she blinked. Whatever she had assumed Doc had meant about having "found them a ride," she had not been expecting *that*.

"Tiny?" She let out a quiet laugh. The enormous iron dragon was lying down in the grass, the opalescent glow from his eyes out. He was sleeping. Hearing them approach, the dragon let out a loud metal-on-metal grumble and lifted his head, his eyes flaring to life.

The dragon peered down at her as they walked up to him. He let out a grunt that was more of a *thud* and lowered his head closer to them.

She reached out and placed her hand on his nose, petting the metal panel. It felt weird, petting an iron dragon, but it was clear that he was saying hello to them. Eod was barking up at the dragon, wagging his tail happily in his own greeting.

"Hey, buddy." She smiled sadly. "Your dad's gone and gotten arrested. He's standing trial at Camelot. Can you bring us there, please?"

"You're asking it?" Doc arched an eyebrow at her.

"It's a *he,* and I'm asking *him*, yes." Gwen rolled her eyes in response. "They have souls, you know. Besides, it doesn't hurt to be polite. Especially when they can eat you." She smiled at Tiny. "Right, big guy?"

The dragon let out another grumble-thunk and lifted his head. She'd take that for a yes. Climbing onto the dragon's back, she remembered how terrified she was of him the first time she saw him. To be fair, it had been a terrible day—and Mordred hadn't helped.

And now here she was, flying off to save the man that she

had been so scared of. Funny how things had changed. Doc sat down behind her, muttering something about how much it was going to chafe. Tiny laid down his head and opened his jaw. Eod jumped inside, lying down—clearly something he had been trained to do. Mordred had planned for everything.

That had been his job, though. Plan for things. Right until Gwen showed up and ruined it all. Sighing again, she shut her eyes. "Let's go, Tiny. Camelot."

The dragon let out a metallic *harumph* and took to the sky. Normally, she'd find it endearing how seeming lazy the large, bizarre creation was. But today, she wasn't in much of a mood to feel anything except grief and anger.

The view of Avalon from above, dotted with the shadows of clouds, didn't even cheer her up.

"Buck up, kid," Doc shouted over the wind as he patted her on the back. Apparently, it was bad enough that he noticed. "It'll all work out."

"Really?" She shot him a look.

"I thought you wanted me to lie." He smiled cheekily.

"I want to push you off this dragon *so badly* right now." She glared at him over her shoulder.

"Yeah, yeah. But you won't." He glanced down at the ground and made a face. "Shit, I hate heights."

Shaking her head, she stared back ahead at the world as it flew by her. Luckily—or unluckily, as the case may be—it didn't take long before Tiny was circling lower toward the ruins of Camelot. As they landed with a heavy *thud*, she saw figures in the trees, all standing warily in the shadows. Elementals, she assumed.

It was weird, knowing she was being stared at. It was a hideously uncomfortable feeling. She'd had a nightmare once, about going to prom naked, and this was basically that, only real. She climbed off Tiny with Doc not far behind her. The dragon let Eod out of his mouth before finding a bigger spot to curl up and nap.

All right, it was kind of endearing. Big, terrifying, evil-looking dragon, just wanted to be left alone to nap. *What a mood.*

Eod wagged his tail as he ran up to her, licking her hand. She smiled, scratching him on the head. Folding her wings around her like a cape, she decided it was best to just get this over with. Straightening her shoulders, she braced herself for what was to come as she walked into the decrepit ruins.

The last remains of the life of King Arthur. Wooden beams were rotting away and falling, resting on stone walls that were crumbling and overgrown with vines and ivy. The last time she had seen it, it had been cloudy—before the Iron Crystal had been destroyed. Now, it was weirdly picturesque with the morning sun casting rays of sun and shadow through the cracks and across the beams.

The castle was crowded. Groups of elementals, as wild as anything she could have dreamed up, were lining the space. Creatures of rock, lava, ghastly things that looked almost like ghosts—and everything in between. One woman looked as though her eyes were made purely of electricity. Her hair was a shock of white, cut short and left spiky and sticking out at all angles.

She smiled at Gwen.

Gwen smiled back, if faintly.

Maybe they aren't all terrible.

Then again.

There was Lady Thorn, leaning up against a column, her arms crossed over her chest. She was alone, glaring down at the floor between her bare feet.

Near the center of the great throne room stood Mordred, surrounded by his knights—or what remained of them. Galahad was standing with Zoe, which left Mordred with Gawain, Percival, Tristan, and Bors.

None of them looked happy.

Walking up to Mordred, Gwen reached out and touched his arm as she approached.

He turned his head to look down at her with a faint, weary smile. "Good morning, firefly."

"Right." She let out a half-hearted chuckle and hugged him. "Are you okay?"

"Of course not. But I will survive." He looked exhausted—deep dark bags under his eyes revealed he likely hadn't slept. Or he'd been tortured by Zoe and that necklace. Or both.

The issue was, they didn't know if he would survive. That was the whole problem. Frowning, she glanced at the four knights. Percival was glaring off into the middle distance. "What happens to them, if..."

"I do not know. Likely, my magic shatters—and frees them from their service to me." Mordred's expression turned cold. "I expect they will vote against me." He didn't even bother to drop the volume of his voice.

Right—they were elementals. They all received a vote, same as everybody else. Frowning, she glanced at the four knights. Would they really do that? Vote to kill Mordred out of spite?

Yeah. After centuries of magical servitude. Yeah, they probably would.

Sighing, she wove her fingers between his. "What about Galahad?"

"I do not know. He is... a friend, but he holds honor and the law above all else. I do not know how he will cast his vote."

"It has to be unanimous, right?"

"Correct."

"Then—then I'll vote against, and you'll be fine." She smiled, hope briefly sparking in her chest.

"You are not an elemental, Gwendolyn. You are a wizard,

though you may share our gifts." Mordred shook his head. "I am afraid you shall not have a say."

"Fuck." She shut her eyes and let out a ragged breath. "*Fuck.*"

"As much as I would like to, now is likely not the time."

She glowered up at him, but he was smiling—breaking through the darkness of the moment. She couldn't be mad at him for it. Going up on her tiptoes, she pulled him down into a kiss. When it broke, she fought the urge to cry. No—this was not goodbye. This was not the end. They would get through this. Somehow. Some way. "I love you."

"And I love you, my firefly." He stroked a gauntleted hand over her hair.

"What if you and I just..." She lowered her voice to a whisper. "I don't know, fight them off. Between the two of us, we could take them, right?"

"To what end?" He frowned. "You cannot leave the isle, and neither can I. We would be fugitives—hunted for all time by a pack of slavering wolves. If I am sentenced to death, and I escape, it would be only a matter of time before they won. Even I cannot take on all the elementals at once." He chuckled morbidly. "It seems they are capable of agreeing on something, even if it is their hatred of me."

Wiping a hand down over her face, she thought about their options. There really weren't any. All of them were terrible. "I'm not going to let them—I can't. I just can't."

"I know." He squeezed her hand gently. "There is nothing we can do at this moment in time. We must wait to see how the matter progresses."

The Gossamer Lady floated forward, taking a place at the top of the stairs that must have once led to a throne, long since rotted away and reclaimed by nature. "We are all in attendance. We stand in judgment of Mordred, Prince in Iron, for his crimes against the elementals of Avalon. He is accused of grievous torture, imprisonment, and murder."

"*Murder?*" Mordred laughed. "And who have I murdered, Gossamer Lady?"

"Lancelot, the Knight in Silver. Grinn, the Ash King. Both were elementals. Both died by your hand—"

"Bullshit!" Gwen stepped forward. "The Lancelot thing wasn't about him being an elemental, and you were all fucking on board with Grinn dying right up until this moment—"

Mordred placed his hand on her shoulder and pulled her back to him. "Lancelot was felled in combat—in war—and there is an exception for such a thing. As for Grinn, if I am to stand accused of murder, then both you and Lady Thorn must stand trial for the conspiracy behind it."

Zoe sighed. "All those who wish to try Mordred for the murder of Grinn, say aye."

Silence.

Gwen let out the breath she was holding.

"As for Lancelot—" Zoe looked as though she were about to burst into tears herself. It was clear that all of this was very, very much against her nature. "There are witnesses who say that you killed him in cold blood. That he was defeated, and you took his life regardless."

Mordred laughed. The sound of it was empty and cruel, and bounced off the stone walls around them, giving the illusion that he was everywhere. "Is this how you betray me, Galahad? Is this how you would see it done? To see me pay for the death of that *traitor?*"

"It was me."

Percival.

Mordred snarled in rage and went to lunge at the Knight in Copper. Gwen got in between them, knowing that if she didn't, Mordred would rip Percival's throat out.

"How *dare you?*" Mordred shouted.

"You have grown weak. Weaker by the day. Weaker by the moment, ever since *she* showed up." Percival glared at Gwen. She rolled her eyes. "If you can't do what needs to be done, then what good are you?"

Mordred snarled and paced away, clearly doing everything in his power to calm down. Shutting his eyes, he took a deep breath and squared his shoulders. "The matter between Lancelot and me originated long before we came to Avalon. It was a matter settled by us as human men, not as elementals. He would not have stopped his efforts to see me in a grave—it was a matter of self-defense."

Percival snorted.

Gwen fought the urge to set his underwear on fire.

Maybe later.

Definitely later.

"All those in favor of finding Mordred guilty of the murder of Lancelot, the Knight in Silver, say aye."

Half the room, give or take, spoke up.

"All those against, say nay."

Silence. Until Galahad lifted his head. "Nay."

All eyes went to the Knight in Gold.

"As someone who served beside them both for the better part of two millennia—and as a man who prides himself upon his honor—I cannot say that Mordred's actions were out of line. Unfortunate as the situation might have been... Lancelot's death was not murder."

Gwen smiled at the knight, relief filling her. It wasn't unanimous. That meant that Mordred would live! Right? *Right?*

"Very well. The matter of Lancelot's death is dismissed," Zoe said with a nod. There were unhappy murmurs in the crowd, but nobody spoke up. "Now," she continued, "is the matter of the Iron Crystal. All those who wish to find Mordred guilty of the wrongful imprisonment of the elementals of Avalon, say aye."

The room responded at once. Including Bors, Percival, Tristan, and Gawain. Galahad said nothing.

"All those against?"

Silence. Zoe looked up at Galahad, who simply shook his head no. He was clearly recusing himself. Which was as good as saying yes, in the end.

Fuck.

Fuck!

Zoe shut her eyes. "Then it is decided. Mordred, you are hereby found guilty."

"No!" Gwen clenched her fists. "You can't do this—you *can't*—he was trying to save this island. What about all the innocent villagers and the normal people of this island that you elementals had been terrorizing? What about all their murders?"

Zoe's eyes creased in sadness. "They are not elementals. Therefore, they are not held to the same code. Their deaths are... unfortunate, but not illegal."

"Oh, that's *fucking* rich." Gwen stepped forward again. "What a bunch of power-mad, childish hypocrites! You treat everybody else like they're garbage, and you treat each other like you're angry toddlers fighting over a bucket of toys. Galahad—Galahad, you can't be serious. You can't let this happen."

The Knight in Gold frowned. "One crime does not condone another. The deaths he was trying to prevent, however noble his efforts, came at too high a cost."

Mordred shut his eyes.

Zoe shook her head. "Forgive me, Gwendolyn. I understand your strife—and I do not disagree. But the laws of our people have existed long before—"

"Your laws are shit!" Gwen couldn't take it.

Mordred chuckled. He placed a hand on her shoulder and gently pulled her back again. "It is all right, Gwendolyn. This is expected."

"Fuck *that*, no." She was fuming. And her hands were smoldering. She had to take a breath to keep from exploding into fire again. *At least I kept the metal clothes. At least I won't really be reliving my naked prom nightmare.*

Mordred kissed the top of her head.

She was shaking, she was so angry. She didn't know how he could be so calm about it.

"Is this how people become murderers?" she murmured to Mordred. "Because I'm about to test the theory."

"Shush, my firefly." He kissed the top of her head again, gently wrapping his arm around her.

"By the laws of our people, as... valid or not they may be," Zoe's voice cracked with sadness. "I find you, Mordred, the Prince in Iron, guilty of wrongful imprisonment of the elementals of Avalon." Zoe shut her eyes. "And the sentence for your crime, is death."

TWENTY

Gwen's heart fell into her stomach. She knew that was likely what they were going to say, but it didn't feel real. This couldn't be happening—this could *not* be happening! She whirled toward Mordred, eyes wide and in a panic. She grabbed his arm. "We have to—"

But Mordred was smiling.

It was an expression she rarely saw him wear when she was around. It was one of those moments that made her realize that her Mordred was not the one that most people were accustomed to dealing with. That version—the one that was staring at Zoe as though he was imagining exactly how she would look with her limbs pulled off—that most of Avalon was familiar with.

"Interesting. Is that so?" He chuckled. "Then I have no need to spare all your lives. Consider them forfeit."

"Wait—wait—" Gwen stepped in between Mordred and Zoe. The Prince in Iron was about to go on a bloody rampage, whether or not the Gossamer Lady could drop him quickly enough. There was no telling how many of the elementals he could kill before she managed to stop him. And she'd be left either trying to protect Mordred or to stop him. And she had no idea what she would do. She had no interest in finding out. "Stop. Just give me a second."

Mordred didn't take his eyes off Zoe, but he didn't move or speak.

Gwen's mind scrambled for options—anything, *anything* she could latch onto to avoid the room turning into a slaughterhouse. "Zoe—can I ask a question?"

"Of course," the Gossamer Lady replied.

"In Avalon... does the punishment suit the crime, with a trial like this? Death for death, and so on?"

Zoe paused for a moment, her brow furrowing. "Yes. Why?"

Mordred was watching the scene with interest, but he still stayed quiet. He truly looked the part of the dark lord. His molten, rust-colored eyes showed just the barest hint that he might be *enjoying* this.

"So... if Mordred is guilty of imprisoning people, then... shouldn't he be imprisoned?" Gwen couldn't help but let the hope leak into her voice.

Lady Thorn swore. Galahad sighed and shut his eyes, though his brow smoothed in the barest sign of relief, maybe.

Gwen was onto something. She kept herself from smiling. "Death isn't a fair punishment. Imprisonment is. Eye for an eye."

Zoe glanced to Galahad. The Knight in Gold simply nodded. It was Zoe's turn to sigh. "It has fallen upon me to sentence him. And I... see the sense in your words."

Lady Thorn swore again. "The bastard must pay for what he's done!"

"And pay I shall," Mordred snapped at Thorn. "Or would you rather admit to all in attendance that what you are here for is not *justice* but *revenge?*"

Thorn spat on the ground. "Bastard!"

"I am quite aware." Mordred pulled the hood of his cloak

up over his head. "I will retire to my keep, and there I shall remain. We are adjourned, and this farcical matter is concluded."

"We are not done, prince," Zoe insisted. "And you are not in charge here."

"A poor prison." An elemental by the wall spoke up. He looked like he was half lizard, half made out of water. "That is your home. No, you should be made to suffer as we did!"

"Yes—" Thorn took a step forward. "Precisely. We were not in chains. We were not languishing around our castles. We were being tortured—suffering every second in that terrible place. Eye for an eye, as the child said." It was her turn to smile cruelly. "Eye for an eye."

Mordred grimaced. "And how precisely do you propose such a thing take place?"

Thorn turned her attention to Zoe. "Put him in his own Iron Crystal. Make him suffer one year for every year we lost."

This was going from terrible, to bad, to worse, very quickly. Gwen didn't know what to do—she felt helpless. Like watching a trainwreck in slow motion. "Mordred," she murmured. Though he was not paying attention to her.

He was staring a hole into Lady Thorn. "You wish to imprison me... within my own magic. And how, precisely, do you think that shall work?"

"You put yourself in. Willingly." Thorn lifted her chin in defiance. "You have spoken about how *sacrosanct* our laws are. How much you value and respect them. Then you will obey them. Of your own volition."

"And if I do not? Not even Zoe's stolen power in the necklace can force me to do such a thing if I do not wish to do it." Mordred's jaw twitched. This wasn't going how he wanted it, that much was very clear. "I defeated you all once before. Do not tempt me to do it again."

"You see? How quickly he resorts to threats of violence."

Thorn laughed. "He is no better than any of us! But very well. You want more incentive, bastard prince? Commit yourself to the Crystal willingly—or the girl dies."

Mordred clenched both fists. "She is innocent in all this. Harming her—" His words were seething in rage.

"She is not an elemental. She is not covered by our laws. We can do what we like." Thorn's lopsided yellow and black teeth were on full display as she grinned at Mordred in triumph. "And she cannot escape us all."

The more time Gwen spent with elementals, the more and more she was starting to take Mordred's side in things. She unfurled her wings and let herself ignite into flames. "Try me, you snaggle-toothed bitch."

Mordred paused again for a stretch. "Very well."

"*What?*" Gwen couldn't believe what she was hearing. "You can't possibly—"

"I said *very well*." Mordred turned to face Gwen; his expression drawn. His voice lowered so only she could hear him. "You are too young. Too inexperienced in your power. We cannot defeat them all, she is right. This is the only way forward."

"But—but no—I can't do this without you. I can't—what am I supposed to do?"

He gently cupped her cheek in his palm, uncaring for the fact that she was still ablaze. "I have faith in you, my firefly." Lowering his hand, he turned to Zoe. "Three hundred years within the Crystal."

"No. One year for every year suffered by all of us. *Together.*" Thorn cackled. "Three hundred years by how many of us? A hundred and more? Thirty thousand years in the Iron Crystal shall do it!"

Mordred growled. "You have lost your mind if you believe I will agree to such a thing!"

"That is unreasonable, Lady Thorn," Zoe interjected. "I am not in favor."

"One thousand," Galahad spoke up, his deep voice carrying through the halls. "Will you serve one thousand years, Mordred, Prince in Iron, for your crimes?"

Mordred's jaw twitched. He whirled from the proceedings, his cape flaring out around him. He paused, halfway out of the room. "I ask for one day and one night before I surrender."

There was coldness in his voice—a deep darkness that would probably have been terrifying to Gwen, if she hadn't known it for what it was.

Grief.

Tears slipped from her cheeks, sizzling as they hit the stone beneath her.

"Come, Gwendolyn."

Gwen looked around the room. At all the elementals in attendance. Most were watching her with curiosity, some with thinly veiled hatred. Some with almost a look of sympathy —almost.

She debated how to react. Cuss them all out? Tell them all where they could sit and spin? Set the place on fire, see how many she could take out before they overpowered her? Shaking her head, she decided it wasn't worth it.

She followed Mordred, putting out her fire. She caught up to him as he reached Tiny. He was petting the dragon's nose.

"What... what'll happen to them, if you—" She couldn't imagine it. She really couldn't picture him gone. Trapped in that Crystal. *Better that than dead, I guess.*

"They shall remain." He let out a heavy breath. "You must look after them."

"I—don't talk like that. I said if. *If.* There has to be a way out of this. A loophole, a—"

"There is no way out of this, Gwendolyn. If I do not surrender, they will unite against me. Against us." He shut his eyes. "I will not see you harmed."

She wanted to argue and say that she could take them on—but he was right. She really couldn't. She could barely figure out how to fly, let alone defeat a hundred pissed off elementals. "I don't want you to go."

He smiled at her weakly. "Neither do I wish to." He held his arms out to her. "Come here, my love."

She half ran into his embrace. He held her tight, lifting her feet off the ground as she clung to him, her arms wrapped around behind his neck. He kissed her, not caring that she was crying.

This couldn't be goodbye.

It couldn't be.

A thousand years isn't that long, right?

Right?

* * *

Mordred held Gwendolyn close to him as his dragon took them back to his home. He would spend his last day and night in his keep, securing matters for his long departure.

A thousand years.

A thousand.

How strange, it was less than the time that had lapsed behind him. He considered it barely more than a blink of an eye, in some ways. But now that he knew the number that reached ahead of him, it felt like an *eternity*.

Perhaps it was the company he would be lacking that made the proposition so sour. For it was not the absence of Avalon that he would mourn—it was the absence of her. The young woman who was sitting sideways in front of him so that she could tuck herself closer as they flew.

He remembered how terrified she was the first time she

rode the ill-named creature. So frightened she panicked and lost consciousness. Now, it was as though they were merely atop a horse. He supposed having wings of her own helped abate the fear of falling at least.

How he wished to see her fly.

How he wished to see her transform into the force of nature that he knew she would become—that the island of Avalon itself recognized in her. But he would have no such luck. That was robbed from him, along with all the rest of the world that he would miss as it passed by him.

Would she fall in love with another?

Would Avalon collapse into warfare and chaos once more?

He would only be left to wonder, alone in that empty void. Alone without any other screams to keep him company—for better or worse.

His would be the only voice that would whisper in that void.

He would have plenty of time to ponder his theories as the days and years escaped him like grains of sand upon a beach. Impossible to count—yet not infinite. Only appearing that way.

A thousand years.

It would come. And it would go.

And he would be left to pray that when he emerged, she would be there to greet him—that she would be there to *free* him.

But these thoughts were for the future.

For the moment, for the *now*, he had blessed little time to spare. And he planned to spend every second of it with her. With the woman he loved so very desperately.

She would be the only thing that kept him sane in that darkness.

Love.

He was willing to die for it. Nearly sacrificed himself from the absence of it. And now, it would be the only thing he had left to cling to in the agony that was about to befall him.

Part of him wished he had listened to Percival—life would indeed have been simpler without Gwendolyn in it. The Crystal would be whole and filled with souls that were *not* his.

A simpler life, perhaps.

But hardly a life at all, in the end.

I will wait for her. And she will set me free.

He kissed her. Savored the feeling of her lips on his. Tried to imprint it into his soul. He would get precious few kisses before it was time for them to part.

What is a thousand years for those of us who do not age?

Sand on the shore.

Nothing more, nothing less.

TWENTY-ONE

Gwen had barely managed to put her feet on the ground inside Mordred's keep before he had half pulled, half pushed her into his bedroom. She didn't know whether to laugh, cry, or slap him as he peeled off her chainmail clothes and threw her onto his mattress face down.

The warlord was in a *mood.*

And Gwen was here for it.

They had a lot to work out in a short period of time. She was furious with him for killing Grinn—he was furious at her for lying about being on Avalon. But none of that mattered. None of it at all. Because they only had twenty-four hours until they would have to part for a thousand years.

Tonight was about their mutual anger. But it was also about their desperation not to have to say goodbye. And more importantly?

It was about their love.

Their *need.*

Mordred's clawed gauntlet fisted in her hair, pulling her head back sharply. She hissed in pain, but the sting felt wonderful as the thrill of it went straight through her. She felt his weight settle onto the bed behind her as he straddled her legs. His breath pooled against her cheek as he hovered his lips by her ear.

"I am going to make certain you never forget me," he murmured to her. "I am going to make certain that any lovers you take in my absence will *pale* in comparison."

She shivered at his words. At the way they were little more than a dusky growl as he made her both a promise and a threat. He pressed her head back down to the mattress. The instruction was clear—stay. *Yes. Yes please.* She wanted to feel his strength, his certainty. She wanted the warlord. Not despite his darker moods, but because of them.

He hefted her hips up until she was on her knees with her shoulders still on the mattress. When his claws trailed up over her thigh, she broke out into goosebumps. How could he ever think that she'd forget the man with knives for hands?

"So beautiful," he said through a breathy exhale, his hands running up her body, following every curve, tracing the small of her back and the hollow of her spine as it trailed up between her shoulders. She had vanished her wings the moment his intent had become clear—there were just a few moments where they got in the way. And this was one of them.

Shutting her eyes, she let herself savor the sensation of those sharp tips roaming over her, just hard enough to make themselves known but not hard enough to hurt or scratch her. It was the danger of it, the thrill of playing on the edge, that did something to her that she still couldn't quite believe. She never even considered anything like this.

How far she'd come from the farmer's daughter.

Now she was a... well, whatever she was.

Doing this.

With the dark Prince in Iron.

And all she wanted was *more*.

The sensation of sharp iron changed for the rough pads of

his hands as he dismissed his gauntlets. The reason why became perfectly clear a moment later as his fingers trailed over her core, teasing her, exploring her—making her whimper before pressing a thick digit inside.

She moaned, biting her lower lip as she did.

His chuckle from behind her was amused as he tutted. "Eager, are we?"

She mumbled something into the sheets that wasn't exactly flattering.

"Well, I plan to take my damnable time with you." He slowly worked his finger deeper inside her, making good on his threat to go slow. "I want to hear you beg for forgiveness. For mercy. For *me*."

When his other hand came down her ass cheek with a hard *crack*, she yelped in surprise more than she did out of pain. The warring sensations muddled in her, the sting and the pleasure. A second finger joined the first, slowly but not gently. Methodical, but unflinching. When his fingers reached the knuckles, he pressed, trying to somehow seemingly force them deeper than they could possibly go. The pressure sent her back arching as she cried out in pleasure, lifting her head from the sheets.

"No." His other hand grasped the back of her neck and pressed her down to the sheets. "You shall stay as you are until you are told otherwise. This is your penance for your lies."

Turning her head to rest on her cheek, she kept her eyes shut as he slowly pulled his fingers from her, only to repeat the pattern. Her head was spinning. "And what about you? What about your penance?"

"I think if you understood precisely how badly I wish to rut you like a wild horse, you might understand that our suffering is mutual." His hand came down on her ass again, before squeezing the offended spot, kneading the flesh in his hand as he worked out the sting that he had just paid her.

It wasn't long before she found herself pressing back against his hand, desperately searching out more of him, her body seeking more than what his fingers could deliver. She didn't know how long she was supposed to hold out, but she knew how long she'd last. Not very, was the answer.

A third slap, and her head was spinning with conflicting sensations. "Mordred, please—"

"Mm. Not yet. You have to ask for forgiveness first." His thumb brushed over her sensitive ball of nerves, and she let out a frustrated wail as pleasure lanced through her—but not *enough*. He laughed, quiet and dark, clearly loving every second of this.

Each time she thought he would bring her to a peak of ecstasy, he backed away, denying her release. She pounded her palm into the mattress, grasping the sheets in a fist. Her antics made him chuckle just a little louder.

"Ask, and it shall be granted."

She tried to hold out. Tried to make a worthy fight. But it was pointless. She knew she was going to lose; she might as well get it over with. "Mordred—forgive me, please—I'm sorry—" She breathed out each section between thrusts of his fingers that were still too slow, still not hard enough. "Please—"

"Tell me you are mine. Tell me that no one else shall have you. Tell me that the stars would blink out and die before you would surrender your heart to another soul."

"Yes—god, yes—" She moaned. "I love you. I'm yours. Please, Mordred—"

His fingers retreated, and his weight shifted until he was kneeling between her knees behind her. She felt him lean down over her, one hand, clawed once more, pressed to the mattress beside her head, the metal digits of the other tightening around her hip. "Then I shall give you something to remember me by."

That was the only warning she received before he rammed himself into her like a machine. She opened her mouth to let out a cry, but all breath had been robbed of her as her mind went white with ecstasy. He buried himself as far as he would go, using his weight and his strength to burrow deep. It ended her in that moment—but the dance had only just begun.

Mordred was going to take his time with her.

But that didn't mean he was going to be kind about it.

Her thoughts were nothing but white noise as he set a relentless pace, pistoning inside of her as though he were trying to make a permanent home for himself. She couldn't think. She could barely breathe. She could only feel. Hear his heavy breathing and grunts of pleasure over her mixing with her own mewls and cries as he made good on his promise.

She would never forget him.

And no one could ever live up to him.

His hand at her hip tightened, digging the tips of his claws just enough into her skin to sting. God, it felt so *good*. How could she go for a thousand years without this? How could she live without him?

When had she started begging for more between thrusts as he railed inside of her? But it was true. She wanted more. Wanted it harder. She begged him for it, barely audible, her voice nothing more than breathy sounds that vaguely resembled words.

He snarled and gave her what she was asking for. His weight shifted back, and he lifted her shoulders up from the bed. He grasped her wrists in his hands, yanking her back into his thrusts.

"Fuck—ah!" There was her voice again. Each impact sent a jarring flash of *everything* through her body. She was going to have bruises from this. *Screw it. I heal fast now.*

How long they went, she didn't know—she didn't care. But not even Mordred could go forever. He threw her back to the bed, collapsing over her, his thrusts becoming erratic and desperate as he pounded into her like the wild animal of his metaphor.

He pressed her to the sheets, her hair once more fisted in his hand, as he bottomed out and held himself there, surging inside her. Claiming her. Making her *his*. The heat of it all, the sensations, sent her reeling into her own release again for the umpteenth time.

When she came back down to reality, barely able to fill her aching lungs, he was kissing her cheek, resting his weight on his elbows as he murmured words of love and praise to her. The next few moments were muddled. When she blinked her eyes open again, she was lying on her side next to him.

He stroked the back of a metal knuckle over her cheek. "There you are. I thought I had lost you for a moment."

She only grunted. "Fuck."

"That is accurate, yes." He chuckled and kissed her forehead. "Please forgive me."

"I wanted it." Not that she wasn't going to be sore, healing be damned. She nuzzled closer to him.

"Not for that." He wrapped his arms around her. "For everything."

"Of course I forgive you." She tucked her head beneath his chin. She was suddenly exhausted. Gee, couldn't imagine why. "I love you, Mordred."

"And I you, my firefly. And I you."

It wasn't long before she fell asleep in his arms.

Perhaps for the last time in a very long time.

No. I can't give him up. I can't let them win.

"I'll find a way," she murmured, half-asleep. "I'll find a way to free you. I promise."

* * *

"I'll find a way to free you."

Mordred smiled, heartbroken, as Gwen sleepily vowed to

free him from the Iron Crystal. He would like to believe her—and he had faith in her sentiment. She would try. But she was so very young in comparison to the other elementals. Barely two decades of life compared to centuries and, in some cases, millennia.

She did not stand a chance.

But how he wished to believe that she would defeat the odds and free him from his imprisonment. But it begged the question—if she *did* destroy the Crystal, then what would follow?

It would be total war.

The elementals, learning of his early freedom, would wish to see them both put to death for the crime. They would have to stand against the elementals, united with his iron army, and defeat them. And this time, there would be no third Iron Crystal waiting for them. He would put them in the grave instead.

Avalon would choose new elementals in time. It always did. And those would have to be dealt with as they made their motivations known.

But for a time, the death and war would lead to peace. Gwendolyn would be safe from harm—free to be with him. A veritable Queen of Avalon.

He smiled faintly. *I would finally have my throne. But it would be built from bone and ash. Would that make me no different than Grinn, in the end?* No. Grinn sought the destruction of all Avalon. Mordred would seek only the death of the elementals.

A hundred lives, versus tens of thousands.

Shutting his eyes, he let out a sigh, feeling the tiredness encroach on him. It had been a very long day, and it was late into the night now. They had one more day and one more night to spend together before it would be up to Gwendolyn to decide what to do.

He could not strike now. Gwendolyn would never agree to such seemingly wanton destruction.

No, she had to make the choice. Between his imprisonment and his freedom. Between peace and war. Between the lives of others and their life together.

He would be certain she understood what would come to pass if she made good on her half-conscious vow to save him.

But there was one thing now in his mind that was made very clear. He was the bastard everyone believed him to be. He was the portrait of a dark, cruel lord that the peasants painted of him. Why?

Because he would see them all reduced to dust before he parted with the woman in his arms.

But he could not pull her into the darkness after him.

She had to follow.

We shall wait and see, my love, if your heart will turn dark enough to see it done.

I, for one, pray that it shall.

TWENTY-TWO

Gwen didn't know what to do with herself when the sun rose on their last day together for a thousand years. Mordred was still asleep, which gave her time to lie there and watch him without the weight of the world pressing on him. It took the age out of his features, the creases by his eyes and in his brow that were always there when he was awake.

God, he was so damn handsome.

She couldn't help but reach out and gently stroke the line of his cheekbone. How could she say goodbye to him? How could she be without him for a *thousand years*? It felt like nonsense—just as much as his age felt like nonsense. Nobody could be that old. Nothing could last that long. It was just a number. It didn't feel *real*.

Not until right now.

Not until she was staring down the reality that she might not see him for a thousand fucking years.

There had to be a way to stop it. Somehow. Maybe she could plead with Zoe—fall on her knees and weep and say that she loved him, so Zoe couldn't go through with it.

Yeah, well, Mordred kept Galahad and Zoe apart for three hundred years.

"You are scheming," Mordred muttered. It almost made her jump in surprise.

"Badly," she chuckled, leaning in to kiss him. "Morning."

He grunted and rolled onto his back. "It is deeply ironic to me that I slept well last night."

"Maybe you just needed to tire yourself out." She smirked and pushed herself up onto her elbows to watch him.

"Perhaps. Or perhaps you are the cure for my sleeplessness."

Her smile faded. "For as long as it matters."

His eyes opened and focused on the ceiling, swirling rusted colors that changed as she watched. "Yes."

"There has to be a way."

"There is. But it involves total war between us and the elementals. And there is only one way that war ends with us both alive and free." His words were quiet, but they didn't need to be loud to express the weight of them.

She knew what he meant. Scooting back close to him, she rested her head on his chest, wanting to hear his heartbeat and feel the warmth of him. "If they all die."

"Yes."

"But... the island'll just make more, right?"

"And I would hunt them down and put them to the blade before they could rise against us."

That sounded like tyranny. She let out a wavering sigh. "I don't know if... I don't know if I can be a part of that."

"Which is precisely why I have not suggested it. Let them think of me what they will, but if your heart turned cold in the wake of the destruction I could cause them—if your love for me faded—their deaths would be for naught."

"So—wait." She lifted her head now to look at him, brow furrowed. "You're putting this on *me*? This is *my* decision?"

He finally met her gaze. "Yes. Forgive the cruelty of it."

She dropped her forehead onto his chest. "Fuck."

He chuckled. "Such an eloquent creature you are."

"I haven't had coffee yet, so this is the best you get." Sighing, she rolled away from him, getting out of bed. She needed to walk. And get dressed. Finding her metal clothing, she slung it back on, tying the skirt around her waist. "I—you're asking me to condemn them all to death so that we can be together."

"Yes."

"I don't—there's no other way? There's no third option?" She shook her head. "There has to be a third option."

"I commend you for believing that." Mordred also climbed out of bed with a grunt. She was distracted by watching the muscles on his back move as he found his trousers. Okay, she was also distracted by his ass—but now wasn't the time to comment on it. "But the world is not so kind."

"No shit." She tried to fight the urge to cry again. It wouldn't help anything. She needed time to think. *You have about a thousand years to think.* Fuck. Just, fuck. She shut her eyes and tried to steady her breath.

Mordred walked up to her, gently catching her cheek in his metal palm before tilting her head up to capture her lips with his. When he parted, a sad smile graced his features. "If I must wait a thousand years, so be it. I will love you no less. It is your kind heart, your desire to give all souls more sympathy than they deserve, that is part of why I adore you. But I cannot be the one to make the decision."

"I get it. I know." It'd be easy to just tell him to do it—to just murder everybody. But those deaths would be on her head. And she didn't know if she could handle it. Part of her wished he would just *do* it without her asking him to, but he was right. She didn't know what that would do to them, knowing that he had slaughtered a hundred-something elementals just so they could be together. Why did he have to be so goddamn noble? She hugged him, her arms barely making it all the way around him. "This sucks."

"Again, I stand in awe of your command of the English language." She could hear the smile in his voice.

"Shut up." But she was smiling.

There was a fast and insistent knock on the door. "Get up and eat before breakfast goes cold! The least you could do would be to get out of bed and let me feed you!"

It was Maewenn!

Smiling, Gwen ran for the door. The poor cook still likely thought that Gwen was on Earth, banished by Mordred what felt like ten years ago. She threw open the door and hugged the metal woman.

Mae let out a yelp of surprise. "Gwen—Gwendolyn? Oh, my dear girl! I heard rumors, the knights were muttering to themselves—but I didn't believe—" The cook's voice cracked. "Oh, who do I have to thank for this? And look at you—back to your fiery self."

"Kind of. I'm not an elemental. I'm a wizard." Gwen laughed. "Or a witch, maybe? I don't know. I don't know how you all classify things here." She finally let go of the cook, but Mae wasn't quite ready for that and hugged her instead. "The island wanted me to stay."

"First good decision this stupid rock has ever made." Mae sniffled, which was funny, seeing as she didn't really need to breathe or, y'know, use her nose. But mannerisms like that were probably hard to shake, even with the metal body and all. "I am just so *happy*. But—but also—"

"I know." Gwen sighed. "I know."

Mordred was pulling on a black linen shirt over his head. Gwen tried not to stare, again. "The keep will belong to you in my absence, Gwendolyn. You are now Lady Gwendolyn, in truth, if perhaps no longer a princess."

Right. That whole thing. She had forgotten that she had

been a princess for a hot second while all the other people were locked up in the Crystal. It really hadn't mattered. "I'm fine being Lady Gwendolyn. I guess." She smirked. "Still sounds weird, though."

"You will come to accept it in time." Mordred walked up to them both and looked down at Mae with a playfully stern expression. "Though you will have to endure Maewenn's incessant pestering. We will both spend a thousand years in suffering, I suppose."

Mae huffed and shook her head. "Insolent, arrogant—" She sighed, her shoulders falling with a small clank. "I am going to miss you terribly."

"And I you." Mordred smiled, if faintly. "Come. Let us eat. I have only the day to have my affairs in order."

Gwen followed Mae and Mordred as the three of them walked to the dining room for breakfast. Eod was already there, sitting at Doc's feet, tail idly swishing over the wood floor as he begged scraps from the wizard.

The other people in attendance were surprising. Galahad and Zoe sat at the table, along with Bors, Gawain, Tristan, and Percival. She was surprised especially that Percival had the balls to walk back into the keep after the incident at the trial.

Probably didn't have a choice. He's still bound by magic to serve Mordred. Which raised the question of what the fuck was going to happen to the knights while Mordred was trapped. She knew that he had freed Galahad already, but what would he do with the other four?

Whatever it was, Mordred opted to keep it to himself as he walked to the head of the table and sat, motioning at the seat next to him. Gwen took her spot, her stomach grumbling in hunger at the sight of the meat pies, fruit, and various cheeses laid out in front of her. Right. She hadn't eaten in a long while.

Talk about an awkward breakfast, though.

Everybody just sat in silence.

Well, almost everybody.

"Sooooo—" Doc broke the stretch, grinning in his usual way that marked that he was about to say or do something extremely inappropriate for the sake of causing chaos. "What're you planning to do with these chucklefucks?" He gestured at the four knights at the table.

Mordred shut his eyes, stabbed a grape with the pointed end of his claw, and took his time eating it. He sat there in silence for a painfully long stretch before answering. "We shall see."

Doc grinned and took a sip from his coffee. Gwen would put money on the fact that he had slipped some alcohol into it. She couldn't decide if he was a low-functioning or high-functioning alcoholic, but she also couldn't say that she blamed him, considering how much he had going around in his head.

"I really hope I don't wind up like you eventually." She shook her head.

Doc barked a laugh. "Just you wait and see. I give it five hundred years."

"Charming." Mordred reached for his cup of tea. "I see I will have something to look forward to."

"I'll do my best not to become a total looney with an alcohol problem." Gwen smiled, weakly, trying to find the humor in the situation. "But no promises."

Mordred sat there in silence for another long stretch. "I am surprised you dare show your face at my dining table, Gossamer Lady."

"I..." Zoe sighed, her shoulders falling. She had a vegetarian breakfast in front of her, which wasn't a surprise. All fruits and vegetables arranged artfully around. Mae had done her best to accommodate. "I will not shy away from the tragedy of what I have been tasked with. I will not hide my face. I understand what you are both losing."

"And you understand what will happen in my absence,

yes?" Mordred sneered. "The elementals will turn on each other. The slaughter of whole villages will resume."

"I hold out hope that you are wrong," Zoe replied. "Though I would not be surprised if that were to come to pass."

"Yet you have no problem with this?" He arched an eyebrow.

"It is the natural way of our island. It is how Avalon has always been, and always shall be. Seeking to impose order upon chaos is a particular conceit that you and I do not share." Zoe shrugged.

Galahad was staring down at his food as though he were at a reception for a funeral. It was clear he hated everything that was happening but had no idea how to change any of it. Or maybe no desire to. Honor above all else, and so on.

Gwen let the conversation pause for a moment. "What happens if, say, he escapes early? What're the laws about that? Say, like, the Crystal is faulty and just... falls apart, or... something." God, she was shit at lying.

Zoe smiled in understanding. "He would remain a fugitive from the law. And if it was discovered that he was aided in his escape, those who helped him would be as well. The punishment for running from the justice of the elementals is death."

"Of course. Death. Naturally,' she mumbled into her coffee. "Why the fuck not?"

There went that idea. She knew the answer before she asked the question, but she had to ask it, anyway. Just in case. She was going to test every corner, poke at every wall, until she found a loophole. Some way, some chance, that she didn't have to be separated from Mordred for a thousand years.

The rest of the meal went by rather uneventfully. The knights were silent, likely dreading whatever was going to befall them. None of them had voted in Mordred's favor, after all.

Mordred spent the rest of the day poring over papers and discussing matters with Galahad. She was glad at least that he wasn't holding a grudge against the Knight in Gold. Gwen listened in, trying to absorb every detail. The keep was going to be her home, and she wanted to help protect it.

Eod punched her in the leg about an hour in. "*Bored.*"

"All right," she muttered to the dog, ruffling his ears. She decided it would be good to stretch her legs as well. "Let's go throw a stick."

"*Stick!*"

And off he went. Smiling, she followed the big doofus dog out of the room and down the hallway. It wasn't long before she bumped into a familiar half-finished guard.

"Tim!" She smiled and ran up to him, hugging him. The soldier clearly didn't know how to react at first before picking up his hand and gently patting her on the back. "I missed you. Are you doing all right?"

A long pause, and then a squeaky nod.

"I'm glad." She smiled. "It's good to see you. I'll—I guess I'm in charge of the keep once Mordred is—is—" Her words choked off. She had to not think about it. She shook her head, not knowing if she could finish the sentence.

Tim's shoulders drooped. Reaching out, he pulled her back into a hug. Gwen choked back tears as she returned the gesture. It didn't matter that she was hugging a suit of armor, which felt exactly like trying to get sympathy from the back end of a Buick. It was the thought that mattered.

"I have to do something. I... I'll think of something." There wasn't another option. And she had plenty of time to come up with a plan, after all.

Eod barked from down the hallway.

"Yeah, yeah, I'm coming." She squeezed Tim's hand as she turned to leave. "See you soon, Tim."

If Eod understood what was happening, he didn't let it show. The animal's joy at chasing after a stick was infectious. It at least was a small bit of normalcy in an otherwise upended world.

To be fair, it wasn't like her world had ever been—uh—un-upended? *Would that just make it "ended?" English is weird.*

But after a while, it caught up with her. Sitting down on the steps to the keep, she wiped her eyes as the tears finally broke free that morning.

Eod sat at her feet, licking her face, trying to cheer her up. At least there were dogs in this world. She hugged the animal, burying her face in his fur, and just let herself cry. Something told her she'd be doing a lot of that in the centuries to come.

* * *

A day and a night. Not nearly enough time. Mordred's affairs were easily set into order—he did not live in a state of disarray. But it was not enough time with Gwendolyn. It was not enough time with those he cared for—those he could finally admit he *did* care for.

So much wasted time.

But for every Maewenn, Gwendolyn, and Galahad—there was a Knight in Copper. He stood in his throne room, staring down the four knights who had "served" him against their will for centuries. Bors, Gawain, Tristan, and *Percival.*

Three had done nothing that Mordred would consider treacherous. He had not expected their support in the matters at the trial. But the fourth? Ah, yes. The fourth. Percival, the Knight in Copper, had attempted to see him put to death over Lancelot.

Attempted, but failed.

There was no reason to spend time recounting the incidents in question. No point in explaining his actions to the four men. They knew. Mordred had blessed little breath left to spare.

Approaching Gawain, Mordred reached out his hand and

pressed it over the man's chest where the crystal was embedded. Unlacing the magic from the man's flesh, he watched as Gawain's face contorted in pain, and then relief, before he collapsed to his knees.

One at a time, Mordred freed two others. Bors and Tristan. Each one watched him with a look of shock and confusion. They likely expected him to take their lives.

I do not need to stand trial for four more "murders."

And it was for that reason alone that he stopped in front of Percival, and wished with all his might that he had a reason to kill the Knight in Copper and have it be excused as having happened in the heat of battle. But this was cold blood.

Percival watched him, angry and uncertain, eyes flicking back and forth as he sought any hint of what was to follow.

The Knight in Copper would be free.

He would live.

But perhaps he would wish he did not.

Mordred lifted his hand, placed it over the shard of crystal in his chest.

And detonated it.

Percival screamed, falling to his knees, the magic lancing through his veins, setting his flesh alight. He howled in pain, collapsing to the ground, as the power dissipated, but not before the stench of burning flesh filled his throne room.

It had crawled up along his chest, covered part of his face and his throat, and likely left his torso in quite a state. He was alive. But he might not wish he was.

Mordred stared down at him coldly. He would not take pleasure in the man's pain. He would not laugh or rejoice. It was nothing to be proud of.

It was merely penance paid.

Mordred turned from the four men and left the room. He prayed he would never have to see their faces again.

* * *

When morning came, Gwen didn't know what to expect. But she expected a little more pomp and circumstance than what seemed to be in store.

The Iron Crystal—suspended from a giant, seven-legged iron *spider*—loomed outside the keep's walls.

"Holy—holy fuck—" She couldn't help but stare at it as she walked beyond the keep's walls with Mordred, Galahad, Doc, and Zoe that morning. It resembled Tiny in its style, with strange, twisted, tangled, almost vine-like construction of panels of armor that made no sense that they could move the way that it did. It was at least thirty or forty feet tall, with the Crystal shard hanging from its rib cages by wires. Its eyes were glowing the same opalescent and eerie tone that all Mordred's creations had.

She glanced at him. "Dude, you need therapy."

He chuckled quietly, but he said nothing. His eyes were fixed upon the Iron Crystal. Gwen couldn't say she blamed him.

There was motion by the woods—elementals, come to watch the proceedings. Come to watch Mordred be imprisoned in his own creation.

"I will take the Crystal somewhere safe," Zoe announced. "It shall not remain here."

At that, Mordred turned his attention to the Gossamer Lady. "And why not?"

"I fear I do not trust Gwendolyn's intentions." Zoe looked at Gwen mournfully. "She is stubborn and in love. Two of the most dangerous things a person can be. And to be honest... I know what I would do in her place."

Mordred sighed. "Very well. It will make no difference to me."

"Can—can I visit it? From time to time? I—" Gwen didn't

like the idea of him being hidden somewhere out in Avalon. At the very least, she wanted to be able to sit outside his cage and know that he was in there, somewhere.

Suffering.

"I will bring it forth at your request," Zoe replied.

Mordred took a step toward the Crystal. "Let us end this."

"Wait—" Gwen ran toward him, her vision blinded by tears. "No—"

Mordred turned to her, and she saw his own eyes were glistening. Throwing her arms around his neck, she was hefted off her feet as he caught her lips with his own. He set her back down, resting his forehead against hers, one metal gauntlet stroking against her cheek. "I must go, Gwendolyn."

"I—please—don't—I—" Her voice choked off. She couldn't find her words. There were only three that mattered. "I love you—"

"And I you." He kissed her forehead, his voice lowering. "Do not make me endure a longer parting. I will not shed tears in front of my enemies."

Nodding weakly, she supposed she could let him keep his dignity. She sniffled, wiping her eyes. "I... can't."

"You can. You will be strong." He stroked her cheekbone with his thumb. "You already are." He kissed her. One last time. For a very long time. "I will see you soon."

Soon.

Right.

Mordred turned from her, pulling the dark hood of his cloak over his head. He walked toward the Iron Crystal.

It happened quickly. And not like Lancelot. For that, Gwen was relieved.

One moment he was there.

The next moment he was not.

The Iron Crystal shuddered, the giant spider stumbling with the change of weight, as if some terrible burden had just been placed on top of it. Or within it. The Crystal flared, the cracks glowing with opalescent power, before quieting.

The first Iron Crystal was always leaking, he had said. Something told her that, as a prison for one, it wouldn't have the same problem.

Gwen fell to her knees and wept.

Mordred was gone.

EPILOGUE

Mordred was gone.

And Gwen was drunk.

Doc really was a terrible influence. The four remaining knights were gone. Galahad had stayed behind to check on her, but she didn't want to see him. He, too, would leave soon. The Gossamer Lady had taken the large iron spider and gone *somewhere* with it, and Galahad would not be parted from her for long.

Gwen sat in Mordred's study, in his chair, curled up by the fire, a bottle of wine next to her and the dog sprawled out in front of her.

Doc was sitting in the chair next to her, silently working on his own bottle.

Mae had fussed over her until she had eaten something. She supposed she didn't want to get blackout, puke-it-out sick. So she picked at the tray of food next to her from time to time between downing glasses of red wine.

And she thought.

And schemed.

"If I free him, he takes his army against the elementals, and everybody dies." It was a statement, not a question.

"Yep," Doc confirmed. "Total bloodbath."

"If he stays in the Crystal, the elementals start their bullshit again, and innocent villagers start dying again."

"Yep. Total bloodbath."

She shut her eyes. There had to be a third way. Two armies —elemental and Mordred. How could she disrupt that? How could she get in between them and keep them from murdering each other?

A third way. A third option.

Her eyes flew open. She jumped up to her feet.

A third way. A third option.

A third army.

The only way she could stop them from killing each other was if she *actually got in between them.* But she couldn't stand against Mordred's army, or the elementals, on her own. She was just one idiot witch-wizard-whatever, pitted against two groups who despised each other.

So she'd need help.

A lot of help.

And she kind of thought she might know where she could get it. *The villagers of Avalon are probably super sick of getting murdered.* Maybe they would help her, if they thought they stood a chance.

She reeled toward Doc, almost falling over from the alcohol.

He was grinning like an idiot.

"Doc." She caught her balance and her breath. "I—I need an army. I need an army to save the world."

He downed the rest of his glass of wine. "I thought you'd never ask."

To be continued...

A LETTER FROM KATHRYN

I want to say a huge thank you for choosing to read *To Break a Dark Cage*. I hope you enjoyed it and are looking forward to the rest of the series! If you did and want to keep up to date with all my latest releases, just sign up at the following link. Your email address will never be shared and you can unsubscribe at any time.

www.secondskybooks.com/kathryn-ann-kingsley

There are several kinds of writers out there in the world—those who are happy to tell their story to a blank page, and those who thrive on hearing about how their readers engage with their tales.

I am definitely the latter.

I love to hear from you and hear what you think of the Iron Crystal and Mordred and Gwen's adventures in Avalon. Please leave me a review or stop by one of my many social media spots!

I absolutely love hearing from my readers—you can get in touch on my Facebook page, through X, my website, or even join my Discord (link to join on my website) to interact with both me and other fans.

Stay Spooky,

Kathryn Ann Kingsley

KEEP IN TOUCH WITH KATHRYN

www.kathrynkingsley.com

 facebook.com/thesocietyofunder

x.com/vodriel

instagram.com/kathrynannkingsley

ACKNOWLEDGMENTS

Thank you to Jack, my ever-patient, ever-attentive, and wonderful editor. Thank you for putting up with my bizarre schedule and strange life events that threatened to put a spanner in the works for this series.

Thank you to my husband, for putting up with me.

And thank you to all of you, dear readers, for enjoying the Iron Crystal series.

PUBLISHING TEAM

Turning a manuscript into a book requires the efforts of many people. The publishing team at Bookouture would like to acknowledge everyone who contributed to this publication.

Audio
Alba Proko
Sinead O'Connor
Melissa Tran

Commercial
Lauren Morrissette
Jil Thielen
Imogen Allport

Cover design
Daria Klushina

Data and analysis
Mark Alder
Mohamed Bussuri

Editorial
Jack Renninson
Melissa Tran